COMING OUT

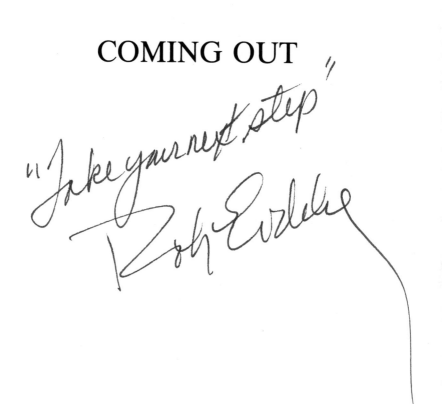

"Take your next step"

Rob Eichberg

COMING OUT:
AN ACT OF LOVE

Rob Eichberg, Ph.D.

A DUTTON BOOK

DUTTON
Published by the Penguin Group
Penguin Books USA Inc., 375 Hudson Street,
New York, New York 10014, U.S.A.
Penguin Books Ltd, 27 Wrights Lane,
London W8 5TZ, England
Penguin Books Australia Ltd, Ringwood,
Victoria, Australia
Penguin Books Canada Ltd, 2801 John Street,
Markham, Ontario, Canada L3R 1B4
Penguin Books (N.Z.) Ltd, 182–190 Wairau Road,
Auckland 10, New Zealand

Penguin Books Ltd, Registered Offices:
Harmondsworth, Middlesex, England

First published by Dutton, an imprint of New American Library, a division of
Penguin Books USA Inc.

Distributed in Canada by McClelland & Stewart Inc.

First Printing, October, 1990
10 9 8 7 6 5 4 3 2

 REGISTERED TRADEMARK—MARCA REGISTRADA

Library of Congress Cataloging-in-Publication Data
Eichberg, Rob.
    Coming out / Rob Eichberg.
        p.   cm.
    ISBN 0-525-24909-5
    1. Gay men—United States—Correspondence.   2. Gay men—United States—
Family relationships—Case studies.   3. Interpersonal relations—Case studies.
I. Title.
HQ75.7.E43   1990
305.38′9664—dc20   90-33689
                                                                                CIP

Printed in the United States of America
Set in Times Roman
Designed by Soloway/Mitchell Design Associates

Grateful acknowledgment is made for permission to reprint lyrics from "Stand Up
for Truth" by Jerry Florence. Copyright © 1988 by Go with the Flo Music.

To my family,
and to
lesbians and gay men
who are taking their next step
in the process
of coming out
and the families and friends
who love and support them.

STAND UP FOR TRUTH

Stand up, stand up, stand up for love for truth
Stand up, stand up, stand up for truth.

There's a call coming out to all of us, it's time we lend a hand
It's a call to peace, a call to truth and with dignity we stand
As once again, we the people choose our destiny
Answering the call to truth we pledge our unity.

Stand up, stand up, stand up for love for truth
Stand up, stand up, stand up for truth.

The children of the world are counting on us to learn to
live in peace
Let's give to them the gift of life and let the fighting cease
As fear and war and prejudice are left behind we say
Let's move into a brand new age and let love lead the way.

Stand up, stand up, stand up for love for truth
Stand up, stand up, stand up for truth.

—Jerry Florence

CONTENTS

ACKNOWLEDGMENTS

I have been blessed with the unconditional love and support of my entire family, and for this I am profoundly grateful. My mother, Shirley Eichberg, has been particularly support-ive of my work, as have my cousins Babette Markus and Jack Weir.

While it is impossible to adequately acknowledge all of the people in my life who have contributed their love and support to me over the years, thereby playing a major role in the content of this book, several must be highlighted. My dear friends Joan Darling and Bill Svanoe gave me the key to preparing this manuscript and have provided daily en-couragement. Michael Parish and Don Brown read drafts of the manuscript and made many helpful suggestions. My agent, Jed Mattes, has provided continual encouragement and guidance; and it has truly been a pleasure working with Susie Rogers and Gary Luke, my editors at New American Library/Dutton. For their early contributions to the preparation of this book, I also thank Steve Siporo and Bonnie Barron.

I thank Sally Fisher, whose work with people with AIDS is an inspiration, for loving me madly and for helping me create the space to write this book; Stephen Kolzak, for encouraging and inspiring me; Harvey Fierstein, for coming out boldly, proudly, and lovingly; Doris Mandelker, for giving the world her late son, my dear friend Philip; and Tom Drucker and Marcia Seligson, for helping me understand the creative process. I thank Byron Nease, Scott Eidson, and Stephen Matthews for believing in me and providing consistent support, as well as Jerry E. Berg, Jim Proby, Jim Hormel, Larry Soule, Bob Sass, Philip Greenberg, Jeffrey Banks, John Benecke, and Wes Wheadon for being my brothers and friends.

The Experience is produced throughout the country by graduates who volunteer their time to support and expand this work. This could not happen without the dedication of Steve Sabin, a man who has never faltered in encouraging me (strongly) to make The Experience available to more and more communities, and Larry Falk, who regularly calls to give me a little push. In making this work available to others I also thank all those who have served on local production committees and my co-facilitators: Dr. Paul Kent Froman, Fred Bronson, Jay Allen, Dan Osborne, and particularly Honey Ward, who not only facilitates The Experience superbly, but has been the National Coordinator for several years and a constant support in my life since 1979.

I lovingly remember my colleague, partner, and mentor, David B. Goodstein, whose extraordinary passion and vision gave birth to The Advocate Experience and to many other projects serving the gay community. While often misunderstood, his deep love of humanity and dedication to service had a profound effect on the lives of a multitude of people.

Many were responsible for the success of The Advocate Experience, particularly our facilitators and staff, including: Tom Watson, Rich Bogan, Frank Ker, Durk Dehner,

Dorothea Patrick Sargent, Cheryl Capitolo, David Delp, Eric MaGrath, and Donna Becker. Thousands of people have participated in these workshops since 1978. Each of them has provided me with new dimensions of growth and added insight. Among those whose contributions to society have inspired me to expand this work are: Larry Kramer, Rev. Troy Perry, Alan Emery, Randy Klose, Catherine Coker, Vic Basile, Ginny Apuzzo, Steve Endean, Murray Salem, Vivian Shapiro, C. Robert Holloway, Jim Corty, Mike Grossman, John Thomas, Mary Franklin, Dr. Robert Brooks, Robin Tyler, Duke Comegys, Paul Kawata, Bill Misenhimer, Louise Hay, Armistead Maupin, Vince Chalk, Richard Kaplan, Torie Osborn, Steve Smith, David Russell, and Michael Nicola. I am particularly grateful to Jerry Florence and Alliance, whose inspirational music has added great value to The Experience, for granting permission to include the lyrics to "Stand Up for Truth" in this book and for assisting me in the production of my audio cassettes.

I want to also thank everyone who has sponsored National Coming Out Day since its inception in 1988. Jean O'Leary, co-founder and co-chair, deserves special recognition for her dedication, vision, inspiration, and friendship. Pilo Bueno (1989 coordinator), Lynn Shepodd (executive director), the late Keith Haring, publisher Niles Merton, and the staff of *The Advocate,* as well as Gabriel Rotello and *Outweek,* have all made major contributions to NCOD's success. My sincere gratitude to Oprah Winfrey and to one of her producers, Dianne Hudson, for their extrordinary and ongoing support in reaching out to the public.

Caldwell and Arlowyne Williams, Jordan Paul, Jeanne Meyers and Phyllis Shankman all participated in my growth and development as a group facilitator. I want them, and all those who participated in DAWN (Developing Adolescents Without Narcotics), to know that my work in the gay community has been an extension of the work we did together from 1967 to 1972.

My commitment to writing this book has frequently been sustained by the memory of close friends who supported this work and who have died of AIDS during the past decade. They are Philip Mandelker, Edward Dunn, Matthew Gotbaum Sargent, Vern Black, Michael Levy, Steven Baker, Michael Hirsch, Stephen Blunck, Robert McQueen, Clyde Cairns, Mark Feldman, Mickey Talbott, Lee Troeger, Sam Puckett, Colin Higgins, Barry Lowen, Michael Marshall, Justin Smith, Anselm Rothschild, Sheldon Andelson, Jon Sims, Zohn Artman, Jim Graves, Michael Barnes, Scott Roberts, Howie Dare, John Sheridan, Enrique Delgado, Jerry Vaught, Michael McMahan, Martin Gonzales, Burleigh Sutton, Peter LaParne, Tom Proctor, Paul Jasperson, Peter Scott, David Quarels, Bill Gassaway, Bill Herder, Richard Romero, and, unfortunately, many, many more.

Finally, I acknowledge all of those Experience graduates who submitted letters for inclusion in this book. It is clearly *our* book. You are my heroes and I love you!

FOREWORD

Dear Abby,
I am a gay man with the AIDS virus and am over-
whelmingly frustrated—fighting with the insurance compa-
nies, the federal and state governments; having my safe-to-take
over-the-counter Japanese drugs seized by the FDA due to
pressure from American drug companies; spending my life
savings to fight this disease; and fighting growing discrimi-
nation which impedes compassion and research for a cure.
My wonderful companion of 5½ years died this past sum-
mer of AIDS, not to mention all the truly great friends, ac-
quaintances, and talents we've all lost. And this past week
two more friends were just diagnosed. I am simply com-
pelled to write and get this off my chest!
Gay men are the highest risk group in this country for
AIDS and it is the gay and lesbian minorities who suffer
discrimination, which now has been extended to people with
AIDS. We're a unique minority in two ways: One, it's easy

xv

*for us to hide out "in the closet" because our skin color, an-
atomical features, or religious beliefs don't give us away.
Two, although we represent a conservatively estimated 10
percent of the population we reach into every home and business in the country. I believe that we as a minority are
perpetuating discrimination long after the time society is
ready to give it up. If every one of us "came out" to our
families and co-workers—the people in our lives who are
important to us and whom we love—a new age of understanding and love would be inevitable. This includes our
politicians, clergy, professional athletes, and celebrities. Prejudices would end because no one would be untouched. And
today with AIDS, not unlike early Nazi Germany, silence
does equal death!*

*I had dozens of good sound reasons for not telling
my family and friends I was gay. "They won't like me.
I'll lose my job. I'll lose my inheritance. I'll be disowned.
My mother can't handle it. It would kill my dad—you know
he has a bad heart. I'll lose love. And besides, it's not that
important."*

*For something "not that important" I was expending
an inordinate amount of time and energy lying to hide the
truth. What did it matter if my dad "died" if he found out?
Lying and withholding the truth about who I am sepa-
rated and distanced us—our relationship had become a slow
death anyway. There are consequences for lying and for
telling the truth.*

*Love, as all great spiritual masters have taught us, is
unconditionally accepting people the way they are. Once I
learned to love and accept myself, telling the truth was inevitable. I felt empowered and free! It is sometimes uncomfortable. Risk-taking often is, but that's where I've found the
golden egg.*

*My parents are and continue to be extremely conser-
vative individuals, but their love for me superseded their
own biases and we have grown and educated ourselves together. It hasn't been easy, but they were there for me when
Peter died and they love and support me now. And as an
adult I know I can always get a job where it's OK to be*

who I am. As an adult I'm capable of nurturing open and honest relationships where I love and am loved.

We literally must heal our lives and the planet by telling the truth. Time is running out! I encourage everyone to make it safe for the people in your life to tell the truth. I appeal to all gays and lesbians to love ourselves enough to be first-class citizens of the world and let ourselves have the life and relationships we deserve. Coming out is an act of love.

Thank you, Abby. I'm feeling better already. I love you.

Scott Lee Eidson

COMING OUT

INTRODUCTION

This is a book about coming out, telling the truth, and being powerful in your life. It is a book about being gay and about knowing and loving someone gay. It is a book about you and me and our families. Most of all, it is a book about love.

Throughout the book there are quotes from letters written by participants in a workshop that I created in 1978 known then as The Advocate Experience and now called The Experience. Many of these letters are included in Parts I and II in their entirety, while others are only briefly quoted. In order to let these men and women speak for themselves, I have interwoven their statements with my own as together we talk about coming out, being gay, the coming-out process, unconditional love, self-esteem, and our lives.

If you are lesbian or gay, this book is intended to support you to look at your own life: what role being gay plays in your life, how open you are with others, how

1

integrated your life is, the quality of your relationships with friends, family, and co-workers, your feelings of self-worth and self-esteem, functioning powerfully as a whole and complete human being, and your relationship to social and political issues currently confronting people who are gay.

If you are heterosexual, this book is intended to give you more insight into your own life and your beliefs about sexuality in general and homosexuality in particular. Though you may not be aware of it, you probably already know and love a lesbian or a gay man. You very likely have a homosexual as a relative, co-worker, fellow church member, or friend. This book is intended to support that person to be more open with you, and to support you to be better able to understand and cope with that openness.

I do not wish to debate with you. I cannot make anything wrong or right, good or bad for you. And you cannot for me. What I can do is share my thoughts and experience with you so that hopefully your frame of reference will be widened.

                                     —Bud, to his father; p. 106

Part I is a call to action, urging more honesty and truth. Part II is about coming out powerfully—coming out in a manner that allows you to give and receive love while learning and growing in the process. Chapter 10 is a relatively didactic chapter that provides tools so that you can become more conscious and powerful in all aspects of your life, tools that I hope will be applicable to you whether you are homosexual or heterosexual. Chapter 11 shows how these tools can be applied specifically to help you come out powerfully and focuses primarily on coming out as a lesbian or a gay man. Specific issues relating to coming out individually and as a community are then discussed. Part II concludes by encouraging you to take your next step in your personal coming-out process, whatever that step may be.

I don't expect someone who is not gay to understand fully. . . . I am not doing this, I would not do this or

anything to hurt you. . . . You are my parents and I will
always be your son.

—Joe, to his parents; p. 228

This book also contains several exercises in order to give you an opportunity to look at your own experience. They invite you to examine your childhood and adolescent decisions about yourself and your relationships; your reasons to come out or stay hidden; and what you would communicate and how if you choose to be more open with others.

To offer some background, in 1977 I was a co-founder, with a number of friends, of a gay rights political action committee in Los Angeles—The Municipal Elections Committee of Los Angeles (MECLA). When we formed MECLA, part of the game plan was to create an organization in the gay community with which successful and professional gay men could identify. We wanted to present a public image of the gay community that was different from the image presented through Gay Pride parades and the media. We did not feel that the images of what it was to be gay, in 1977, were an accurate reflection of who "we" were, though they did indeed accurately represent some parts of the community. Rather than wasting our time criticizing those who were already active, or trying to get them to represent us better, we decided to represent ourselves and put ourselves forth visibly in the political community. This was a major step in our coming-out processes, and each of us dealt with it a bit differently. Those of us who started MECLA spent a considerable amount of time together raising our own consciousnesses and reached a high degree of comfort with ourselves as gay men.

In September 1977, at the invitation of David Goodstein (then the owner of *The Advocate*) and Jerry E. Berg (a San Francisco attorney), I trained a group of gay men from San Francisco to do effective fund-raising and be more successful politically in the Bay Area. To accomplish this I created a weekend retreat that involved a number of activities designed to support these men to become more comfortable telling the truth about who they were, how they felt about themselves and their sexuality, and how they felt about coming out to family, friends, and co-workers. This was a truly wonderful experience for all of us, and many of the men in that group have gone on to make major contributions within the gay community and as openly gay men within mainstream society.

After completing that retreat, David Goodstein asked me to be his partner in taking these activities on the road, and together we created a workshop called The Advocate Experience. During the past decade I have made several changes in the workshop, softening the methodology and focusing more on the concept that *all we have to give and receive is love.*

The AIDS epidemic had not started when we founded The Advocate Experience, but now it is an important aspect of life for all of us. While not focusing specifically on the experience of AIDS, more healing techniques have been added to the workshop, including visualizations, affirmations, and meditations, in addition to other processes aimed at supporting participants to "let go" of the hurts of the past (of childhood and adolescence) and be willing to be powerful adults. These workshops are produced throughout the country by graduates who volunteer their time and energy in order to share this work with others.

A cornerstone of all of these workshops are letters, written by participants to those who are most significant in their lives. Regardless of how one feels about one's parents, I always suggest that the first letter be written to parents (alive or dead) in order to be open and honest with them. Our relationship with our parents is generally the fundamental model on which we base all other relationships, and unless we are willing to be adults with them it is often difficult to be whole and complete adults anywhere else.

These letters are written after a great deal of time has been spent discovering decisions made during childhood and adolescence about self-worth and about being willing to give and receive love and support. We have also explored a model of consciousness that allows us to move from an experience of powerlessness or depression, through several states of consciousness toward becoming more powerful and loving. We have examined our own barriers to giving and receiving love, to trusting ourselves and others, and to feeling good about who we are—including our sexuality—and being responsible for our lives and relationships. Toward the conclusion of the workshop the letters are written, and people are encouraged to either send them after The Experience, or find some other appropriate way to deliver the communications they contain.

This is the letter that you didn't want to get and the letter that I didn't want to write.
—Michael, to his parents; p. 232

Many of the letters in this book were collected between 1978 and 1980. During the past few years I collected more letters in order to capture some of the issues involved in coming out during the AIDS epidemic. The more recent letters are often more political in their nature, reflecting some fundamental changes that have occurred during the 1980s, and the added sociopolitical significance of coming out at this particular time.

The letters in this book provide insight into who we are—sons and daughters, parents, brothers and sisters, friends.

Contrary to many beliefs, gay people are no different than heterosexual people. We have the same hurt, love, feelings, and needs as anyone else in the world.
—Bob, to his children; p. 251

Most of the letters are from men, since during The Advocate Experience the majority of the participants were men, and by far the largest number of letters submitted were from men; however, during the past several years, The Experience has had an increasing number of both lesbians and heterosexuals in each workshop. I can only hope that in talking about the coming-out process—from my personal experience and from the experiences shared through these letters—what is presented herein captures the essence of your experience and is relevant in your life.

I thank the courageous men and women who submitted these letters, and the many more who submitted letters that have not been included, for their willingness to share themselves openly and honestly with you.

PART I

TRUSTING, LOVING, AND TELLING THE TRUTH:

A CALL TO ACTION

1

BEING GAY

Some of us are heterosexual and others of us are homosexual and no one really knows why. Though many people might desire to do away with homosexuality in themselves or in others, there are now, have always been, and always will be lesbians and gay men. Being attracted to one's own sex is as natural for someone who is homosexual as being attracted to the opposite sex is for someone who is heterosexual. Much like differences in the colors of our hair, eyes, or skin; the shape of our bodies; or being right- or left-handed; it is not good or bad, right or wrong, or better or worse to be homosexual or heterosexual—it just is.

Please understand if you can—that I have no more choice about being gay than about any of the other attributes I mentioned earlier—I am gay, I am a good, loving man and I want you to know me and to love me.

—Andrew, to his mother; p. 37

9

Most lesbians and gay men experience little or no choice about whether or not they are gay. It is a sexual orientation that is generally present throughout one's life and is no more and no less conscious a choice than is being heterosexual. What we *can* consciously choose is how to act and how to live in our relationships with others and in relationship to our sexuality. We can also choose whether to attempt to do away with and deny our differences or to celebrate these differences.

> I can choose to act gay, I cannot choose to be gay!
> —Michael, to his parents; p. 232

Even as children, most gay men and lesbians had some awareness of being different from others. Though perhaps not consciously, family friends and teachers frequently responded to them in a somewhat different manner from the way they responded to the other kids. This may have conveyed the message that they were somewhat special, out of the ordinary, and perhaps even a little unusual. This could be interpreted as good or bad (better or worse) depending on many other subtle or perhaps overt messages received about how OK it was just to be oneself—just to be alive.

> When I came to this planet to live I brought many gifts with me, but there was one gift that was quite separate from all the rest, a gift so special that it would take a large part of my life to understand it, and then all the rest of my life to completely give it away.
> I was excited about this gift, because I knew that it made me happy and it would make a lot of other people happy too. But early in life, about the age that you are now, I began to be aware that other people had brought gifts also, each one of them priceless, necessary, and filled with joy and happiness. As I grew older, I realized that some people considered their gifts to be better than others; in fact, some of them insisted with loud voices and angry faces that their gifts were right and

*good and that my gift was bad and evil. It wasn't long
until I learned that some of them even hated me for my
gift and if I tried to share it they would make things very
unpleasant for me.*

*I began to be afraid, especially when I learned that
some other people whose gifts were like mine had been
killed, or put in prisons, or treated very meanly. It was then
that I decided to hide my gift rather than face all the
trouble.*

—Gerald, to his four children; p. 246

Most people—homosexual and heterosexual alike—
were taught that homosexuality is a sin, a crime, disgusting,
an aberration, or an illness. If you are heterosexual, consider how it might feel if you were told that the type of
people you found attractive and wanted to have relationships with (romantically and intimately as well as sexually),
were not OK for you to associate with.

- What would you do?
- How would this affect your life?
- Would you behave as you were taught, and if so,
  how do you think you would feel? How would
  you feel about life? How would you feel about yourself? How would you feel about those who told
  you you shouldn't relate to the very people you
  most want to relate to?
- If you decided to act on your attractions, and not
  do as you had been taught, how would this feel?

Perhaps answering these questions honestly for yourself will give you some modest notion of what it would feel
like to be homosexual. Now add to this picture what it
would be like to have been dealing with this issue from the
time you were very young (as many gay men and women
have) and try as you may, you still find yourself attracted to
those you were told you shouldn't be. What now?

While each of us is brought up by parents who express themselves differently from one another and have different views on child rearing and different abilities (financially, emotionally, physically, and spiritually) when it comes to raising a family, some aspects of life are similar for most of us. For one thing, with very few exceptions, we are brought up by heterosexuals, taught that it is best not to be homosexual (if homosexuality is mentioned at all), and grow up in communities and in a society in which there has been a very clear and pervasive message that being different is bad and being "queer" is the worst kind of different we can be. Given these circumstances, it is not at all surprising that if someone begins to feel "different" they may also begin to feel "not OK." One might feel as if something is wrong, and almost everywhere one turns there is reinforcement for that belief.

For those of us who are gay males: our parents may have told us that we should be better at sports. We usually got stuck playing right field in Little League (if we were willing to play at all). The other kids frequently called us a sissy, a fairy, a queer, a fag (and we didn't notice that they called lots of other kids that as well, since somehow we sensed that they were right about us). Our teachers in religious school told us we would be forever damned if we turned out "like that." For gay women: it might have been great to be good at sports, but not so great to play pitcher or short stop (which of course many of my lesbian sisters have assured me was their most frequent position). A premium was usually placed on being "more feminine" or on being a "little lady." Again, religious authority figures told them they would be forever damned if they turned out "like that."

When someone first begins to recognize that they may be homosexual, the feeling of not being valid as a human being is often overwhelming. Consciously or unconsciously they may decide to hide aspects of themselves that they feel are not acceptable to others. If one starts to recognize as a child or adolescent that he or she might, in Gerald's words, "have a special gift," it is not uncommon to make a firm decision not to tell anyone.

Gays often fear that their survival, both literally and figuratively, is at stake if anyone finds out about their homosexual life-style or even about their homosexual desires. This fear of being discovered or of having some secret found out can diminish one's self-esteem. This may be compounded by feeling that you are not even courageous enough to tell the truth. Not standing up for yourself—as a child, adolescent, or adult—has broad ramifications for one's self-esteem and may lead to isolation and to developing a solitary world—perhaps no bigger than a closet.

There are, of course, lesbians and gays who overcompensated continually and made a point of being the very best they could in every way. This is the story told in John Reid's novel *The Best Little Boy in the World*. Yet even those "best little boys" and "best little girls" always felt that they might be exposed as a fraud. They were always afraid that someone might discover their secret and tell others, tease, or inflict hurt in some emotional or physical way.

Perhaps the worst fear is that if someone finds out who you really are they won't love you anymore. *People often feel they are lovable only if they are the person others want them to be.* Some people are concerned about being popular and fear that if others know the truth about them they would no longer be liked. Some people are afraid their favorite teacher won't accept them anymore or are terrified that God will not love them and accept them into the kingdom of heaven.

For many people—regardless of their age—parents pose the biggest threat of all. It is ironic that the very people who we are told "should" love us no matter what are also those whose love we most fear losing. This threat is expressed in a varieties of ways. If your parents discover that you are acting in a manner they don't approve:

- They might forbid participation in certain activities.
- They could withdraw financial support.
- The shock might kill them.

- They might disown or disinherit you.
- They might withdraw their love.

Fear of losing parental approval is common for all children. When it comes to being gay there are even greater hurdles to overcome than for other minorities: stereotypes, ignorance, and irrational fears. Within other minorities parents, other family members, and even entire communities share the way in which they are different from others, but for homosexuals such support and camaraderie are not available. As a result, someone who is gay is very likely to hide this information even from those whose support they should most be able to count on.

While homosexuals develop what seem to be very sound reasons for hiding and very clear strategies for surviving, it is also true that many people, whether gay or not, grow up not feeling good about themselves and fearing that love will be withdrawn *if* . . . Most lesbians and gay men have grown up believing that this was a unique problem for them, and it was their sexuality alone—first and foremost—that had to be hidden. Although learning to hide differences (or those aspects that we feel others won't approve of) is not unique to gay men and lesbians, societal expectations can make revealing one's homosexuality extremely difficult.

We still live in a society, though it is in the process of changing, where homosexuality is looked down upon. People have a great deal of difficulty dealing with sex in general, and when "homo" is added, we have usually entered a taboo area. If we are ever going to create a healthier environment for ourselves it is essential that we be able to talk more openly and realistically about sexuality. Sexuality in general and homosexuality in particular are not problems—repression and oppression are. It is not homosexuality that can destroy families or societies—it is ignorance and fear.

When we hide a part of ourselves—for example, hiding our sexual identity—that which we hide takes on a much more significant role in our lives than it might otherwise.

Even though my gayness has been a major issue at times, the reality is that my gayness is just a layer of who I am. On one level, I have been dealing with my Self as a gay man, but I'm not just a gay man, I'm a human being.

Nicholas, to his mother; p. 19

As long as we hide our sexuality it takes on extra weight and added significance. Sexuality is a very important issue to everyone—not just to people who are homosexual. The relationships you get into and how you function socially have a great deal to do with your sexuality and sexual orientation. Whether you are homosexual or heterosexual consider:

- What a significant part your romantic relationships play in your life.
- What it might be like to feel you had to hide your interest in someone you were attracted to.
- What it would be like to get into a relationship and not be able to share it with those close to you—to have to hide it.
- What it would be like to be living in a committed relationship with someone (a marriage for example) and have to keep your relationship a secret.
- How your relationships would be different if you could not celebrate the milestones in them with your family and friends.

Establishing positive relationships that work is difficult, but it is easier to do in the open than it is in a closet. Historically, much of what we consider to be the "gay life-style" has grown out of years of hiding and being told by society that being gay is not OK. Some examples of what I mean by this are:

- Gay bars get crowded very late at night, probably because it wasn't safe to go into a gay bar during daylight because one might be seen.

- People who have clandestine sexual contacts (in baths, parks, etc.) may have convinced themselves that this is exciting and fun. Since homosexual sex has not been acceptable, it has not been all right to make contact in publicly visible places. Clandestine contacts are often an expression of not feeling all right about homosexuality and the result of years of being told, and believing, that it isn't possible to have intimate, stable, and acceptable homosexual relationships.

- The gay community for many years defended and even promoted nonmonogamous relationships. Yet what the majority of people I talk to say they want and fantasize about is a committed, long-term love relationship. Rather than state how we really want our relationships to be, lesbians and gay men have reacted against society's standards of monogamy, since society had little or no room for supporting homosexual relationships.

- Some lesbians present themselves as "butch," denying their femininity rather than being more playful in their range of behaviors.

- Some gay men present themselves as feminine and refer to other men as "girls." Others dress in conventional clothing during the day and wear leather by night.

Rather than being an accurate reflection of homosexuality, these ways of "being gay" may be no more than a "position" that has been taken in reaction to how society has limited our self-expression. As we enter the 1990s, and as a reflection of the greater visibility of lesbians and gay men during recent decades, much of this behavior is in transition. As more people tell the truth about their sexuality, a clearer picture of what it is to be homosexual will emerge. Simultaneously, homosexual life-styles will also be free to change and to reflect more accurately the wide diversity of people who identify themselves as gay. This is evident already in the large number of homosexual couples adopting children and the increase in gay families.

None of us are experts on how to be homosexual or heterosexual—but we are all experts on how to be ourselves. Most lesbians and gay men do not neatly fit into the stereotype of being gay. Many are "passing" daily as heterosexual—living by values that make them virtually indistinguishable from their neighbors, families, and co-workers. If we were all to tell the truth about ourselves—including our sexuality as one aspect of our identity—I believe a far different picture of homosexuality would emerge than the one that currently exists. This process would build upon itself:

- More visibility would lead to more accuracy about what it means to be gay.
- Replacing stereotypes with the truth will lead to more understanding, acceptance, and respect.
- More acceptance and respect will allow more diverse role models to come forth.
- Diversity of homosexual role models will encourage more expression of individuality.
- Greater expression of individuality will further broaden the spectrum of what it is to be gay.

In this book I am calling on all of us to be willing to come out further. I am calling on us to express ourselves more fully and be more willing to say who we are and what we value. If you are homosexual and "pass" as heterosexual, I am asking that you disclose your homosexuality and realize that by hiding your sexual orientation you have contributed to the prevailing stereotypes of what it is to be gay and can make a major contribution in changing those stereotypes. If you are heterosexual and know and love someone who is gay, I am asking that you come out as well. You too have supported oppression by not stating that you have a son, daughter, mother, father, cousin, friend, or acquaintance who you care about and who is gay.

This book is a call to action!! I call on you to take your next step in your own coming-out process. I call on you to help clarify what it really means to be gay. I call on us collectively to create a society in which it is safe to be a lesbian or a gay man and safe not to hide who we are. I call on us to create a world in which diversity and difference are celebrated—not ridiculed. I call on us to simply tell the truth and be willing to stand up for the truth rather than perpetuate stereotypes, myths, and lies.

Nicholas, to His Mother

Dear Mom,

I begin my twenty-seventh year on the planet tomorrow, and life gets more fascinating and rewarding by the moment. I believe that I have learned more this past year than any other, and I must say, I am happier and healthier than ever.

Growing up has been a complex, joyful, and ongoing process, and I know now that I will always be growing, learning, changing, and meeting new challenges.

I want to express my love and appreciation to you for all you have done for me over a quarter of a century. I know that I have been self-absorbed almost all of my life and that I haven't taken the time to recognize fully the countless people, everyone I have known, but especially you, for helping to give me the tools of growth and survival coming from the seeds of your love.

The reason that I am more fully able to acknowledge and appreciate and love you is because I can now see that I love my Self, that I am a beautiful human being, and that I am worthy of loving and being loved.

I am glad to realize that my most powerful connection with anyone on the planet is with my Self, and I am glad to share this with you, because, next to my Self, you are the person that I am most powerfully connected with.

I believe that you and I are a lot alike, and frankly, I am proud of that fact. You have survived some very painful struggles in your life, learned some (many) things and today you are thriving.

Although many of my learning experiences have been different from yours, they have been the same at the basic level—learning to find and love our Selves in the confusion of our lives, learning to face the challenges and stand up for truth.

I know that I have learned a lot from you for which I am grateful.

You taught me to be independent (I'm still learning), to be compassionate toward other people, to be a great conversationalist, a diplomat, and so much more! I hope that you realize that all of the qualities that you like in me are also qualities that you possess.

Something that you and I have dealt with, to different degrees on some levels and to the same degree on others, is my gayness.

Even though my gayness has been a major issue at times, the reality is that my gayness is just a layer of who I am. On one level, I have been dealing with my Self as a gay man, but I'm not just gay, I'm a human being. My gayness has been a powerful catalyst for me to become a person of much greater love, truth, and integrity. I have learned to take responsibility for who I am, the good and the areas where I want to grow. My increasing responsibility in all areas of my life is proof to me of the value of purity of heart on levels of love and integrity.

The difficulties that I have experienced, I have experienced because I had not accepted responsibility for my Self. I know now that one of the reasons I have stayed in a pattern of financial dependence, until recently, is because that is the way I was able to illicit validation from you—love from you. That was a way that I could somehow keep you involved in my life.

I have seen what has happened in my life by denying truth, by denying reality, and I'm not going to do that anymore. I love you, and I'm going to keep expressing that love, and I'm going to continue to stand up for who I am. I know that you love me very much—I know this now more than ever.

Love,
Nicholas

TELLING THE TRUTH: THE FIRST STEP IN COMING OUT

Telling the truth is the first step in coming out. It is also the first step in liberating yourself to be a whole, complete, and powerful adult—the authority figure in your own life. Withholding the truth from others, as well as from yourself, generally leads to depression and feelings of powerlessness. Often someone is not being truthful because of fear of being unable to cope with the consequences of the truth. They are afraid of others' reactions and of their ability to function effectively in the face of these reactions. Withholding the truth tends to be self-perpetuating, since once a false image is created there is then the added fear of what might happen if that falsehood is exposed.

It is common for people to believe that in order to tell the truth they must trust the person (or people) to whom they are telling it. However, it is far more important to trust yourself. Telling the truth is difficult, if not impossible, if you do not trust yourself to cope effectively with the consequences of the truth. *It is not someone else's reaction and response you must trust, it is yourself.*

> *I do not want to get stuck in the why's of who I am . . . nor do I want you to. Be it genetic or learned behavior for whatever set of reasons or circumstances, I am who I am. There is no fault or blame. It simply is. And the most important consideration is acceptance and dealing with that truth.*
>
> —Bud, to his father; p. 108

If you have not been truthful in the past, or are not being truthful now, this probably stems from a decision you made early in your life that you would be safer not being truthful. Through my work in The Experience I have seen many people re-experience early decisions—decisions made as an adolescent, or as a four-, five- or six-year-old (and sometimes even earlier)—not to be truthful and open. Usually such decisions are not conscious ones at the times they are made, though they tend to be reinforced over the years by incidents where telling the truth hurt someone else or oneself.

You may recall particular incidents in your life when you decided that it was best not to tell the truth. Such a decision probably seemed like a good idea at the time, and may even have felt essential in order for you to survive. At the end of this chapter, I have included an exercise that will allow you to observe decisions you have made that may have had an impact on how you handle yourself today. It is important to notice whether the decision not to tell the truth is working well for you now. If you decide that it is not and that you want to be more truthful, make a decision now to trust yourself. Your willingness to tell the truth rests on this fundamental decision.

Gale, to Her Parents

Dear Mom and Dad,

I first knew I was gay when I was twelve years old. I used to look in psychology books in the library about the subject of homosexuality. I was intrigued about it and thought my secret made me different. I withheld that from you. I knew it would make you angry and you would make my life miserable for me. In my twelve-year-old mind I locked that part of me from you for fourteen years. It was my secret and it made me different and I clammed up so no one could know me that way. The burden I carried—silence and fear of ridicule.

Kathy and Marcie used to spend the night when I was twelve. I had such a crush on Kathy. She was the first girl I ever had physical contact with. Sometimes she would lay on top of me. She would act like she didn't know what she was doing. I pretended that I didn't know either. I made a colored picture sign that said "I love Kathy" and I showed it to her and she reacted like there was something wrong with me.

Linda used to like me. She and I cut out pictures of women from magazines and showed each other our collection. I didn't have access to *Playboy* or anything like that. I would go into old issues of *National Geographic* and cut out pictures of African and Polynesian women showing their bare breasts. At that age (twelve) I felt lustful toward girls. Boys interested me only in a social way because that was expected of me.

When I was fourteen, I started going steady with boys and I joined Girl Scouts that year. Bigger girls aged fifteen to eighteen were around there. What a paradise and such a quiet, unassuming secret I carried with me—the casual touching with the girls . . . the way Cheryl would put her arm around me (of course she liked boys but I'm sure she was attracted to me). It was fun to go to the Girl Scout dances. I used to fantasize about being with Penny. She was very attractive to me. I would fantasize that I was a boy and then she would really like me. It was paradise at Girl Scout camp outs. I would have romantic fantasies as we lay together in our sleeping bags at night. You never knew, Mom and Dad, and I didn't feel it was your right to know because you could only see how BAD I was and I would need professional help.

Seventeen years old—I discovered the *Free Press* newspaper. There were ads in there about gay women wanting to meet other gay women. I wrote to one. She was twenty-three years old and I told you, Mother, that I met her through *Teen Magazine*. This was to be the first of an endless list of lies to cover up my gayness.

The gay woman came to our house when I was seventeen. I was very nervous about it. I made sure she would arrive sometime when you took my brother to Junior Achievement, Mother. But, Mother, you thought there was something funny going on so you stayed on a little longer. And the gay woman was introduced to you. She wasn't at all the way my friends usually looked—she was older, and big, and wore some kind of leather jacket. She visited with me in my room and I was shocked at her language. And I did not see her again for some years after—about five years later I had a brief affair with her.

I had my first sexual experience with a woman when I was nineteen years old. Her name was Gail, and I met her through the *Free Press* and had been corresponding with her for a while. Never in my entire life was I so totally turned on to someone. I was having these tremendous orgasms and she was just sitting next to me. I loved going to bed with her. She was small and delicate and soft. I knew that I was gay and women were what I wanted.

Since then I've been in several relationships—some of whom you've guessed about and some of whom you've never known about. That's where all my lies to you came from—places I went and who I was with.

Now I'm in a permanent relationship with Roberta. She is my family. I love her totally and I will be with her in this relationship forever. We are married in all senses of the word. You will need to accept it and the only thing you can do is accept it because it is the TRUTH.

I love you,
Gale

Many people function in adult bodies, living much of their lives based on decisions made in childhood or adolescence. Even though you might not be consciously willing to let an adolescent or child control your life today, as long as your early decisions go unexamined it amounts to the same thing. If you repeat patterns of behavior that are not constructive, it may be because you haven't re-examined decisions that you made early in your life. Most of us have a major investment in the rightness of the decisions we have made over the years. We seek evidence to validate that we were right in making those decision, so they often seem as if they are rational today. However, *your "right" decisions may now be holding you back.* You may be defending some non-productive decisions by piling on more and more reasons to justify what you did in the past, and how you are living now.

If you are using such a strategy, examine it. If you spend a lot of time wishing your life was different, you can begin to make it different today.

Anne, to Her Parents

Dear Mom and Dad,

I have many things that have gone unsaid for too long that I find I need to say to you now. This summer when Mom sent me clippings of clothes I realized something— that neither of you know who I am. That realization has been strengthened recently by some work that I am doing. What I know is that you don't know me because I don't show you who I am. I don't share with you the fullness of my experience.

I came out to you ten years ago. Formally, I mean.
I said, "I am a lesbian." You didn't want to hear it then
and I suspect you don't now either. Nonetheless, that is who
I am, or rather part of who I am. I am not my sexual
orientation, just as you are not yours. I am the sum total
of all my experience and personality. Being lesbian was
not a choice, no more so than your heterosexuality. It is
who I am, it is my sexual orientation. I use orientation
because that is what it is. It is not my preference—preference
implies choice. My sexuality is not by choice, it just is.

I realize that you are shut out of a large part of
my life. I realize I have acted out of rebellion and anger
at your lack of understanding of who I am. But how could
you know when I didn't show you? Rather, I have re-
belled, taken extreme stances to prove to you that I am not
what you want me to be.

My purpose in writing is to clean up some things and
to really "come out" to you in totality of who I am. Yes,
you know I am a lesbian but you don't know me and I don't
want to hide any longer.

Being a lesbian is a fundamental part of who I am
and how I interact in the world. It's interesting to me how
much I hide from you, from your friends, and our family—
not because I have anything to hide but because you do.
I am a very out person in my life. I was out at law school.
I helped found the Lesbian/Gay Legal Society, an organization I am very proud of. I am out to friends—gay and
straight. I'm out to doctors, my dentist, and vet. I'm out
to the people I work with. I'm out to almost everybody,
except my extended family.

I was a member of the board of directors of the Lesbian Resource Center for one and a half years. I strived
to make it a better organization and believe I did an excellent job. Dad, you may get your wish about me going into
politics soon—probably not in the way you envisioned, but
it is a way that I feel proud and positive about. I am being
considered to be appointed by the mayor of Seattle to the
mayor's lesbian/gay task force. It is a volunteer position.
The task force advises the mayor and city council of the con-

cerns of the gay/lesbian community, makes proposals, and implements programs. As you can see, I am a vocal, visible lesbian seeking to better her community.

I am a happy person. I have a wonderful partner in Carla. I love her very much and look forward to going through life with her. Perhaps one day we will have children and if we do, I hope that they will know their grandparents and that Carla and I will instill in them many of the things you taught me—confidence, the desire to succeed, good manners, compassion, gentleness, love, respect, and honesty.

Honesty is something I've been thinking a lot about. What I remember growing up, and even today, was/is mixed messages about honesty. I was told to be honest yet was also raised with a Scandinavian ethic that teaches us not to share our feelings. I was told not to feel what I was feeling as an adolescent so as not to get Dad angry or whatever with me. Since I came out, I've been told to be honest, but not about my lesbianism.

What I have decided is to be truthful, it's the only way I can be. For example, the past two to three months have been very difficult for me with this job search and money situation. I float in and out of depression. But I have started to tell the truth. If I'm fine I say so, if I'm not I say so. Either way it's OK.

So what does that have to do with this letter? I can't lie anymore. It takes too much energy to edit out the things that I think you may not want to hear or have family/friends hear. Plus, I'm lying. That is a stance I can no longer take. This is not to say that I don't understand your concerns and fears. I love and support you in your process of letting go of your fears or of holding on to them. I will no longer be a part of your being able to foster them. I've been lying for a long time for you—and for me. For me out of the fear of losing your love and respect, your support period, you period. What I realize now, though, is that I was losing myself by being dishonest and I was enabling you to stay in your fear and denial.

I may lose your love and support by being out, but I

will have my self-respect and I will always have the qualities I have learned from you. I am a considerate, caring,
gentle woman. I am concerned for the people and planet
around me. I am generous, giving, and successful—I make
a difference in the world and in the lives of the people I
know. I have humor and laughter. I can build a house, cook
a meal, and argue a case. I take risks because I've seen
you do so.

I want to share with you the totality of who I am. In
that way I am being truthful and allowing myself to know
you better as you get to know me better. I think as I let
myself be me around you, that you'll find someone who
is less extreme than I have sometimes been with you. It's
like I've been trying so hard to prove that I'm not heterosexual, I'm never going to be Jane Pauley, I don't like
make-up or dresses, etc. . . . that you haven't seen the
person who is soft, gentle, funny, playful, both masculine
and feminine, tough and sweet. I am all of that and more.

With much love,

Anne

*Invest in a vision of who you can be rather than
reinvesting in who you were in the past.* Create a clear vision
of who you are now, and who you will become, and tell the
truth about it. When you tell the truth, some of the consequences will be positive and some may be negative. Not
everyone will like the truth. Trust yourself to effectively
handle all the consequences. This will involve taking some
risks. Usually, we play it safe, maintaining things as they
are. But when things remain the same they often seem to
get worse and worse. Taking risks is part of what makes life
interesting and generally leads to personal growth.

*These three sons of ours are the greatest reward I
have in life, and I no longer feel I should lie to them. Our
sons should have the opportunity to understand and
share their love with their father for what he is as a person, and not a living lie.*

Paul, to his former wife; p. 166

EXERCISE: BECOMING AWARE
OF YOUR EARLY DECISIONS

This exercise is intended to give you the opportunity to bring to consciousness decisions you made about yourself and your relationships early in your life. Pay particular attention to those decisions about trusting yourself and others. Many of those decisions were made instantaneously as a result of one or more incidents in your life as a child or adolescent. They were often made unconsciously, and you may still be functioning today based on some of those spontaneous and unconscious decisions.

The first step in releasing yourself from those decisions is to become aware of them. Then you can observe how they are operating in your life today and whether they are appropriate for you now. If you are letting some of your early decisions play a role in your life, you then have a choice as to what role you will let them play from this time forth.

If you notice some of your decisions are inappropriate for you today you can choose to inhibit them—to not base your actions on them in the present and future. Since you are likely to be comfortable functioning out of your old decisions, they may resurface frequently. It is helpful to know that this is very common, but also that you can—at each moment—choose to inhibit them.

You may notice some of the decisions you made in the past are so comfortable to you now that they keep reappearing, even if they are not in your best interest at this time. In order to re-examine these decisions you must be aware of what they are and of when and why they were made.

Give yourself a period of time, perhaps as much as an hour or more, to be by yourself in a quiet setting and review your life as a child and an adolescent. I will provide some specific suggestions as to what to look for, and it is your choice as to how deeply and specifically you will examine your own life. Give yourself permission to observe closely those things you may have wanted to forget and allow yourself to experience any feelings and emotions that may be present. After you have completed your self-examination, you will probably find it helpful to write down your main observations. If you like visualizing, you might read over this exercise and then give yourself some time to close your eyes, take a few deep breaths into the center of your chest, and relax deeply. You may observe your life in a meditative mode. You may even choose to play some soft music in the background. There is also an audiotape available (see p. 274), *Living Powerfully—Releasing the Past,* if you prefer to do a guided visualization on this theme.

Remember yourself as you were as a child. Get as clear a picture as you can of the "little you." See if you can recall how little you felt, including that child's emotions. When you get a clear sense of little you review little you's life incident by incident, making observations about the following questions:

- What did the world look like to little you?
- Did the world look safe?
- Who were the most significant people in little you's life?
- How did little you feel with them?
- Did little you feel safe with them?
- Did little you feel supported by them?
- Did little you feel nurtured by them?
- Did little you feel loved by them?
- Did little you trust them?
- Did little you feel trusted by them?
- How did they treat little you?
- What kind of things did they tell little you about himself or herself?
- How did they express emotions to little you?
- What did they express to little you?
- How did little you feel about them?

- How did little you treat them?
- Was there anything little you wanted to express that little you was afraid of expressing?

Once you have examined the life of little you, observe any decisions little you made as a result of his or her interactions with these significant people.

- What decisions did little you make about relating to others?
- What did little you decide about accepting support?
- What did little you decide about trusting others?
- What did little you decide about being trustworthy?
- What did little you decide about trusting himself or herself?
- What did little you decide about the wisdom and safety of expressing his or her feelings?
- What did little you decide about being lovable?
- What did little you decide about being worthwhile?
- Did little you decide there was anything he or she had to do, or be, or say in order to be worthy of love?
- What did little you decide about telling the truth?

After you've made all the observations you can about little you's life, take some time to write down what you observed, especially the decisions that little you made about being able to trust himself or herself to tell the truth in relationships and to deal with the consequences of telling the truth.

Now let yourself relax again. Remember yourself as you were as an adolescent. Get as clear a picture as you can of the "adolescent you." See if you can recall how you felt, including that adolescent's emotions. When you get a clear sense of adolescent you, review adolescent you's life incident by incident. Then allow yourself to make observations about the following questions:

- What did the world look like to adolescent you?
- Did the world look safe to adolescent you?
- Who were the most significant people in adolescent you's life?
- How did adolescent you feel about them?
- Did adolescent you feel safe with them?
- Did adolescent you feel supported by them?
- Did adolescent you feel nurtured by them?
- Did adolescent you feel loved by them?
- Did adolescent you trust them?
- Did adolescent you feel trusted by them?
- How did they treat adolescent you?
- What kind of things did they tell adolescent you about himself or herself?
- How did they express emotions to adolescent you?
- What did they express to adolescent you?
- How did adolescent you feel about them?
- How did adolescent you treat them?
- Was there anything adolescent you wanted to express that adolescent you was afraid of expressing?

Once you have examined the life of adolescent you, observe any decisions adolescent you made as a result of his or her interactions with these significant people.

- What decisions did adolescent you make about relating to others?
- What did adolescent you decide about accepting support?
- What did adolescent you decide about trusting others?
- What did adolescent you decide about being trustworthy?

- What did adolescent you decide about trusting himself or herself?
- What did adolescent you decide about the wisdom and safety of expressing his or her feelings?
- What did adolescent you decide about being lovable?
- What did adolescent you decide about being worthwhile?
- Did adolescent you decide there was anything he or she had to do, or be, or say in order to be worthy of love?
- What did adolescent you decide about telling the truth?

Observe the life of adolescent you and the decisions that adolescent you made. After you've made all the observations you can about adolescent you's life, take some time to write down what you observed, especially the decisions that adolescent you made about being able to trust himself or herself to tell the truth in relationships and to deal with the consequences of telling the truth.

Now let yourself relax again and examine your life and relationships as they are now. Notice both the similarities and differences that might exist between the way you are today and the child and adolescent you just observed.

- How do you feel today about relating to others?
- How do you feel today about accepting support?
- How do you feel today about trusting others?
- How do you feel today about being trustworthy?
- How do you feel today about the wisdom and safety of expressing your feelings?
- How do you feel today about being lovable?
- How do you feel today about being worthwhile?
- Do you feel that there is anything you have to do, or be, or say in order to be worthy of love?

- How do you feel today about telling the truth?
- Do any of the decisions made by little you or adolescent you play a role in your life today?

Once you've completed your observations, write down any of the ways in which little you or adolescent you, and the decisions that they made, play a role in your life and relationships today.

Now you are in a position to examine the decisions you have been functioning out of and to notice which ones support you in being a happy, satisfied, and powerful adult and which ones do not. If you want to function more powerfully, stop yourself from acting out of those decisions that do not support you. Simultaneously, make some new decisions that are appropriate to your life today which will redirect you in creating your future.

If you have been letting your child or adolescent self control parts of your life, it is not constructive to spend additional time punishing yourself for this, or punishing them. Simply recognize it and move on. You may even notice that you can acknowledge and love your child and adolescent selves. Each decision they made seemed like a good idea at the time. Each was made to protect you from perceived pain. The real issue is whether or not it is still appropriate to operate out of those decisions.

Andrew, to His Mother

Dear Mom,

Many years ago you asked me a very important question —I think it was in 1970 when I first moved out of Loomis Road to a very small room on Farwell in Milwaukee.

You had followed me around the house looking very grim, on the verge of tears—somehow I knew what you were going to ask, and it frightened me. I was half moved out and it was a terribly impractical time for a confrontation.

You said you had something to ask me but you were afraid to ask; you asked me if I was *"becoming a homosexual."* I must have turned white as the proverbial sheet, and I answered with only a small piece of the truth—*"no* (I'm not *becoming* a homosexual), what in the world makes you ask?" It was a terrible "cop out," a withheld communication that's been bothering me for at least *nine years*!!

For nine years of my life I've been dishonest with you—and punished myself for it—and punished you because I perceived that you had caused me the pain that came with the dishonesty—the distance—not sharing something so central and essential (and precious!) in my life. Feeling I had to keep this "terrible secret" brought up a lot of real anger against you—a logical sort of process, like a chemical equation—

> You think gay is evil
> You made me gay
> You told me gay is evil
> You told me I am evil

Well I'm *NOT evil*!!! I am gay, and while you deserve a lot of the blame/credit for what I am—you don't deserve 100 percent of it. I don't *really* know *why* I'm gay—I expect it is a combination of a lot of factors, among which is your upbringing of me. After all, until I went to UWM you were my whole life! I didn't have friends in high school or before. Children of your friends don't count.

I wish I could believe that you could get the message I'm trying to convey! *I love you*—very much. I want you to love me unconditionally—no matter what I do or what I am—I am your son—neither of us can change that even if we wanted to. I don't want to change that.

I went through hell—*hell*—when I "came out" (acknowledged my being gay). You had a lot to do with the pain. I had to come to the realization that I was a composite of all you had told me was evil—or at least, I was all those nasty men you warned me against.

Don't you remember when I was going to Sacred Heart School and innocently asked you what I had to fear from talking to strangers, you said they would "put a stick in my 'poopa,' " my rectum. I remember that I could not figure out why anyone would do something so strange! I didn't really fear it because it was just *too* weird for anyone to really do that to me. Why would some man take a twig off a tree and put it in my rectum?

Of course now I know what you were talking about. You believe(d) that absurd myth that gay men are child molesters—and so there was danger of some man raping me. I know you meant it out of love—you cared about my safety and so wanted to protect me.

You cannot imagine the impact that and other comments I may not remember quite so vividly had on my entire twenty-nine years of living.

With that and other methods of communication you made it infinitely clear that being a homosexual was about the *worst* possible thing that could be part of my life—in your opinion.

Having that bit of motherly "wisdom" planted in my brain—can you possibly imagine what I felt when I finally acknowledged that I am gay and had been as far back as I could remember?

Well, I felt horrible! I thought I was the most loathsome creature on earth and deserved to die. I spent a lot of energy trying to think of a way to commit suicide. A way that would be sure, painless, and save you grief and embarrassment. (God forbid my pain and death should embarrass you!) I wanted to die! You had given me the tools to hate myself enough that I was going to kill myself for you and to end my anguish.

When I think of all the time and energy I spent wanting to hate you—hating this supposed curse of being gay— what a waste of a life. Did you make love to Dad, conceive me, give me life, and mold that life for twenty years just for me to end it? I'm sure you didn't.

I want you to love *me*. I want you to love me as I am and always will be—what you like, and what you don't like too. How can you love me if you don't know *me*?

Do you have any idea how much pain you mothers

bring into the lives of your children by planting the concept that being gay is something awful—rather than something
normal and good—as good as my brown hair, my blue eyes,
or being right-handed! Can you conceive of the pain of
thinking your own mother could not love you if she really
knew you!

I love you—but I hate the pain you gave me—the
wasted years, the opportunities passed up because I thought
it was part of my life to fail—that it was part and parcel of
being gay to have a mediocre life at best.

Please understand if you can—that I have no more
choice about being gay than about any of the other attributes
I mentioned earlier—I am gay, I am a good, loving man and
I want you to know me and to love me.

I will always love you.

Your son,
Andrew

Mickey, to His Family

Dearest Family,

For the last two days I have sat in a consciousness-
raising group of men and women and shared with them,
and they with me, sorrows, trials, joys, lies, truths—all the
small and large things that make us unique . . . that make
us human. It has felt so rewarding, so gratifying, so cleans-
ing to tell it how it is, open all doors, open that which is
truly me and to be totally committed to being honest!

As I have sat here I have heard horror stories of childhood and parenthood that just bewilder me, and hurt me,
because of the cruelty involved. Locked doors, slapped faces,
divorce! Through it all your faces were right there with me.

I felt my Daddy standing next to me, caring, strong,
resolute, proud. I saw him and his birds, pounding two
walnuts together to call Halfshot. I saw him talking to me
of building my world, help better the existing world. My
Dad, in a coffin of wood on a clear, balmy December day.

I have memories of childhood, adolescence, manhood. Memories . . . memories . . . memories.

I see my mother always compassionate, always strong, always an answer. My mother, Sunshine Lady, prisms dancing on a Blue Ridge floor. I see my, our, mother unswerving in devotion, my biggest fan, reveling in the name of Grandmother. Memories of a cut finger, 4-H, plays, Cub Scouts, Easter eggs, reupholstering chairs, memories, memories, memories.

I see my sister always vulnerable and trying, though five foot two, always to be six foot tall and succeeding. I see her bearing children, fighting to survive. I see her suffering, always emotional, caring, selfish as hell, greedy as hell, giving as hell, sharing as hell! Love is my sister . . . like the rose . . . like her name.

LUCKY LADY, LONELY LADY
SEEING LADY, BLIND LADY
MEMORIES . . . MEMORIES . . . MEMORIES.

I see my brother, redheaded, skinny, stubbed, crushed fingers, cocksman, child lover, male chauvinist pig, wicked, bewildered, lost and shut away, redeemed, Gale, Matthew and dear, dear Chris. His little boy, his junior, one of our dad's truest memories. Dad's funeral—Mom and "Spark" —the true and noble.

I see dear Charles, my other brother. Bull-headed, red-necked, bigot, religious zealot, compassionate, loving, lonely, hard worker, wanting to succeed, powerful, handsome, hurting, self-possessed, Debbie, "Chipper" Patty, church, beloved Jesus, Bible, trying, trying, trying.

I think on all the people we have known (a man cries like a wounded animal in the background even as I write), all the pets we have loved, all the spring days and winter nights of little children, growing, growing.

BAD DAYS, SAD NIGHTS, RAINBOW DAYS,
RAINBOW NIGHTS

I see how I have hurt, how I have loved, how I have ignored, and forgotten you. I see my vast sense of selfishness and I am ashamed. My vast dishonesty flies home to me.

Perhaps your individual faiths, beliefs, dreams, ha-
treds, won't allow me to tell you of that which is me! My
hand shakes and falters even now and my usual good grasp
of words is stifled for fear, for being afraid that you will
consider me second class, low rent, or wanting me to get
out of your lives.

Simply, I am gay, a homosexual. I know, Mother,
that you and Rosemary, and perhaps all of you, have known
for a long time and yet you kept silent out of what I hope
was not disgust, or fear, but out of your respect for my
privacy.

I am not ashamed of being gay, but society has de-
clared us misfits, sick, abnormal, perverted, purveyors of
little children.

TO HELL WITH THAT!!!

I am not abnormal, or perverted but simply a man
who desires to love another man.

True, now you can say how did this happen? What
did I do wrong? But those questions are, to me, the true
perversity, the real misfits, the true sickness.

Realize, I am a grown man, who works, eats, goes
to the bathroom, makes love, buys, sells, cares, loves gets
hurt and smiles just like you. I AM NO DIFFERENT!!!

I hope not to get negative feelings from what I have
written to you, and would hope that you will never fear
to bring my wonderful little nephews and nieces to me.

The simple truth behind all of this is that I simply
wanted to tell you that I love you all and to let you know,
exactly, what is really me.

> *Much love,*
> Mickey

Mickey was a beautiful and loving human being, and my
friend. After completing the workshop, he joined the staff
of The Advocate Experience. He died of AIDS in 1983, and
I miss him.

3

THE COMING-OUT PROCESS

Coming out is a process and not a singular event. The expression coming out is frequently used to refer to one's first same-sex experience, yet coming out is much more than that one experience. Coming out begins with a very personal inner core of thoughts, feelings, and impressions. It progresses through a private sharing of those personal aspects of one's life and may ultimately lead to a public phase where one is open and free to be exactly who she or he is.

Progress through these phases is not linear, but cumulative. In the private phase, where a person shares who they are with others, there are still personal issues to deal with. Even in the public phase, where someone is open and free about who they are, there are still both private and personal issues to deal with.

To draw from my own experience, I am very public

40

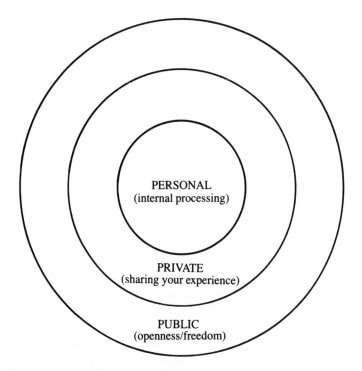

PERSONAL
(internal processing)

PRIVATE
(sharing your experience)

PUBLIC
(openness/freedom)

about my sexuality. Not only do I share freely this information with others, but I also have been quoted often in the press and frequently am heard on radio and appear on television as an openly gay man. Nevertheless, each time I sit next to someone on an airplane, or talk to someone at a gym who does not know who I am, I come out privately with that person through sharing who I am and what I do professionally. Furthermore, each time I share myself with someone new I have a personal experience. Sometimes I experience a moment of concern or apprehension as to how a person might react. Other times I may start to hold myself back, and feel myself creating distance. No matter how public I am about my sexuality, I still continue to have personal reactions to sharing myself with others. Even the process of putting myself further out in the public through this book generated personal resistance for many years. I had to become more comfortable with myself and with my ability to accept other persons' reactions to me in an open way, before I allowed myself to write this book.

Regardless of whether the issue you are coming out about is your sexuality or some other secret you have been carrying around with you, the process is basically the same. It is a process of becoming comfortable with yourself and sharing yourself freely with others.

PERSONAL PHASE

As long as the decision is to hide yourself, not acknowledging who you really are to another living being, and possibly not even to yourself, you remain in the personal phase. This is the least conscious phase of the coming-out process and is often quite a long one, frequently taking years. The personal phase is the one in which you are coming to grips with who you are, how you feel about that, and what you are going to do about it.

The personal phase may be painful and involve hiding and denial. Because your self-esteem is negatively affected, you can feel depressed and powerless. You may also feel self-pity, regret, shame, grief, sadness, self-abasement, hopelessness, unworthiness, embarrassment, numbness, fear, despair, terror, or resentment. You may feel angry with yourself or with others because of your perceived need to hide and your fear that you will not be accepted if you tell the truth. Your anger, however, is likely to be expressed in a covert manner, since you may fear that expressing it directly might generate a confrontation with another person and may lead to more self-disclosure than you are ready for. You might become cynical or sarcastic or distance yourself from others in some way (i.e., I'll reject them before they can reject me).

If you are gay, notice whether this has been a part of your experience. I suspect that it has. You might also notice how long you remained in the personal phase, or even if you are still functioning in that phase now. Whether you are homosexual or heterosexual, you might also take a moment to notice whether there is some other issue in your life that you have been in this personal phase about. For example: withholding the truth about being unhappy in a relationship, thinking about having an affair, having an affair, or being unhappy on your job. Notice what results are produced by not talking about your feelings. Do you feel powerless or powerful, restricted or free flowing, closed or open?

Usually when you are hiding something about yourself you approach life with an attitude of shame, condemnation, numbness, helplessness, weakness, loneliness, apprehension, dread, worry, humiliation, suspicion. You may tend to perceive the situations you are in as overwhelming, burdensome, and perhaps even as a trap or a threat.

It is common, when struggling with some aspect of life that you are not yet willing to share with others, to feel like a victim. On the other hand, you may be afraid that if you share yourself with others you will be in some way persecuting them or threatening to harm them. You may see yourself as wanting them to rescue you and make things better, or that you will have to take care of them if you open up to them and they are hurt by your disclosure.

> *After being bar mitzvah, I used to pray for forgiveness and hoped I could change, although I knew that it wasn't possible. . . . All I really wanted to do was to be what you wanted me to be.*
> —Richard, to his parents; p. 224

When you are functioning in this very personal and internal way, you don't trust yourself to open up because you fear that you aren't ready or capable of handling the consequences of your self-disclosure. While you are in the personal phase you may not feel ready to add more interpersonal dimensions to your life.

If for any reason you decide to face another person, to let someone else in, to add the interpersonal dimension, you enter the private phase of the coming-out process.

PRIVATE PHASE

It is often easier to tell people the truth when you don't have a great personal investment in their reaction. For this reason, the first people told "our secret" during the private phase are often not the people who are the most important to tell. You might, for example, talk more openly with a new friend or a casual acquaintance. You may seek out a professional counselor or therapist whom you pay in order to continue your personal exploration without fear of being rejected.

Feedback received from others is often used to determine whether it is safe to continue the coming-out process. When coming out as gay, the first discussion of this often takes place with someone who is also gay. For some, the first person with whom they have a same-sex encounter is also the first one they talk to about their homosexuality. How and what you choose to communicate in moving through the private phase will be a function of how much you have worked through your own feelings and this will affect how others react to you. (This will be discussed more thoroughly in Chapters 10, 11, and 12.)

If the first responses you receive are negative, or the manner in which you deal with them is negative and produces painful results, you may stop the progression of coming out. You may use such experiences as validation that you ought to keep to yourself.

When the initial responses you receive are positive, or you perceive them in a manner that allows you to grow and expand, you are likely to continue moving through the private phase of coming out.

As you continue to tell the truth to more and more people, moving in the direction of becoming more public, you eventually get to those people in your life with whom you have the greatest personal investment. These are the people whose love, respect, or support you are the most concerned about maintaining and the most scared of losing. Most of the time these are co-workers, employers or employees, old friends and parents. Parents are usually among the last to be told.

> *Dad and Mom, I know of no other way to be than just as I am. Yes, in your eyes, I am different. I want you both to know that I am different and yet very much like anyone else. I am gay and I am very, very happy. If I had to do it all over again, I would choose to be who I am now. . . . It has not always been easy being gay and hiding, lying to you, pretending I was not what I am.*
>
> —Jim, to his parents; p. 98

Several other people are generally told before parents, since most often there is concern about "hurting" Mom and Dad, or fear that they will reject us. The decision made in childhood that survival depends on their acceptance and support often gets in the way of being fully truthful with them.

Until you trust yourself to stand on your own, it may be very scary to run the risk of alienating your parents, regardless of how old you are. Because so many people are afraid of losing their parents' love, it is not uncommon for lesbians and gay men to live their lives distant and apart from their natural family rather than risk being discovered. Whatever the reasons one gives for not being more truthful with one's parents, not coming out is virtually always based on a fundamental personal belief that it is not all right to be gay. Lesbians and gay men, unwilling to tell someone else because they believe the other person won't accept their homosexuality, generally don't really feel good about it themselves.

If you feel good about who you are, you will present your sexuality as just a part of yourself. When you feel good about yourself, and have told those most important in your life that you are gay (or shared whatever the personal withheld communication is for you), you are able to move into the public phase of the coming-out process.

PUBLIC PHASE

The public phase equates with freedom and liberation. Your sexuality is integrated into your daily life and into who you are professionally, familially, and intellectually. This simply means that your sexuality is a part of who you are, and your sexual orientation is no longer something you have to hide. This does not mean that you have to take out an ad in a newspaper or appear on radio and television.

> *Until I was in college I denied my gayness, lied about it, was afraid of it, and in short did about everything but deal with it. I was making myself miserable with a double life by living one thing and feeling quite another. It has only been in the past two years that I have come to terms with who I am and how to live constructively and responsibly with that. I feel free, serene, content, and happy. I live one day at a time with as much responsibility, creativity, integrity, and honor as I can muster.*
>
> —Bud's reply; p. 107

Bud's experience is similar to any self-disclosure. If, for example, you haven't disclosed to anyone the fact that you are having an affair, when you move into and through the private phase your spouse is very likely going to be one of the last people you choose to tell. Once this is done, you can breathe more freely because others finding out does not have the same ramifications as it did previously. You are free to come to terms with this aspect of your life and determine how to live constructively and responsibly with it.

Even once you are in the public phase, there continue to be private disclosures and personal feelings. Every step you take toward being more public will produce personal reactions, and most of those steps involve some form of private self-disclosure. If you already feel good about yourself, that feeling is likely to be reinforced each time you come out to someone new.

The process of coming out and ways of taking your own next step will continue to be discussed throughout this book. Given the degree to which this process may have the potential to make you or others uncomfortable, you might be asking yourself: why come out in the first place? Although this is addressed in the next chapter, I suggest you take some time to pause here and answer this question for yourself. You may even choose to write down some of the personal benefits that would derive from moving through this process.

Dominick, to His Adult Children

Dear Kids,

This letter is about lies, lies of evasion and lies of omission. My entire life has been governed by these day-to-day lies, and I am so facile at telling them that I don't have to even think about them, so easily do they fall off my tongue. The other night at dinner I told you I was taking est this weekend in San Francisco, a lie of evasion. What I am taking is a seminar called The Advocate Experience. I would like to tell you about it. I first heard about it some months ago from a friend who took it, and I knew it was something I must do. But I didn't. Then recently another friend took it and told me about it and I knew again it was something I had to do. Instead of taking it in Los Angeles, which would have been easier, I came up here to do it, away from running into anyone I would know. It's an intensive for gay people to deal with being gay. Part of the program is writing to someone in your family to tell them that you are gay. What I have to tell you, my dear children, is that I am gay. What I want to say at the same time is that I love you all and am so proud of the way that you are living your budding adult lives. I hope that the love I know you have for me will help you to understand what I have to tell you, for the task of writing this letter is agonizing for me.

The fact of the matter is that I have always been gay, but the sense of shame that accompanied this knowledge was so great that I have never been able to deal with it. It has been like a giant cancer eating its way through my body for forty-five or so of my fifty-three years. I have never discussed it with any of my brothers and sisters, and certainly neither my mother nor father before they died. I have always felt that the reason my father hated me so much, as he was a reasonable man to others, was because he knew, even before I knew, what I was going to be. His way of dealing with it was to mock me in front of my brothers and sisters for being a sissy, imitating the way I spoke, the way I threw a ball, the way I gestured, filling me with shame for my very being. In order to escape this mockery that was so humiliating I started at a very early age the masterful cover-up that has ruled my life. My speech, my walk, my gestures, I changed so as to be like the other boys. Eventually I grew to accept this acquired identity and I became quite successful at living it. I even managed to convince myself that I was not what I was, that I was really like everybody else. It was the most important thing in my life to be like everyone else, so a few years after college, when all my friends were getting married, that's what I knew I had to do. And that's when I met your mother. She was getting off a train when I first saw her. She was so beautiful and so much fun and so glamorous, like a Fitzgerald heroine, and I fell in love with her and she with me and we became engaged. My family was ecstatic and so was I because here was proof positive that I was not what I was. And we got married, and you kids came, and I got successful and life was going to be happy ever after, but that's not the way it worked out. The guilt I feel toward your wonderful mother is too painful for me to write about except to say that I love her still and will always love her, but it's a different kind of love now than it once was.

The burden of living a double life finally became too great. First came impotence, then the development of a secret life that became dangerous and furtive, then the divorce that so devastated all of us. But still the cover-up continued. I can't go on with that cover-up any longer. I want you to know me as I am. However you decide to think about me, it's OK. I love you all.

Dad

4

WHY COME OUT?

There are many sound reasons for telling the truth about who you are, and the appropriate reason for you is likely to depend on what phase of the coming-out process you are in. You are not likely to move into the private phase if you are still uncertain about your own sexual identity or about how you feel about yourself. You're certainly not likely to move into the public phase if you are still threatened by the possibility of your family or co-workers finding out about you.

There are so many things about my life I want to share with you . . . but I withhold most of them from you because they are connected to my sexual orientation.
—Doug, to his parents; p. 178

While many of the reasons for coming out discussed in this chapter are personal ones, some are of a political nature and may seem detached from your life if you are still in the personal phase of the coming-out process. You're not likely to focus on making a contribution to society if you are dealing with your own survival or if you feel isolated and apart from others. If this is the case for you, coming out further, exploring who you are more actively and letting others in on it, will allow your energy to flow more freely. Until you have done this you are not likely to be ready to take a close look at the broader social picture.

It is difficult to do good things for yourself when you don't feel you are deserving. If you are hiding who you are it is unlikely that you will be able to develop meaningful intimate relationships, since you will always wonder whether these relationships will continue once the truth is known about you. It is also likely that the personal struggle you are going through will affect your physical health. It is very stressful, and we are more susceptible to disease when we are holding back parts of ourselves. Good health involves a natural and comfortable flow of energy through our bodies.

One of the surest ways to discover more about yourself, and your feelings, is to begin expressing what is true for you now. As you express those things that are most obvious—pain, fear, or even anger—you start to discover other feelings you perhaps never knew you had. It is a bit like standing in line at a salad bar where there is a stack of plates, and as you remove one another one pops up. So it is with our feelings. As we express the first one that is apparent to us, another, previously unseen one, begins to surface.

Rather than just sitting and thinking, meditating, or dwelling on your feelings, it can be helpful to express them verbally or in writing. Talking to yourself may seem rather strange, so I recommend writing down your feelings as they reveal themselves to you. You might do this in a journal, so that you can notice any changes that take place over time. It is probably going to be more helpful to express yourself to someone else so that you receive some direct feedback, but this requires you to share your feelings with another person and is the beginning of the private phase of coming out.

It is most valuable to express your feelings to those toward whom those feelings are directed. As you enter the private phase of coming out this may be too threatening, so it is helpful to identify someone you feel you can trust. The more isolated you have become the harder it will be to identify someone you trust, but there is always someone out there. If not, seek professional support, or talk to someone with whom you have very little invested emotionally.

Each step you take, no matter how small, will add to your personal growth and provide you with a broader base from which to grow. It may not seem necessary or desirable for you to be public. It may be, however, that you are not fully trusting yourself to open up to some important people in your life—perhaps co-workers, family members, or old friends who you think already know everything about you. You may be sure they've suspected for years, but if you haven't actually discussed this openly with them your relationship isn't of the quality that it could be.

When you don't openly discuss your sexual life-style with someone important in your life, you must constantly avoid discussing other things as well. For example, you may change the name of the person you spent the weekend with, not quite tell the truth about where you were on Saturday night, or even keep separate bedrooms in a long-term relationship in order to avoid a confrontation with others. If you are functioning like this you may say that it isn't important that they know, and besides, nothing will change. If it truly wasn't important, you would not spend so much energy withholding the truth. If you really felt nothing would change you would be comfortable being open and honest.

The rewards for being truthful are great and the self-respect and self-esteem that follows cannot be explained until you experience it for yourself. If you have already come out to a number of people, just notice the effect that this has had on you. Who do you want to spend the most time with, the people who know the truth or those who don't? The assets of coming out to someone important in your life are many:

- You can share more of yourself and your life with others.
- They have a greater opportunity to know you as you really are.
- You have more of an opportunity to validate your own life and your own life-style.
- You give the important people in your life a real opportunity to support you, and you become far more available to them as well.
- Love flows more easily between you and others because some of the barriers you've constructed in your relationships are removed.

Ken, to a Friend

Dear Bobbi,

I want to first thank you for being who you are. Since we first met, I have experienced you as a wonderful, alive, and open individual. We have had many incredible times, and I always enjoy being able to be there when you need to talk with someone about your children or your divorce and its impact on your life.

But, our experience of each other has been lacking because I have held back a part of myself that is very important to me. Remember all the times we would have an early breakfast before one of our meetings and exchange stories about the night before or I would tell you how much fun I had the past weekend with a young lady friend I had recently met.

Well, the first few stories may have been true because when we first met I was still seeing women. You were there whether you know it or not (and I suspect you do) when I experienced my personal coming out. The coming out I am referring to is my acceptance of the fact that I am gay. The stories I told you were true except you have to replace the *hers* with *hes* and the *shes* with *hims*. I told you how great my weekends were—they were!! They were great because I was able to express myself fully through touching, holding on, and loving sex with another man. That experience is truly beautiful for me. Our relationship the past few years has been distant, and I believe my lack of openness is the reason why.

You represent a lot of what I was told I was supposed to want by our mostly heterosexual society—a young beautiful woman, strong enough to rear healthy children and brave enough to go out in the world to experience your own feelings of individuality.

I know my gayness is not going to matter to you. I just had to share it with you so we can get on with a real experience of each other—an experience of awareness, sharing, and love.

Ken

It is because we often withhold the truth from our families that we may be uncomfortable around them and spend so little time with them. I have long felt that the reason there are gay ghettos or gay meccas is that many lesbians and gay men haven't yet come out to their families and are not comfortable in their hometowns. San Francisco, New York, Los Angeles, and other major metropolitan centers may be more exciting and fun than some areas of the country, yet they are also places where we can go to be anonymous. Most gay men and women I encounter have a desire for a deeper sense of family yet often feel estranged from their natural family. They usually don't notice that they have erected their own barriers to the very families and communities from which they come.

On the other hand, when we come out, what if those important people in our lives do what we most fear? What if they reject us, damn us, disown us, and don't continue to love us? This concern is based on our lack of trust in them or in the genuineness of our relationship with them. It is also based on a lack of trust in our own ability to survive such rejection.

If you are afraid that someone important will withdraw their love when they know more about you, do you feel genuinely loved by them in the first place? You might ask yourself the following questions:

- Is the cost of maintaining their love, as it is, worth it to you?
- Is their current love for you based on who you really are or based on their beliefs about who you are?
- How much have you contributed to their beliefs about you?
- How much have you had to manipulate in order to receive their love?
- How much energy has it taken to create a pretense about who you are?
- Do you really experience the quality of love you want and need from this person?
- What will happen if a crisis develops in your life where the truth comes out (if you contract AIDS, if you have an accident and your lover or gay friends show up at the hospital)? Will they still be there to support you?

If you are afraid of someone rejecting or disowning you, it is an indication that you don't really trust them or the quality of your relationship with them. It may be that they really can't be trusted. In my experience, however, when you let someone know the truth about yourself they usually are supportive. Sometimes this takes time, as it should, for they have their own process to go through as will be discussed in Chapter 7.

What happens if you were *right all along and your parents, friends, or co-workers do disown or reject you?*

While I know that this is a very real fear for many and may actually come to pass, if this happens it too can truly be a most liberating experience.

- You need no longer work to maintain a relationship with parents or friends that is based on a lie.
- You need no longer be struggling to work productively on a job where you were never really able to be comfortable.
- You are free to establish closer relationships with others who will genuinely be there for you.
- You are free to find a job where who you are is appreciated and you are likely to find yourself happier, warmer, more spontaneous, and more productive.

Every apparent loss in life can be used as an opportunity to learn, grow, and expand. Successful and powerful people already know this. As I hear from person after person, the rewards for confronting fears and moving beyond them are great, regardless of the outcome. People whose worst fears don't come to pass have miracles to share about how much better they feel and how much more comfortable they are in their lives. People whose worst fears do come to pass frequently are liberated by the discovery that they survived after all, and now they feel freer to create an affirmative life for themselves.

In a discussion about coming out at a conference in San Francisco, one of the participants told us that he had been married and had been a doctor with a thriving practice in a relatively small town. When he disclosed that he was homosexual he lost his wife and his practice. He was now building a life for himself in a new community, as an openly gay physician. It would have been easy to respond to the losses that he suffered and use those as evidence that he should not have come out in the first place. However, when I asked him if he would do it again he said, without the slightest hesitation, "Absolutely!" His growth and freedom far outweighed his losses.

When someone has had great apparent losses as a result of coming out, they may focus on these—partly for the sake of the drama it creates and the reactions of sympathy they get from others. The important question to ask is: If you could do it over, what would you do? Virtually every time I ask that question I discover that the person who came out would not go back into the closet if he or she had that option. The freedom that accompanies coming out, even when it involves losses and challenges, is worth it.

Of course, I want to be clear in stating that most of the time these losses are not present. Even people who feared imagined losses often discovered that there is far more support for them than they ever dreamed possible. A psychologist who was resisting coming out to his family because he has two young sons, lives in a small community, does family therapy, and was certain his family and his practice would suffer recently changed his mind and let his wife know he was gay. Concurrently, he also explained that he loved and respected her and that many of the communication problems that existed between them, as well as his sexual neglect, had little to do with her and were primarily the result of his hiding his homosexuality. To his surprise, she has become his best friend and strongest support. They are communicating better than ever and have established separate homes, within blocks of each other, so that they can accommodate both of their needs without creating great distance in the family.

John, to His Father

Dad,

Today I am sitting in a room filled with beautiful men like me who are gay. Prefacing this letter with that first sentence takes courage.

Our facilitator just related the story of when he came out to his father and all the pain and discomfort that it held for him. It evoked tears that haven't left me yet. I remembered my childhood and my experiences growing up with you and how different we were as people. I never knew why I was so different from you, but I was. My feelings of inadequacy were augmented by the fact that I didn't live up to most of your expectations of me. I had no interest in hunting, fishing, or sports. You were the opposite of me in so many ways.

As I grew older I began to realize that I loved boys in a way that was purely sexual. The more I saw myself as a "queer" the more I hated myself and truly believed that I was unworthy and disgusting. I hid my feelings from everyone for most of the rest of my life until most recently.

I feel like a child who is telling the truth to his parents for the first time in his life. This is the most painful thing I've ever done. I can't stop crying. Forty years of hiding from you and most everyone else is indeed painful.

I never believed I'd ever be doing this. I thought you'd go to the grave never knowing me. Now I don't want that. I want you to know who I am and what I am.

I am a loving man who loves men in a very natural way—natural for me and my gay brothers. Because I have held myself back all my life, I have not become a full person even as a gay man. My relationships with other gay men have been incomplete because of my feelings of inadequacy. Suffice it to say that my relationships with women have been even less complete. Why? Because I never felt whole with them. Living up to society's expectations of me has left me drained and unfulfilled.

I reached a point in my life this year that I was no longer going to be an incomplete person. I gave up everything I had to move to San Francisco in order to experience being gay in an environment where other people like me are searching out themselves for similar reasons. I'm scared and at the same time prepared to take any risks required to become the full person I so richly deserve to be.

The experience of this seminar has brought up all the pain and suffering I have witnessed for forty years. Right now I don't care if the whole world knows that I'm gay. I won't live in a vacuum any longer, afraid of being who I am or what I am. And I don't have to flaunt myself to be me either. No job, no position, no relationship, is worth the risk of losing myself, my dignity and self-worth.

Seven years ago when I ended my "marriage" to Verda, it was because of my being gay. Verda knew it and she accepted me totally. She supports and loves me as I do her today. The boys know I love men, and they accept it as natural in me. I wouldn't have it any other way with my family. However, disclosing this to you is not as easy. Why? Again because of the rejection that stems from my childhood experiences and the notion that you won't accept me as I am.

For forty years we have kept at a distance from one another just as if you already knew this about me. So what's the difference now? If the distance has to exist, let it be because I am leveling with you at last. At least now it's out in the open, and you can accept me or reject me legitimately.

I want you to know that I am a real person with all the love, warmth, and tenderness that anyone could possess. I want to share myself completely with others without being afraid of disclosing myself. It's taken me all my life to begin to accept myself as normal. Childhood was too painful for me anyway, notwithstanding being gay from infancy.

I knew I was different from the moment I could remember. With each passing moment of time I withdrew myself, hiding my feelings, terrified that someone might discover that I had pictures of men's bodies secreted away in the deepest, darkest corners of my bedroom. No one ever discovered me and my pictures. Today I'm still living in a world of pictures, and these pictures out of the past prevent me from getting close to other men like me. This is why I am here today. I want to rid myself of all the shit I've carried around for forty years. I'll take any necessary step available to unleash myself, to unlock the doors that have kept me entombed in the dark recesses of the closet.

I want out of the closet and into the world. I want to be proud of being gay. I am part of a new movement that is enabling all of us to experience ourselves as truly worthwhile, truly beautiful and truly natural people in a world that has too long rejected us. I feel the necessity to express myself as all of us do, so that the world will envision us as just plain, ordinary people just like you.

I love you, dad,
John

Most people consider their sexuality to be very personal, and believe that it should be neither a public nor a political issue, but being gay is a political issue whether we like it or not! Coming out isn't making homosexuality an issue—it already is. As long as we do not have full protection under the law, being gay is a political issue. As long as we can be discriminated against, being gay is a political issue. As long as we require attention and support from government health agencies, being gay is a political issue. As long as we require public agencies to engage in our health and welfare problems, being gay is a public and political issue.

If the AIDS epidemic hasn't been enough of a learning experience to teach people who are gay that they must take a stand for themselves, what will it take? The government was able to ignore AIDS, and politicians were able to distance themselves from AIDS, because it was primarily affecting groups (intravenous drug users and male homosexuals) isolated and/or alienated from the mainstream of society.

Homosexuals are not disliked because of who we are but because of the beliefs that people have about us. Most people don't think they know anyone gay, and that's because lesbians and gay men have been so good at hiding.

There are many stereotypes of gay men I am sure you have seen. Unfortunately, what is most widely publicized about homosexual behavior is not at all my ex-

perience. It is a part of the gay world, but certainly not all or even most of it. For me, being gay is simply a matter of loving someone of the same sex. I do not lisp or swish, or dress up like a woman, or molest children, nor do I have any leaning toward that extreme behavior.

—Bud's reply; p. 109

In reality, most people not only know someone gay, they actually love and respect someone who is gay. Unlike any other "minority group" in our culture, gays are everywhere. That's not just a slogan we made up—it's the truth. Gays are in most families, careers and businesses, schools and social groups. From the standpoint of changing society's attitudes toward homosexuality, then, let's look at the opportunity that coming out presents.

Everyone who is gay has heterosexuals in their immediate family. All lesbians and gay men have heterosexual co-workers and friends. If we are passing for straight we are allowing the existing stereotypes of what it is to be gay to continue and flourish. If we come out, openly and lovingly as who we are, we disabuse people of their stereotypic beliefs and lay the foundation for a broader view of what it means to be gay—and ultimately for a change in individual and societal attitudes, understanding, and acceptance. If homosexuals were out openly and publicly, major gains would be made on legal, health, and social issues. Gay men and lesbians are not out of the mainstream of society—they are hidden within the mainstream.

It is time to take responsibility for this situation. While there have always been many good reasons for coming out, I believe that there are even more reasons now— with an AIDS epidemic that has clearly been dealt with badly in large measure because of our own unwillingness to be open about who we are and to take a stand for ourselves.

I am pissed that your stupidity is helping to let my friends and lovers die!

—Michael, to his parents; p. 236

Each and every one of us (homosexual and heterosexual) is responsible for the way AIDS has been dealt with by society, as well as for the way homosexuality has been dealt with. If you are gay and passing for straight, you may be thinking how comfortable your life is and that you ought not to come out because it isn't safe or isn't necessary for you personally. While there will be personal gains to you that you may not see at the moment, you are also personally responsible for how homosexuality is perceived in your family, place of employment, religious institution, social organizations, community, and society. All of us together, you and I, can make it safe for each of us to be who we are.

Lesbians and gays are in many positions of power in the world. This is true in politics, economics, science, health, entertainment, and the media. Far too often, rather than being valuable role models that can effect social change, they cannot be counted on to support gay and AIDS-related issues. Paradoxically, these lesbians and gays may be so frightened of being public that they take stands to the detriment of their brothers and sisters and to society as a whole. It is unfortunate that we must often rely on heterosexuals, who are more secure about their positions, to be the ones to speak out for civil liberties and for adequate AIDS funding.

I realize that you may reject the entire notion of being more public. You may not feel that this is your issue. You may feel that we shouldn't "rock the boat." Having lost far more friends to AIDS than anyone should lose to illness in five lifetimes, I'd like to call your attention to the fact that this boat may be sinking.

Gays are not making greater strides because we are holding ourselves back. I am often angry and frustrated with lesbians and gay men who claim to feel good about themselves and still maintain a position that they shouldn't come out any further. Many of us have had, and continue to have, an investment in maintaining our privacy. We have worked hard to get what we have—why risk losing it? If you hold this opinion, I ask that you re-examine it in the light of what has happened during the past several years. Each of us has a major contribution to make—and the time is now.

I have a lover that I love more than anything in my life. I am proud of him and of my love for him, and of his love for me. I cannot . . . pretend this doesn't exist or feel ashamed of it.

—Gerardo, to his mother; p. 204

It is only when you move into the public phase of coming out that you can truly be free. Everyone has a role to play in shifting public consciousness. Never minimize the power that you personally have—you impact on everyone who knows you, cares about you, and loves you. All of us, individually and collectively, make a difference!

5

FEELING GOOD
ABOUT YOURSELF

While growing up it is rare that any of us—gay or straight—
get all of the love and attention we want or need. People
grow up, have their own families, and are usually ill equipped
to share love freely with their children or even with their
mates.

I never gave a lot of thought to the fact that maybe
you don't think or feel the same as I do, or maybe you
do not have the same resources and experiences to rely
on. Looking at the whole picture, you were not as fortu-
nate as I was. I was given many more tools to build
my concepts and ideas. I am realizing you have done the
best you can, given the knowledge you've been given.
We are all victims of victims.

—Billy, to his parents; p. 229

Real-life families rarely look like the families in "Father Knows Best," "Ozzie and Harriet," or "The Brady Bunch." Dad and Mom are not always home when school gets out, and sometimes they are exhausted after work or are having their own problems. Dad is not always receptive to listening to his kids and providing warm hugs and sound advice. Sometimes he even drinks. Mom isn't always the perfect homemaker, getting everything done so that all she has to do is attend to her child's every need in a warm and nurturing way. Sometimes she's angry, sometimes she's insecure, sometimes she wants time to herself. She may not always be there when she is needed or wanted. Sometimes she even drinks.

Being self-centered, as children are by nature, most people think that how their parents behave and treat them is a reflection of their own worth. When parents don't provide understanding, touch, love, and support, most children think this is because of something they did or didn't do. They decide that they're not good enough in some way.

Later in life, people continue to be the center of their own universe and rarely get the degree of validation that they seek from others. This feeling of unworthiness affects their relationships with peers and with authority figures.

In order to feel worthy, people aspire to, and strive for, success in the form of material possessions and/or social stature. Daily the media exposes us to those with astounding wealth and abundance, and by comparison most of us don't seem to be making it and fail to notice our abundance, focusing instead on scarcity.

People rarely affirm what they have and express gratitude for it. More often they wish for what they don't yet have. For example: you may have a home that was perfectly acceptable to you when you attained it, but now you want one that's bigger, nicer, and in a better part of town. In the guise of this being "motivating," this actually can set you up for feeling as if you are failing. Many of us don't allow ourselves to enjoy what we already have. While striving to attain that next home or that newer car, do you stop long enough to notice that you are probably better off today than you were in the past?

You may be unconscious as to when and why you set your sights on the goals for which you are now striving. For example: do you know when you chose your values? Do you know when you decided that you had to have more and more? Did you, yourself, actually set your own goals or are you working to attain something someone told you would lead to success and happiness?

Most people spend an inordinate amount of time and energy focusing on the space between where they are now and where they want to be. Though envisioning a goal has great value because it can begin the process of manifestation, focusing on what you haven't yet obtained can also be used to invalidate yourself. You may deny yourself the experience of feeling good in the present, under your present circumstances, because you still have so much more to do.

While not feeling good about oneself is not the sole province of lesbians and gay men, consider what it is like to add to the process of living the fact that something about you is clearly not accepted or valued by society. This was the message conveyed to many lesbians and gay men through direct threats, innuendo, and by being called names. The message that it is not good to be lesbian or gay is all around us, both blatantly and subtly. There is a noticeable void when it comes to positive gay role models, particularly in mainstream media.

Do you have any idea how much pain you mothers bring into the lives of your children by planting the concept that being gay is something awful—rather than something normal and good—as good as my brown hair, my blue eyes, or being right-handed! Can you conceive of the pain of thinking your own mother could not love you if she really knew you!

—Andrew, to his mother; p. 36

For someone growing up gay, most of the time the message is that you are not a valuable person. Lesbians and gay men grow up believing that their very survival depends on staying hidden and invisible. They usually don't have support for being gay from anyone in their lives. At early ages, rarely is there support from others because you dare not mention this to anyone else. The sense of shame and isolation can be profound.

Even the most loving and concerned parents often say and do things that convey the message that it is not all right for their children to be gay. Most parents want their children to be happy. If their son is effeminate they think this will lead to unhappiness, so they make comments intended to get their child to be more masculine. If their daughter likes baseball, they may suggest that she take ballet. If they find out, or even think, that their child or teenager is homosexual, they may suggest therapy. All these loving, concerned and well-meaning parents intend to support their child to grow up to be "normal"—for being "normal" will lead to happiness. These reactions are an expression of love yet are likely to be interpreted by the adolescent or child as "the way I am isn't all right".

The only way to be happy is to be happy. The only way to feel good about who you are is to feel good about who you are. You are who and what you are. You are doing the best you can at any given moment. This is what you get to feel happy and good about. We grow when we acknowledge that we are all caught in this dilemma together. For in society today, it still looks like the only way to be happy is to be like everyone else. This, of course, is not the case at all.

Be the adult and the authority in your own life. This starts with telling the truth about who you are and allowing yourself to be presented positively to the world. It is just as easy to be happy being homosexual as being heterosexual (or just as difficult). It is just as easy feeling good about yourself if you are homosexual as heterosexual (or just as difficult).

Be aware that others' judgments are more a statement about themselves than about you. When someone makes negative comments about you it is a reflection of their own biases and not a factual statement that you are or are not valuable. If someone criticizes another for being black, uneducated, homeless, poor, rich, or makes any one of a number of other such comments, this is a more significant statement about the person doing the judging than about those being judged. So too with those who put you down for being gay or for any other aspect of who you are!

I made myself feel sick about it all; worthless, futureless, bleak. . . . So, South High, I'm one of hundreds of your graduates who are homosexual, and that's what's so. Boy, though, did I feel like the only one then.
                                    —John, to his high school; p. 259

Let the past be in the past and take responsibility for today. Love and accept yourself today, as you are, and you will have a far greater capacity to love and accept others. When you acknowledge your own responsibility for who you are and for how you interpreted the messages you heard as a child or adolescent, you will have a far greater capacity to love and accept yourself and others.

The reason that I am more fully able to acknowledge and appreciate and love you is because I can now see that I love my Self, that I am a beautiful human being, and that I am worthy of loving and being loved.
                                    —Nicholas, to his mother; p. 18

Your self-esteem can be enhanced just by taking a stand and being more open and honest. Nevertheless, someone who feels absolutely terrible about being who they are is unlikely to be open with others. When they come out, even privately, what usually comes across most clearly is "I don't like myself." This is the message that will be responded to by those they tell.

I am happy with what and who I am and . . . I wouldn't change a single thing, AIDS included . . . because

*to do so would mean that I might have missed out on one
of the other parts of my life that I hold so dear.*
                            —Chuck, to his father; p. 222

When you approach the process of coming out with
the genuine feeling that you are a whole, complete, and
worthwhile human being, you are more likely to be accepted, and your self-worth will be further enhanced. It is,
therefore, worth taking the time to do some exercises that
can enhance your personal self-esteem and put you in the
right frame of mind for taking your next step in the coming-
out process.

It may be difficult to feel good about yourself if what
you have been declaring and reaffirming about yourself for
years has been negative. It is valuable to replace negative
thoughts about yourself with more positive ones. This can
be done through a variety of methods, one of the most
common being to create positive statements (affirmations)
and consciously replace the negative thoughts with them.
Some people think this is silly, but all you are doing here is
creating a positive image of yourself, or a vision of how you
will function, and planting it in your consciousness so that it
can grow. Rather than declaring the negative, you are af-
firming something positive. Some examples may be:

- I LOVE MYSELF EXACTLY AS I AM.
- I AM WORTHWHILE AND WORTHY OF BEING
  LOVED.
- I AM ATTRACTIVE, PLEASANT, AND LOVING.
- I AM CAPABLE OF SUCCESS.

Taking ten to twenty minutes one or two times each
day to say these to yourself or write them down over and
over can have a strong effect on how you function in your
life and how you feel about yourself. Create affirmations
that are relevant to you personally. If you find that you
don't believe them at first, that is not uncommon. As you
let yourself do this regularly they will start to become more
and more a part of your conscious and unconscious experi-

ence of yourself. If you decide that you are going to take your next step in the coming-out process you may even choose to create some affirmations specifically about that. Some examples might be:

- COMING OUT MEANS TRUSTING MYSELF TO BE AN ADULT. I TRUST MYSELF AND AM TAKING MY NEXT STEP!
- COMING OUT IS AN EXPRESSION OF ACCEPTING AND LOVING MYSELF AND THOSE TO WHOM I COME OUT!
- I LOVE MYSELF AND I WILL LET OTHERS LOVE ME AS I AM!
- SHARING MYSELF HONESTLY IS A GIFT AND I AM GENEROUS!
- I AM TAKING MY NEXT STEP—I'M WORTH IT!
- I AM ON THE PATH TO FREEDOM AND LIBERATION!
- BY COMING OUT I AM BEING POWERFUL AND EMPOWERING OTHERS!
- COMING OUT IS AN ACT OF LOVE, AND ALL I HAVE TO GIVE AND RECEIVE IS LOVE!

A Letter from Marcia's Father

Dear Marcia,

You won't believe how pleased I was to get your letter. In one fell swoop you cut through a barrier that I thought was permanent and you made me feel that you have come to like me and love me the way I had always hoped you would. And I am glad that you seem to have made your transition and are clear as to where you are so that you can begin thinking about what the next phase should be.

Of course I supposed that you were well on your way to the gay life for some time. And, although initially it was somewhat painful to contemplate, I never thought it was an act directed against me. Indeed, during the same time

I had come to know and respect so many people of the same bent that I was becoming quite comfortable with them and in many cases respected their life-style and how they were making it supportive of what they really wanted to do.

So please don't worry about my reaction on that score. Of course, being satisfied with my own straight life I suppose I harbor feelings that others are missing important things, but I can imagine that there are compensations and that there surely are many in both camps to prove you can find happiness either way.

You are right that your teens were a rough time for both of us. I don't suppose we will ever know how much your "fuck you" reactions were due to your own frustrations over dyslexia, etc., and how much over rebelling against the rather different standards that Helga and I were trying to hold up. (Hers being different from mine, I mean.) In any event I always remembered that opposing my own parents (although in much more decorous ways as befitting other times) was an absolutely essential part in my own development and in becoming my own self. In any event, that rocky ride is long past and we have survived. And you have indeed become your own self.

I certainly look forward to spending time together when you come at Christmas. There is lots to talk about, but I must warn you not to expect too much. After sixty years I have built up a lot of protective walls myself, many that I don't even know about. But that still leaves quite a bit of territory to explore.

Your tickets are all set and I shall send them on soon. Autumn is late this year; the leaves are just beginning to turn. I've really upgraded the yard. It looks nicer than ever and I'm sorry you won't be able to see it in that state.

Be sure to vote. And write as soon as the spirit moves you. With love, including all that has gone unexpressed,

Dad

6

COMING OUT AS AN
ACT OF LOVE

There are many ways in which you can come out about sexuality, about your views and beliefs, or about some other aspect of yourself. How you communicate has a great deal to do with how you feel about yourself and your life. When you feel really good about yourself, and love yourself exactly as you are, coming out is an act of love. People who love themselves express who they are in a loving way.

If you're depressed or feeling isolated or powerless, coming out may be a cry for help. If you don't feel good about yourself you will invariably look to others either to rescue you from this feeling or further to validate that you are right in not feeling good about yourself. Someone who persecutes you—perhaps calling you names, rejecting you, withdrawing love, beating you up, etc.—is only providing you with justification for being depressed, isolated, and powerless. You will get to resent them, though you'll still be depressed. Someone who rescues you—perhaps trying to support you and tell you that they love you as you are—is also supporting you, even if you don't believe what they're telling you. You may get to resent them as well, since they can't seem to understand just how awful you feel about yourself.

If you're angry, arrogant, or contemptuous you may come out to someone in order to hurt them. Under these circumstances you may use your coming out in order to start a fight or to prove that the person you are coming out to is the enemy after all. If you are angry about being gay you will invariably set up others as the enemy, and you are likely to generate evidence that you were right all along—that others are the enemy and that you are truly oppressed and have every right to be bitter.

Reactions you get from others are often more related to *how* you express yourself than to *what* you express. You may have been brought up not to express your love either verbally or physically. This would not be uncommon. If you look into a mirror and say "I love you" to yourself, do you believe it? This is the starting point. If you don't love yourself as you are, you will tend to look to others to tell you you're all right. Most of the time they will mirror back your own personal doubts.

The person you get to love is the person you are right now—right at this very moment. Many people are willing to love themselves only when they become the person their parents, or themselves, always wanted them to be. Without loving yourself, you are unlikely to ever become the person you want to be. You are less likely to do things that are good for you and probably don't feel worthy of being all you can be. When you love yourself as you are, you open the door for all kinds of miracles to occur. When you love yourself exactly as you are you may miraculously begin to be the person you always wanted to be. Even more miraculously, you may discover that you are truly perfect just the way you are. Either way, you're the winner.

Once you are willing to love yourself exactly as you

are, it is easier to come out on any issue, sexuality included, because your personal value is not up for a vote. Once you are willing to love yourself, telling the truth is far easier because who you are and how you live is genuinely OK with you.

When you have achieved self-acceptance and self-love, coming out is truly an act of love. It is a clear and present expression that you love yourself as you are. You are confident being who you are and do not depend on being loved by others for validation. But what about those others—those people you come out to? Is coming out selfish? If you love them why should you hurt them? What is the most loving thing you can do for people in your life?

Cheryl, to Her Father and Her Sister

Dearest Dad,

There's one real important thing I want you to know. I love you and what I want to share with you now will not change that. I know that you also love me and I am going to trust in that love to tell you I am a homosexual. It has taken me a long time to feel brave enough to tell you, Dad, because I was afraid of losing you. What I realize, Dad, is that I don't have you and I think withholding this part of me is what stops our relationship from being so much more. I want to give you and me the opportunity to relate in a much fuller way. I can only do this by sharing all that I am, and my homosexuality is part of what I am.

Love always,
Cheryl

My dear "baby sister,"

It is long past that you are my baby sister and I will always lovingly think of you as that. With the passing years our relationship has been special to me. We have become close. I want our relationship to continue to grow and be enriched because I love you very much. I suspect that what I am going to tell you, you already know and if not, I trust your love for me will not change. I am gay. I tell you this now because I think it is in the way of me having the full relationship that I want with you.

Lovingly,
Cheryl

Perhaps the most loving thing you can do is to let people you care about be exactly who they are and let them know you exactly as you are. If your value is not dependent on the reaction you get from them, you are free to love and support them even if they react negatively to your self-disclosure. When you love someone, it is not selfish to come out to them but is a statement that you trust them and love them enough to let them know the real you. It is important to convey this message to them clearly, as Cheryl did in her letter to her father and sister, and not leave it to chance that they will understand this. When you do, the message that you love them will generally be more powerful than the issue you are coming out about.

When coming out is accompanied by a clear message that "I love you and I love myself," acceptance usually follows, and the experience of love is deepened and strengthened.

Fred, to His Children

Don, Brian, Kurt, and Betsy,
    This is probably the most difficult letter to write that I have ever attempted. I send it to you because of the deep bond of love I feel I share with each of you. It is more commonly the kind of letter a son might write to his father rather than a father to his sons.
    Well, here goes. . . . You may have noticed that since

Mom died I haven't dated women very much. The reason is that I have long known that I prefer being in the company of other men. Yes, I am a gay man, a homosexual, bisexual: call it what you will.

Yes, Mother knew. In fact we had discussed it many times together. This I really think helped to make our marriage especially close. As you know, we shared a lot of love together.

But those days with Mom are over. After she passed away, my life has come to have a different meaning for me. I have decided to live the remaining period of my life in a way that will give me most satisfaction.

The expression of love between a man and a woman, two men or two women, to me can be a beautiful thing and often is. I believe in the freedom of the individual to express his choice, and I have made mine.

I have never regretted my marriage, nor the fathering of you children. I consider myself to have been blessed with a rich life surrounded by loving family.

I am writing this letter to you, my children, so that you will know where I'm coming from. It is my hope that your greater understanding of me will even further deepen the love we mutually have always shared.

Love,
Dad

A Follow-up Note from Fred

I sent the letter to each of my children together with a handwritten personal note, which was for that person and that person alone.

The results were heart-warming.

My eldest son, with whom I practice, received his letter (which was addressed to him and his wife) by hand. My other two sons each received theirs in the mail.

Don apparently had shown the letter to his wife during his lunch hour, because in the early afternoon he said he wanted to talk to me privately.

When he came into my private office and closed the door, he said, "Thank you, Dad, for sending me that letter. Betsy and I were very surprised. Even though I am not that way myself, it makes absolutely no difference to us. We love you and will continue to love you as we always have. You have been a marvelous father."

Then, he walked around my desk to where I was sitting and gave me a big hug and a kiss. Boy, that felt wonderful!

As far as my other two sons were concerned, it seems that within a day they had all communicated with one another by phone, because they both reacted the same as my first son. They each even gave me noisy kisses on the phone.

I feel like I have been "on a high" ever since this occurred. About three weeks have passed and everything my children have said and done since seems to confirm their initial reaction.

I am a happy man.

Cordially,
Fred

When this transpired Fred, a physician, was fifty-nine years old.

7

SUPPORTING THOSE TO WHOM YOU COME OUT

How someone reacts to your self-disclosure is far less important than whether you have the capacity to continue to love them regardless of their response. As difficult as it may be to tell someone the truth, it may be equally or more difficult for that person to hear it. People who resist telling others the truth frequently say that they don't want to hurt the people they love. Resisting self-disclosure is more often a reflection of fear of confronting someone else's reactions. When you come out to someone, you are putting that person into their own "coming out" process, and you are responsible for supporting them through that process. You will experience more of your own growth and power as you discover your capacity to provide support.

*This is no doubt going to be the most difficult letter
I've ever written or will ever write. I want you to know
something very important about me because without
knowing all about me, you can't know anything about me.
I am gay and probably have been gay since I was
born. . . . I don't know what your feelings are about gay
people and I know that it is a situation you probably
know very little about.*

—Richard, to his parents; p. 224

If you are telling someone you are gay, keep in mind
that they may know very little about homosexuality. They
may think they know what it is to be lesbian or gay based on
what they have read, heard, or seen in the media. By letting
them know that you are homosexual, you are introducing
them to new information. You are letting them know you
better, and you are opening the door for them to learn more
about homosexuality in particular and sexuality in general.
Talking about being homosexual is difficult, in part, because
openly discussing sexuality is difficult in our culture. As long
as we perpetuate this we are contributing to ignorance and
are responsible for reinforcing the attitude that sex is bad
and homosexuality is worse.

If you are lesbian or gay, remember that you, too,
were once ignorant about homosexuality. It may have taken
you many years to move beyond your early knowledge of
the subject. It probably took many years for you to move
beyond your beliefs, prejudices, and stereotypes to discover
that there are as many ways to be homosexual as there are
to be heterosexual. As more people come out, individually
and collectively, and homosexuality can be discussed more
openly, all of us will discover more about the diversity that
exists. Telling the truth will in the end be a liberating
process.

*I know this is hard for you. It took me thirty-three
years to get here and, believe me, I know it's hard to face
the world with the truth.*

—Gerardo, to his mother; p. 205

When you come out to someone, you put them into the personal phase of their own process. This is a process that parallels your own. By the time you are willing to move into the private phase of this process and share yourself more openly with others, you have already dealt with many of the personal issues. As you come out to others, remember your own experience, and that you probably did not jump for joy or take your realization as good news. Give those in your life the same opportunity for growth that you have had. They may even deal with this information faster than you did.

Most lesbians and gay men have dealt with their sexuality for many years before disclosing it to others. They have usually gone through sadness, pain, disappointment, regret, resentment, anger, and confusion before being ready to responsibly come to grips with their sexuality. It is often many more years before they are able to feel joy about their sexuality or to love themselves as homosexuals. Consider if this conforms to your own experience, and to that of your friends. Keep this in mind when you tell others. They, too, are entitled to have these feelings.

If you are heterosexual, and someone has recently come out to you, know that it is all right to have any of your feelings about this new information. In fact, as you explore your own feelings you will gain a great deal of insight into what it feels like for someone to discover that they are gay.

To be as honest with you as you have been with me . . . I must tell you that these have been the heaviest, saddest four months that I can remember. To know of your involvement is the saddest, most disappointing news that I have ever received. You reached me with more shocking and painful impact than anything I have ever experienced.

—A letter from Bud's father; p. 103

Expressing your sadness, disappointment, hurt, and anger is helpful, for it allows you to move on to other feelings. Withholding these emotions when they are present will leave you in a state of denial. Don't overlook that these feelings can all exist within a context of love.

You are bigger than the hate and disappointment you feel. I know those are your tools in handling this issue.
—Billy, to his parents; p. 230

Parents want their children to be happy. Most people were brought up to believe that happiness rests on falling in love, getting married, and having children. For someone who is lesbian or gay, as well as for their parents, the disappointment and anger that is felt is often related to this shattered stereotypic dream of happiness. If parents want their children to be happy, and being happy means being married and having a family (or living life in a particular way), then they will be disappointed, hurt, and angry if their children don't live that way. This is not because they hate their children—it is because they love them and want them to be happy.

If your parents love you, and you make it sound like you need their approval, they may let you know unequivocally that they do not approve. To them the equation, consciously or unconsciously, works like this:

- My child is homosexual.
- Being heterosexual is the way to be happy.
- If I approve of his/her homosexuality this may be all she/he needs in order to remain homosexual.
- If I withhold my approval, maybe he or she will change and be heterosexual, which will ultimately make my child happier.
- Therefore, I will withhold my approval.

I know it wasn't particularly easy for you to learn that you had a gay son. . . . I hope that you don't feel closeted about being parents of a gay child. . . . Please be proud of all of me, not only the aspects that please you.
—Doug, to his parents; p. 231

The closet is not where homosexuals hide—it is where the truth is hidden until we take it out into the light. Everyone has his or her own closet where they keep their secrets—those things they don't want others to see. If you are lesbian or gay, and come out to your parents or friends, they may put your disclosure in a closet of their own. Look at the situation from another's point of view and remember your own process of discovery. Remember how long it took for you to let your sexuality "out of the closet." Your family and friends may be concerned about what others will think. They will need to work through their own personal feelings before they are ready to discuss this information with others.

Parents and friends need people going through similar experiences with whom to talk openly. Many of us first came out to people we knew or sensed shared our "secret." When we discover our homosexuality we usually seek out others who are going through similar experiences. Parents and Friends of Lesbians and Gays (Parents-FLAG), an organization active in many states, is a wonderful resource and provides support for many thousands of families every year. The Experience, as well as many local organizations, can also provide support and insight. It may take some time before parents are ready to talk. Let them have their own process and support them through it. You are probably further along in the process than they are. If you are proud of yourself, and love yourself, it will be much easier to support them.

Just as we go through a coming-out process—just as those we tell privately go through a parallel coming-out process—so will society go through a similar process. All of the dynamics discussed above also apply to coming out on a collective basis. Homosexuality is talked about far more often today than it was ten or twenty years ago. Part of the reason is the large number of individuals who have already told the truth. There are also many lesbian and gay organizations throughout the country that speak up and support the coming-out process. AIDS has also contributed greatly to the visibility of homosexuals.

As we move into the public phase of the process, the phase in which liberation and freedom occur, we generally experience exhilaration, aliveness, and a sense of well-being. There is a very positive and enlivening experience that accompanies each step of the coming-out process. In the following letter from Bill to his parents, we see an example of someone who has been drifting away from his family as a result of withholding his sexuality from them. He comes out to them because he wants to re-establish his closeness to the family. In his note to me, which I have included, he points out that while his family still has a ways to go in dealing with his sexuality, he feels "like a new person."

Bill, to His Parents

Dear Mother and Father,

Lately, I've seemed to be drifting away from the family. When asked to do things with the family, I have always been able to come up with an excuse to either not be there or limit my time. This has gotten to the point where I want it to stop. It was much better when I could involve the family in every aspect of my life. When things started to fall into place a couple of years ago, I became afraid to include you in everything.

The evening when Sister Mary Theresa was sitting on the couch talking to me, she made a comment that got me thinking about myself. She said that she could not tell why it was, but she saw that I was a much happier person. What struck me was that I knew in part she was right. The problem was that I could not talk to anyone as to why I was feeling that way.

As time passed, some of my friends were seeing this change in me also. Even with them I was afraid to talk about it. As you know, I have never had many friends. Now that I had some, I was afraid that honesty with them would result in losing them.

I had known for quite some time that some of my feelings were different, yet I chose to ignore this. As you taught all of us kids, you must eventually face the truth. That is what I have chosen to do now.

My family has always been very special to me. Yes, there have been times when we have had our problems, but when you compare our family to others it shows just how lucky we really are. This has made it that much harder to tell you what I must now say.

After more soul searching and prayer than most people would do in a lifetime, I have finally accepted the fact that I am gay. At first my response was that I would ignore this fact. All that this did was to worsen the problem. Not until I came out to some very special friends was I able to get a better grip on the situation.

The common thread that always came through was that I could not be happy in this life-style or any other while I was not being honest to the family. Just from the short exposure these friends have had to you, they were able to understand the situation. The response they almost all gave me was that they felt the family would understand and be able to cope with this new knowledge about me.

What I must emphasize is that I am still the same Bill that you have always known. The only thing changed is that now you know me a little better.

You must also know that I am not telling you this because I am being forced to. I am telling you because I want you to know that I am happy, healthy, and ready now to continue on with life. I want the family to be able to continue along with me and me to continue along with the family also.

I have seen just how unhappy a person can be when they choose to live a lie. I cannot do that, and hopefully you will be able to understand and respect my decision. By telling you now, I hope that I can minimize the hurt that this will cause. Prolonging the way I am avoiding the family would only hurt worse.

Please know that I do not want to hurt or embarrass the family. I also hope that you feel the same toward me.

The situation has already been uncomfortable. I only hope that we can build back what has already been damaged.

Just because a person is gay does not mean that they are that different from straight people. Hopefully you will choose to meet some of my gay friends someday. You will see that they are just regular people. In fact you would probably have trouble picking them out.

I also want you to know that I will not force the issue. I have laid my cards on the table. If you choose not to talk to me about it right now I will understand. Just please do not leave it that way. Our family has been through problems before and survived, we can make it through this one as well. I am sure that it will not be the last!

Finally, I do not want you to think that this is due to something that was or was not done in raising me. As I said before, after hearing what some people went through in their childhoods, mine was a bed of roses. This just reinforces how lucky I am to be a part of this family.

Thanks for everything you have done for me so far in this life. Now let's go forward and see what else we can accomplish. If you can't talk to me about this right now I do understand. Just please don't wait too long, it will only get harder.

Still your loving son,
Bill

A Follow-up Note from Bill

As far as my parents' reaction, it could have been worse. At this time my mother does not want to bring my father in on my life-style. I left this up to her at this point, but made it known that he would have to find out sooner or later. At this point in time, there has been very little communication with any family member. I am letting them have some time to think before I bring up the subject again.

As far as the rest of my life goes, I feel like a new person. With the tools I now have, I am going forward with my life and loving the results. The great thing is that I am understanding more every day!

Bill

A feeling of relief, such as the one described by Bill, can also be the experience of those to whom we come out. When you withhold parts of yourself from others they often sense it, yet may misinterpret what you are hiding. They are likely to have a lot of personal feelings about the distance between you and may be saddened and disappointed by that, without ever knowing what it is really about. While I was struggling with my homosexuality I not only distanced myself from my family but was actually belligerent toward my parents—and in some respects toward most people around me. I was frustrated, angry, and not very pleasant to be around. When I finally told my mother what I was going through, she was somewhat relieved because she had thought that perhaps I was angry with her for something she had done, or that I had gotten myself into some kind of serious trouble. While she wasn't thrilled that I was gay, she was relieved to know what was behind my behavior and attitude toward the family.

You won't believe how pleased I was to get your letter. In one fell swoop you cut through a barrier that I thought was permanent and you made me feel that you have come to like me and love me the way I had always hoped you would.

—A letter from Marcia's father; p. 69

It is helpful to disclose your sexuality, or any other withheld truth, in a loving context. What most people will want to know is how this will change your relationship with them. Remember, we all want to love and be loved. The content of the communication may be something one might prefer not to say or hear, but if the context is love, the content generally becomes more acceptable.

I am still your father—who has always been gay— except that I did not share that with you. I still offer to you the deep and lasting love I have for you. God, our Creator, who loves me and provided me with the opportunity to marry your mother and gave to both of us you and your brother, brings us together and binds us with love, providing we open our hearts to each other and let go of the hate man has taught us.

—Paul, to his son; p. 253

In a context of love we allow ourselves, and others, to experience all there is. A context of love is enormous, powerful, and healing. It is large enough to include sadness, pain, disappointment, hurt, anger, confusion, guilt, aimlessness, anxiety, joy, exhilaration, ecstasy, and the truth. When we love ourselves and others we have lots of room to experience the process of coming out and the process of life. Love is not based on right or wrong, good or bad. *Deep in the center of our being we know that when we love someone, we love them no matter what.*

Laurence, to His Parents

Dear Mom and Dad,

As I sit down to write this letter to you, I realized how long it's been since I've written you a letter. It seems the telephone has replaced the need for pen and paper.

Actually, though, this is a letter which I've been wanting to write to you for quite some time. In fact, I did write you about a year ago, but decided not to send it . . . for a number of reasons. But, I'm very pleased now to be sitting here in my sunny upstairs loft on a quiet Sunday afternoon sharing my thoughts with you.

This past year has been an important one for me, and the transition has been fulfilling and exciting. I can't tell you how happy I am to be back in New York. For what-

ever reason (and I'm not always absolutely certain of it),
I know in my heart of hearts that this is where I should be
right now. I am blessed with an abundance of warm and
supportive friendships here, as well as an environment to
explore and develop my personal and professional interests.

Besides the geographic relocation, this year has been
important in a number of other ways—more internally, I
suppose than externally. Though my "journey" is by no
means complete, I do feel that I have made considerable
progress on my own personal path of self-acceptance and
personal understanding. Believe me, it hasn't been easy!
But I feel very good about the progress I've made and no
doubt will continue to make. It's a welcome feeling.

It does seem like the time, therefore, to begin sharing these feelings and personal insights with my family,
which explains why I am writing to you. For whatever reason, our family has never been very much on sharing personal feelings and issues with one another. I've never really
understood this and often have felt very isolated and concerned by the lack of *real* communication within our own
family. I've come to realize, however, that I'm as "guilty"
as anyone, since I, too, have chosen not to be self-revealing
or intimate with my own blood relatives.

So, here I am, committed to taking the first step to
what I'm hoping will be a more honest, open, and understanding relationship between us. Though I have openly
shared most of my life with you, there is a part of me
which I have kept hidden, and I don't think it is serving
anyone, least of all me, to continue to do so.

Which is why it's time to be completely honest with
you and to acknowledge the fact that I am gay. By now
you've probably already pieced it together, given the fact
that so many of my friends are gay and that there have
been no significant relationships with women in my life since
Sarah. But I don't want it to be a "secret" that I can't
talk about with my own family. It is a part of who I am
and not something I want to keep hidden from you any
longer. Quite frankly, I could use your support in all this!

I do understand, however, that before you can be sup-

portive of me you will need your own time and space to
sort it through. Heck, I've probably known I was gay since
childhood, but never really accepted it until I was twenty-
six or twenty-seven years old . . . and I'm still working at
it! So, I am fully prepared to help with and participate in
this process of understanding. It does take time, and I just
hope we can work together at feeling comfortable with
it. If we decide that it is "not something to talk about" or
that "it's been said and there's nothing more to say," I
think we'll be doing each other a real disservice, and I hope
that this will not be the path you choose! It'll only draw
us further apart rather than closer together, which is the essence of why I wanted to share this part of me with you
in the first place.

Maybe I'm assuming incorrectly, but based on the
comments you've made, I'm guessing that you aren't very
well acquainted with homosexuality and the realities of being
gay. Fortunately there is plenty of very good literature
available, some of it written by parents of gay men and
women, which I will be glad to send to you.

In fact, it might help to tell you that one of the primary reasons that it took me so long to accept myself was
due to a lack of adequate information available and the
absence of positive role models—in the community or
through the media. So much of what we hear about being
gay is *false*, biased, and truly misrepresentational. Growing up all we ever heard about being gay was very negative
and misleading stereotypes and entirely incorrect myths
and other bits of misinformation. Only now can I fully appreciate the fact that gay men and women are *exactly* like
straight men and women—except for the fact that we choose
a partner of the same gender, rather than of the opposite
sex.

Like so many others, I spent years wondering *why* I
was gay. Was I born this way? Was it something about
my upbringing? Was it something I brought upon myself in
childhood? Finally, as an adult, I've come to accept who
I am and to realize that the "why" of it really is irrelevant.
(It's like wondering why I have green eyes instead of

Dad's blue eyes. It just is, and there's really nothing we can do about it . . . except enjoy and appreciate who we are.)

If it matters, most research scientists support the notion that we likely are born predisposed to a particular sexual orientation. (In fact, it is no longer referred to as a "sexual preference," since it is not a matter of choice or preference. I didn't "choose" to be gay. I just am!) Some doctors like to compare it to being left-handed. We still don't know why some children are left-handed while the majority of their peers are right-handed. But fortunately society (and those nasty parochial school nuns!) have stopped misunderstanding left-handed children and forcing them to adapt to using their right hand. They get along fine being left-handed, and it's very natural for them to be this way. Well, it's much the same with being gay. We're in the minority, but at least we're being true to our own inner selves and not forcing ourselves to be something we're not, simply because society, as the ruling majority, dictates otherwise. We *all* end up losing when that happens, regardless of the issue.

Actually, it is amazing to see just how large this so-called minority really is. It is conservatively estimated that one of every ten children is gay and that there are nearly twenty-five million gay men and women in the United States. So, it's comforting to know that at least I'm in good company.

When you think about it, even in our own circle of family and friends it is amazing how many gay men and women we know—but don't talk about. I think it's safe to assume that Ron is gay—though that's certainly no reason for "dropping out" of the family as he has. I've always felt that Francie's daughter is gay. And, of course, I was as surprised as everyone when John flew out to D.C. to tell me that he had to leave Jane because he was gay! I hadn't a clue. I guess we both were so fearful and lacking in self-awareness that we never revealed ourselves to one another. Pretty sad, considering that we were best friends for so many years. (Actually, the same surprise came when Michael told me he was gay during our junior year of college. Poor guy still hasn't learned to accept it or make peace with himself, unfortunately.)

I have to admit, though, that for a very long time I said that I would never tell my parents I was gay. I was . . . and still am . . . worried about how you would respond, and since our family never discusses very personal matters of any kind, it's been very easy not to bring it up. I began to change my mind about telling you, however, in the spring of last year. You may recall what a difficult time that was for me. Helen, my neighbor, was very sick and then died so suddenly, and I thought that my position was going to be eliminated due to budget cutbacks. But there was something else going on, which was the hardest of all to handle. Someone whom I was dating for the past seven months and whom I loved very much decided to abruptly end the relationship that February. It hurt me very deeply and still does when I think about it. In fact, you might remember telephoning me one Saturday morning in the middle of all this, and you were able to detect that things weren't well with me, but I was very evasive at the time. Well, now you know why. It was very painful not to be able to talk to my own family about what was troubling me, and I vowed that I would not allow such a "silent" separation to continue. It will be wonderful to no longer have any part of me sheltered or hidden from my family.

I know that this letter will probably raise a lot of questions for you, and I sincerely hope that you won't hesitate to talk with me about them. As I said, I'm fully prepared to participate with you in this "coming-out" process. But please know for now that I am very happy to be exactly who I am and I wouldn't change any aspect of my sexuality, even if I could (which, we know, is impossible anyway). I'm still the same son you've always had, just a little more honest and self-revealing. And, yes, I do hope to eventually make a home with someone special, complete with a fireplace, piano, lots of plants, and maybe even children! But, the only difference will be that it will be another man whom I'll choose as my partner and soulmate.

And, as for this godawful health crisis plaguing the gay community and the rest of society, you need not worry about me or my safety. Though I do often regret that it has taken me so many years to accept myself, I am grateful that when I did finally begin dating I did have the advantage of knowing exactly what the rules were, since the AIDS epidemic was already in full swing. So, I am OK and will stay that way.

I guess that's about all for now. I didn't know when would be the best time to write this letter, but last Christmas I did commit to myself that I would do so before Labor Day. So, I've procrastinated long enough. And I am glad that we may be seeing one another in September. If you'd like, we can talk further about this then. As I said, I will send you some written materials that I have found very useful and informative.

Above all else, please know that I love you both very much, and it is for this reason that I am choosing to share this with you. I'm convinced that it'll only be better for us all to be completely honest and open with one another!

With much love,
Laurence

8

LOVING
UNCONDITIONALLY

Having been brought up on conditional love, it is difficult
for many people to trust their love for others, or others'
love for them. Few people were raised with the simple
statement, consistently given and demonstrated: I love you.
You were probably told you were loved when: you behaved
properly, got good grades, made your parents proud, or
otherwise lived up to some expectation they had for you.

Very few people are raised to give and receive love
unconditionally. Though the conditions for love may have
been clearly laid out, usually they are only alluded to.
Children and adolescents are often correct about the conditions they must meet in order to be loved, and added to this
they often make up their own conditions based on assump-
tions about what others expect of them. You probably were
not raised to love yourself exactly as you are or to love

others exactly as they are. You were probably raised to believe you are not worthy of love exactly as you are, and that if something about you is perceived as a fault it somehow makes you less lovable.

Arlene to Her Daughter and Son-in-Law

To my beloved son and daughter,

True, I told you that I'm gay years ago—and you did give me tacit acknowledgment—but you are truly a no-good son of a bitch (and daughter of a bitch?) in that you are letting that knowledge just lay there and will not *really* face it so that we can get back to the business of truly loving one another.

I am a homosexual—dyke—a queer—I love other women. *Please* say those things—please scream about it and curse it—and hate it if you must, but *please, please* stop ignoring it.

I am still the woman I was—I am still the mother you loved—and who loves you so very much. I felt (and I still feel) that when you became an adult I wanted a relationship with you that was based on our whole beings —I wanted a friendship as well as love—and we can never have that unless you know who and what I am—and I feel really cheated by you because you now say "I love you *in spite* of your gayness," when what I need and long for is "I love you, and that *includes* the fact that you are old— and fat—and bossy—and gay—and opinionated—and whatever other faults and defects you may have."

Because I am *all* of those things—not just the ones you choose to accept and feel comfortable with.

I want more!

So stop being such assholes and let's get on with it.

I love you,
Mom

Arlene was fifty-six years old when she wrote this letter. When she and her husband were married, each knew the other was gay. They wanted a family and Linda was born. Now married herself, Linda and her husband, Fred, participated in The Experience and Linda's letter to her parents follows.

Linda, to Her Gay Parents

To My Most Beloved Faggot Father and Dyke Mother,
I think I always did accept your sexuality—both of you. I just kind of ignored it because it didn't seem important—so what—so I'm straight, so who cares. I never really felt like I was shutting it out, but I can see how a little projecting (fear that that's how I felt) may have made it seem so. Especially after the kind of rejection you'd both felt from such happenings as the Ephrata visit, where I was so wrapped up in my own world that I was oblivious to you.

My completely blind and selfish actions on such occasions put a deep lump in my stomach. It seems to be human nature to only look at the world through tiny slits—always looking out—getting only one perspective—having no idea how much pain and injury we cause as we bumble along gratifying ourselves. The saddest part is that we would receive so much more gratification if we would learn to reach out and climb inside others—and love—and be loved—instead of hurting!

During my teenage years I often had a vision of life as follows: We were, each of us, prisoners inside a tower—like a rook on a chessboard. We were chained deep down at the bottom of the tower and we could never get out—all we could do was to use our sensors to relay information about the universe back down to us. But we, ourselves, never got outside. I used to think this example only had to do with our sense organs and the "we"—our minds—only acted on nerve impulses, interpreting the outside world. I know now that the analogy runs deeper than that. We really are locked inside an impenetrable tower—and our mind is the guard!

I love you both very much and choose you to be my parents. I like you both very much too. The Open Letter which I wrote will give you some further input about how I feel. Thank you for putting up with my shit for so many years—all those years when I hurt you so much. If you had written me off as not being worth it—oh, how I would have missed out!!

With beautiful love,
Linda

Linda's Open Letter appears on p. 195

It is no wonder that so many people have a difficult time being open and intimate in relationships. Most are afraid that if they let themselves tell the truth about who they are someone else will disapprove. Disapproval is equated with the potential loss of love, and they consequently seek to let others know only what they think will get them loved.

The need to love and be loved is a powerful motivating force. Can you ever truly lose the love of someone who really loves you? When someone loves you unconditionally they love you as you are. If they love you only for who they think you are, they have never really loved you to begin with. What they love is an image of who they think you are. You can not lose love you never had.

Many people manipulate others into loving them by presenting a false image of who they are. They may say things that others want to hear, withhold things they feel others will find unpleasant or may judge, or even dress and act in a manner that they believe will get them the most love from someone else. In doing this they may have succeeded in creating, even for themselves, the illusion that they are loved. Since ultimately, consciously or perhaps unconsciously, they know that they have manipulated, they never genuinely feel loved in the first place. When you genuinely feel loved

by someone, you know that it is safe to tell the truth and to
be who you really are.

*It is not my desire or intention to become a burden
to anyone . . . believe me it hurt to lose some friends but
the ones who stick around and love you anyway are
far more precious and important than those who sit in
judgment.*

—Chuck, to his parents; p. 221

What you really risk losing when you are open and
honest with others is not love but the illusion of love. You
risk losing a love based on so many conditions that it may
actually be no more than a control mechanism. Unfortunately, many relationships, including romantic ones, are
based on this same model, which has been learned from
family, society, and religion. Yet anything we have learned
we can unlearn—and if loving unconditionally is your goal,
you can achieve it. Once again, it begins with a willingness
to trust yourself and to tell the truth.

You may not be exactly as you want to be at this
moment—yet it is you, as you are, that you get to love.
Your friend, parent, lover, or spouse may not be exactly as
you want him or her to be at this moment—yet it is she or
he, as is, that you get to love.

Each of us is doing the best that we can with what we
have at every given moment in time. All you need to do is
look at your own life and your decisions from the same
vantage point from which you looked at them as they were
happening and being made. Didn't you always do the best
you could? Guess what—so did everyone else. If you begin
to look at the actions of others from their perspective, you
will surely notice this.

*When love is unconditional, relationships are able
to change forms naturally and lovingly.* Living in an unconditionally loving manner is not always easy. In fact,
most of our relationships are conditional in nature. You
have conditions for who you are "in love with," who

you want to live with, who you want to spend time with. You also have conditions for how you choose to relate to family members. These need not be seen as conditions for love—merely conditions about the form of your relationships.

If a relationship has a fundamental basis in unconditional love, it will continually change for the better. When you are afraid that your relationship with someone will change if that person knows who the real you is, it is possible that you will be right. If your relationship with that person is based on meeting some set of limited conditions, ask yourself, Why are you in that relationship in the first place?

I wish I could believe that you could get the message I'm trying to convey! I love you—very much. I want you to love me unconditionally—no matter what I do or what I am—I am your son—neither of us can change that even if we wanted to.

—Andrew, to his mother, p. 35

You may know that your relationship with your parents is not based on love but on duty, obligation and illusion. You may be afraid of being disowned or even disinherited if they know you as you are. This may be a legitimate concern. If this is the case, at least tell yourself the truth about it. You might also notice that these same dynamics of relationship carry into other areas of your life. It has always seemed to me to be worth the risk of telling the truth. What is at stake is your life and your integrity.

Jim, to His Parents

Dear Mom and Dad,

I'm sitting here in a hotel conference room doing a special weekend, looking at my life. I am doing this with seventy-six other people.

One main thing I need to let you know is about my coming out of hiding and sharing all of myself with you.

There was a real big event in my life, one that I was most unhappy about. I came home one weekend from Detroit to tell you about my sexuality and the problems around this. I was scared, especially of your reactions. I remember, Dad, you told me not to worry, to take an aspirin and it would be all better in the morning. You then went to bed. Mom, you felt so guilty, as if you made me "that way."

I need to finish up that night with you so we all can go on with our lives in honesty.

Dad, I didn't need an aspirin. I needed to hear that you loved me as your son even though you may have never really understood what I was trying to get out.

Mom, you didn't make me "that way." I hurt so much seeing how you reacted. Just as with Dad, I needed to hear that you loved me. You said if I didn't get "straightened around" I would no longer be welcome home.

Dad and Mom, I know of no other way to be than just as I am. Yes, in your eyes, I am different. I want you both to know that I am different and yet very much like anyone else. I am gay and I am very, very happy. If I had to do it all over again, I would choose to be who I am now.

I am not asking you to accept this. I know how bizarre this must be for you both. You believe it is immoral and unnatural. You can continue believing this. My letter is not about changing your beliefs. You have a right to believe in what you choose.

I see myself differently. I am not immoral and unnatural for the way I am. God created me out of love and I am His creation. I know *very* powerfully that God is big enough to love me.

It has not always been easy being gay and hiding, lying to you, pretending I was not what I am.

I don't remember ever hearing you say "I love you just as you are." What I got was "I would love you if you turned out the way you're 'supposed to.' "

Well, I did turn out the way I was supposed to. I turned out gay and it is no one's fault. This is a fact of life. I can no longer pretend it isn't a part of me when I am with you. There is so much beauty in my life and I want to share it with you. And I'm scared to death. I'm scared you won't love me, that you won't want to see me in August, afraid of your own embarrassment. And I also know that getting all this out in the open, off my chest, will make my life much easier.

I also want *not* to tell you that I'm gay. I think it is actually none of your business. But I know that this is the chip on my shoulder, the grudge I held against you from back then, that night, when I came home from Detroit. If I keep the grudge, I will never be at peace with myself. I need to fill a large communication gap between us so I can love you just as you are. As I mentioned, I have so much to share about myself with you, and now I have to leave it up to you to choose.

—You can never welcome me home again.

—We can continue relating to each other without talking about it, keeping the awkward silence.

—You can allow me to be who I am, and most importantly, you can give yourselves the permission to love *all* of me.

However you choose to deal with this, please know always that I love you both so very much and I will always love you because, you see, a long time ago, I made a firm commitment that I would love you absolutely and unconditionally, no matter what came up. Now, I need that same commitment from you.

                              I love you both eternally,
                                             Jim

9

RELIGION
AND SPIRITUALITY

Religion is not my primary expertise and I'll leave religious
doctrine for others to debate. I have included this chapter
because so many people have a difficult time integrating
their sexuality with their religious beliefs—a difficulty that is
magnified when one is homosexual. Most people were brought
up with religious beliefs that had little room for the truth—
particularly if one is homosexual. While the word *love* may
be used frequently in a religious context, it is generally used
so conditionally that it rarely captures the spiritual essence
of love.

　　I have always experienced myself as a deeply spiritual
being, and many people I encounter also have a strong
sense of their own spirituality. Frequently this is kept in the
closet, or not discussed, when it does not conform to the
religious beliefs with which they were brought up. While
growing up I was very religious and simultaneously had a

strong sense of my spirituality. Over the years my spirituality has become far more important to me.

I am deeply moved by spirituality but I have experienced being constricted and socialized by religion. Some of the ways in which I experience dissonance between spirituality and religion are these:

- *Spirituality teaches that we are all one.* Religion teaches that some of us are Catholic, some Jewish, some Mormon—that we are all separate and different.
- *Spirituality teaches that love is unconditional.* Some religions teach that love, even God's love, is conditional.
- *Spirituality teaches that you are a perfect being.* Some religions teach that you are imperfect.
- *Spirituality teaches that we are energy, soul, love, Christ consciousness, and always a perfect manifestation of God.* Most religions teach that we are separate from God.
- *Spirituality teaches that sexuality is a natural expression and that homosexuality is a part of our reality, and a perfect manifestation of God.* Many religions teach that enjoying sexuality is bad and that homosexuality is a sin.

Ideally, religion teaches us spirituality, yet too often religious institutions teach primarily about social order and social control. The ways in which we express ourselves spiritually are beautiful and loving—creating unity and oneness. Frequently, the ways in which we express ourselves through our religions are limiting and manipulative—creating separation and disharmony. I do not believe that the two need to be mutually exclusive, yet frequently they appear to be.

Many people have a great deal of trouble moving through the coming-out process because they are struggling with how to integrate the truth about who they are with their religious beliefs. When the truth is that you are homosexual, integrating this with your religion may be difficult. In recent years, as religious congregations have become more aware of the presence of homosexuals within them, some positive changes have taken place. There are currently both Jewish and Unitarian gay congregations as well as gay and lesbian caucuses of Catholics (Dignity), Episcopalians (Integrity), Mormons and United Methodists (Affirmation), Lutherans (Lutherans Concerned), and others. Additionally, the Universal Fellowship of Metropolitan Community Churches (MCC) provides Christian services throughout the country for lesbians and gay men.

Since the personal cost of hiding one's sexuality is so great, I strongly encourage lesbians and gay men to come out even in the context of their religions. While I realize that this might be threatening, and raise many of the types of fears already discussed in this book, I once again encourage you to trust yourself to deal effectively with the consequences. By doing so you will either create room for your religion to embrace you, or you will create the freedom for you to discover a spiritual basis for your life that has room for you to integrate all of who you are. I do not pretend that this process will be an easy one, since our religious beliefs are often very strong, and many beliefs have been predicated on a fear of reprisal for not adhering to them. Your religious beliefs may not change, though the power that you give to those beliefs may.

Rather than putting a lot of energy into trying to change the beliefs held by one's religion, it may be far more productive to change one's own beliefs about religion. Most people follow a religion not because they examined its principles and chose it but because their parents, and their parents' parents before them, followed that religion. It is not an expression of one's own choice but of indoctrination. Don't give your power away to a belief system that you may not even remember having chosen in the first place. Regardless of whether you are homosexual or heterosexual, take some time to examine the fundamental principles of your religion.

- Does it provide room for you to be all of who
  you are?
- Does it allow you the room to be spiritual and unconditionally loving?
- Does it allow you to be a master, or are you always looking for the answers outside of yourself?

If you discover that your religion does not support
you to integrate your life with integrity you might look to
your own spiritual awareness for the solution. There are
many religions and spiritual practices from which to choose—
there is only one you!

Bud wrote a letter to his father, a minister, to let him
know that he is gay. What follows is his father's response
and then a follow-up letter from Bud. Over the ensuing
years they have grown closer and closer together and continue to correspond on this subject.

A Letter from Bud's Father

Dear Bud,
    You are on my mind and in my heart these days so
much of the time that I must sit down today and express
some of my thoughts to you.
    Four months ago you took me into your confidence
expressing your established choice to engage in homosexual activities . . . as a major ingredient of your life commitment . . . of your sexual life-style as a human being.
    I accepted the openness and painfulness of your spe-
cial confidence with love and understanding . . . because
of my deep love for you as my son.
    You have been in my thoughts and prayers almost
continuously since that time. To be as honest with you as
you have been with me . . . I must tell you that these have
been the heaviest, saddest four months that I can re-

member. To know of your involvement is the saddest, most disappointing news that I have ever received. You reached me with more shocking and painful impact than anything that I have ever experienced.

I have empathized with your hurt . . . with your deep turmoil since your earliest years as a boy . . . with your excruciating uncertainty about your own masculinity . . . with the many early discrediting experiences that you have suffered . . . about your own identity as a human being . . . as well as your early unsureness about your dad's credibility.

I have admired your courage and your persistence . . . in your swimming and your singing and acting . . . in your studying and in your working and growing with responsibility . . . in your compassion for others and in your desire for excellence. You are an immensely valuable human being . . . not only to yourself . . . but also to Mom and me . . . and will always be.

But by submitting to these tendencies, to these inner leanings, to these latent, sexual dissatisfactions . . . you are giving yourself to the distortion of the natural human processes, to the unhealthiness of an immorality that is as ancient as mankind and clearly warned against as sodomy in both the old testament and the new testament.

Despite the experiences that you have had . . . despite the associations that you have had across these recent years . . . you *can* change the balance. Never believe in never! By a total humbleness of desire you can work through these human tensions . . . and discover your maximum possibilities through yielding yourself to the divine tensions of seeking God's will.

Bud, you acquired through your heritage and your early environment a positive, spiritual sensitivity that is a gift of God. The greatest thrill and hopefulness of your life can be realized by taking the steps necessary to sever your relationships with a process that will inevitably become a binding, twisting, narrowing, self-destroying force in you . . . and seek the help of someone who will guide you into a Christ-ethic that will once again open your life to success and happiness and serenity.

You have an inner drive to succeed that is God-given . . . but you will only make it by admitting to your inner self this perversion of the fundamental processes of successful human fulfillment and . . . by redirecting your life to Matt 6:33 . . . "Seek ye first . . . the Kingdom of God . . . and His righteousness . . . and all these things shall be added unto you. . . ."

The *seeking* is the drive . . . that can be the most exciting, challenging, rewarding, fulfilling motivator that you can imagine!

Bud, God has a plan for your life . . . that He wants to accomplish . . . through . . . in spite of . . . and because of all the influences that have been brought to bear on your life. . . . If you will accept His vision for your life . . . He will multiply many times over what you give to Him . . . and unfold in front of you a future of service and accomplishment and personal satisfaction for the next twenty-six years plus that will be astounding.

Although there are many, many scriptures, especially in the Apostle Paul's writings that can assist you . . . initially following the progression of these words of Jesus in Matthew can be personally productive: 6:8, 33; 7:7, 14,21; 8:13; 11:28; 12:33–37; 16:24; 18:3; 22:37; 23:12.

Bud, my deep love for you has prompted me to pour out my heart and mind and life experience to you in this letter . . . dedicated to the supreme worth that God has granted to you . . . and the gigantic, positive possibilities that you can discover in dedicating your life to doing His will.

I am always with you in the strength of caring and hoping and loving and seeking . . .

Dad

Bud's Reply

Dear Dad and Mom,

I have so much to say to you. First and foremost is that I love you. I would never have begun this process last October had it not come from total love, trust, and the desire to share with you all of who I am.

For a long time . . . my whole life . . . I have hidden and suppressed a part of me. The last three years . . . no, the last twenty-six, have been a process for me of finding out all about who I am . . . dealing with it, and even learning to enjoy and capitalize on it. I suspect that I am still in that process. In fact, from all I have learned it seems that this is a process that never ends. I believe that we are always in the process of transformation, both when we consciously are aware of it and seeking it, and when we are not.

In this letter I have several objectives. Most important is to share with you so that you will know me more fully and have a wider foundation of information. Some of this, Dad, I shared with you in October. I want you both to know about my life experiences . . . my dreams . . . my hopes . . . my fears . . . my thoughts . . . my strengths . . . my weaknesses . . . and all of the information I have gathered. I hope that I can ease some of your fears and perhaps some fantasies and misconceptions about a world that is no doubt foreign to you.

While there are a few specific things from your letter to which I do wish to respond, generally, I do not wish to debate with you. I cannot make anything wrong or right, good or bad for you. And you cannot for me. What I can do is share my thoughts and experience with you so that hopefully your frame of reference will be widened.

I received your letter, Dad, and experienced our conversation, Mom, with the grateful knowledge and special sense that we will walk through this together. Believe me, if this were not the case I would have made a different choice entirely last fall.

The primary reason I did not share this with you previously was a fear of rejection. And our relationship is very important to me. I have learned to love and value our special communication across the years and look forward to more. I respect you, I love you, and I value your opinions highly.

I could more easily have gone on indefinitely with the deception I had propagated for some time . . . the half-truths . . . the partial lies . . . the withheld communications. And I chose not to. I am at a place in my life where I do not have room for or energy to spend on that . . . not with you.

Literally for as long as I can remember being, I have known a different kind of need and desire for physical closeness and satisfaction than you experience. My most natural preference and satisfaction comes from experiencing myself with and to another man. The only way I know to share this certainty with you is to compare it to your need and desire to physical sharing with someone of the opposite sex.

Of course, as a boy, I did not realize all the ramifications of my instincts and feelings. But knew they were there . . . even then. The only reason I stress that is because I want you *to know* that this is not something that I have chosen at random as something new, or different, or kinky, or chic; it is a normal, natural part of my function as a human being . . . and always has been.

Growing up with this knowledge is very difficult at best. There is very little support in the world for gay people. Although it does get easier, and better, and more acceptable all the time, it is still difficult. While both the American Medical Association and the American Convention of Psychiatrists have long since taken homosexuality off the books as an illness, aberration, or anything abnormal, many people with less or limited information retain old prejudices and ill feeling. As in anything, fear of the unknown often results in denial and hostility.

I know that to be true for me. Really, until I was in college I denied my gayness, lied about it, was afraid of it, and in short did about everything but deal with it. I was making myself miserable with a double life by living one thing and feeling quite another. It has only been in the past two years that I have come to terms with who I am and how to live constructively and responsibly with that. I feel free, serene, content, and happy. I live one day at a time with as much responsibility, creativity, integrity, and honor as I can muster.

As in the work that I have chosen, I must create my own social structure . . . my own order, because there do not seem to be many good gay models in the world for me. Not that my life is only about my sexuality. Certainly, my world is larger than that. But that part of my life is constantly new frontier . . . for me as a man, and for gay society in the world.

Dad, you mentioned at one point my "excruciating uncertainty about my own masculinity, as well as my early unsureness about my dad's credibility." One thing you both might be interested to know is that I have never been more certain about my masculinity . . . about what I have to offer as a man both inside the bedroom and out. I think at times my sexuality was at issue. But sexuality and masculinity are two very different issues. Secondly, I do not want to get stuck in the why's of who I am . . . nor do I want you to. Be it genetic or learned behavior for whatever set of reasons or circumstances, I am who I am. There is no fault or blame. It simply is. And the most important consideration is acceptance and dealing with that truth.

Again, please know that this is not a tendency, an inner leaning, or a latent sexual dissatisfaction. It is not a distortion of my most natural human process or an unhealthy expression of a natural human tension. It is the most natural, fulfilling, and satisfying way I know to express my sexuality. Keep in mind that I have had some experiences with women as well. The binding, twisting, narrowing, self-destroying forces in me were in control only when I denied, lied about, and was afraid to be fully who I am. The Christ ethic you talk about I believe to be working in my life, as I do my best to express the love I have for myself

and others with openness, generosity, compassion, and
responsibility.

There are many stereotypes of gay men I am sure
you have seen. Unfortunately, what is most widely publicized about homosexual behavior is not at all my experience. It is a part of the gay world, but certainly not all
or even most of it. For me, being gay is simply a matter of
loving someone of the same sex. I do not lisp or swish,
or dress up like a woman, or molest children, nor do I have
any leaning toward that extreme behavior. The Bud I am
with you is the Bud I am all the time.

One of the most difficult considerations for me to
work through has been my uncertainty of the spiritual dimension of this issue. Clearly, I was raised to believe that
homosexuality is a sin. And I had great concern for my
eternal welfare. The struggle between what I had been told
and how I had been instructed scripturally versus my own
instincts and sense of right and wrong was devastating.

One very positive result of this confrontation with
both of you was that it finally forced me to look deep into
my heart, my soul, my mind, as well as seeking some professional assistance to some very specific spiritual questions. I have talked to three men, one of whom is a Catholic
priest, one a Lutheran minister, and the third is Ed Pow-
ers, who co-authored the enclosed study on Human Sexuality for the United Church of Christ. All three offered
essentially the same verdict . . . that I am on solid ground
. . . that this will be the major issue for the church in the
1980s . . . and that what is important scripturally, socially,
and morally is how I deal with who I am and the choices
that I make in that context. So that the criterion is that I
show love, caring, responsibility, compassion, and respect
for and to those with whom I am involved . . . and not that
it is specifically a man or a woman. Of course there will
be as many interpretations as there are denominations, people, and insecurities.

Again, I cannot make this or anything right or wrong
for you. My intention has been to share more of me . . .
all of me . . . so that we learn to live together with dignity,

compassion, pride, and full expression in all parts of our lives.

While I feel it has been necessary to go into some detail, all of this should be held in the context and perspective that my sexuality is only one area, one part of my life. And now you have it all.

I could have withheld this, and I chose to share. Thank you for giving me the space to feel free and safe. I love you both very much and hope that this letter with the enclosed books will help us all down the road to better understanding and richer, fuller relationships.

Bud

PART II

COMING OUT
POWERFULLY

10

BEING POWERFUL
IN LIFE

Being powerful in life means being fully integrated, open, and loving. It does not mean that you are "in control" of others, nor that you are "in control" of every aspect of your life. Control, after all, is merely an illusion. Living powerfully means that you make the most of everything that life offers to you—regardless of your circumstances. Ultimately, you view yourself as the creator of your life. You are not a victim.

You have the power at every moment to choose what to do with what you have. You may even sense that you have chosen this lifetime and the circumstances in it. I believe that we choose our families, our circumstances, and our life prior to entering our bodies. You may or may not share this belief. I have found it extremely valuable (and empowering) to view life from the perspective that I have

113

chosen everything in it and am responsible for it at each moment.

The difference between being powerless and being powerful has less to do with circumstances than with how you experience and use your circumstances. Being powerful is a state of consciousness, a way of consciously functioning in your life that allows you to welcome each moment as an opportunity to learn, grow, and expand.

Powerless people use the circumstances of their lives to validate that they are indeed victims. There is virtually nothing that they can do that will produce a "win" (or a positive outcome) for themselves. They view situations as betrayals, traps, threats, or conspiracies, overwhelming or burdensome. They look to others to rescue them or blame others for persecuting them. They do not see their responsibility for situations they are facing and continually seek validation that they are not responsible for those situations. They drain energy from those with whom they are in relationship.

Powerful people, on the other hand, use the circumstances of their life to learn, grow, and expand. The circumstances may be exactly the same as those for a powerless person, but someone who is functioning powerfully will discover a way to produce a "win" for themselves out of these circumstances. They welcome situations into their lives and experience inspiration and support all around them. They see, or are willing to look for, their responsibility for situations they are facing in life. They continually validate themselves and their power, responsibility, and creativity. They are empowering to those in relationship to them, and energy gets continually regenerated.

Let's look at some specific examples of what I mean. Remember, the circumstances don't change—rather they are experienced differently and therefore responded to differently depending on one's state of consciousness at a given moment.

A woman discovers her husband is having an affair. If she is functioning as a victim she will blame herself, blame her husband, feel trapped, threatened, and burdened. She may become suicidal, emotionally ill, or cry endlessly to her friends and family about how she has been wronged. If she is functioning powerfully, however, she will take responsibility for herself and her life. She will see her husband's affair as an opportunity to improve communication within the marriage or perhaps to leave the marriage and expand her own life. She will look for the positive and create a better life for herself and those she loves.

A person is diagnosed with AIDS. If he is functioning in a powerless way he will feel like a victim. He may blame someone else for giving it to him, society for having done too little and too late or himself for having done something to bring it on. He will look to others to take care of him and a doctor to tell him exactly what to do. He may quit his job and prepare to die. Someone functioning powerfully, however, will take responsibility for how he deals with his life now. He will be inspired and supported by others and simultaneously will inspire those around him to cope with his diagnosis. Rather than affixing blame he will express gratitude for what he has in life and will look at what he can do to care for himself. He will explore options with his doctor and others and will determine the best treatment program for himself. He will not only prepare for the possibility of death but will focus on how to live day by day, continuing to pursue his goals and perhaps create new ones.

A woman tells her parents she is a lesbian and they reject her. If she is functioning in a powerless way she will feel abandoned and betrayed. She will dwell on their rejection for days, months, or years. She may keep trying to change their minds, always ending up frustrated. She may refuse to be happy until they accept her, and consequently she may never be happy. If she is functioning powerfully, on the other hand, she will continue to love her parents and yet realize that she must move on in her life. She will see their rejection as an opportunity to stop living her life to please someone else and will allow herself to establish a life where she is able to give and receive love. She may continue to communicate her love to her parents and remain ready to accept them back into her life if and when they change their point of view and are able to accept her as she is.

Does this mean that while functioning powerfully the woman who discovered her husband's affair never feels hurt or desperate? Absolutely not. She includes these feelings, and probably many more, yet she operates from a higher state of consciousness in which she is able to have and express her feelings yet not be dominated by them. She can continue to love herself and those in her life—even her husband—and function in a way that empowers herself and those around her.

Likewise the person who functions powerfully with AIDS may still have many other feelings as part of his experience, but he continues to love himself and those around him and functions in a way that empowers himself and others to deal with life-threatening illness and their fear of dying. The powerful lesbian who is rejected by her parents may still feel abandoned, hurt, and angry, yet she operates consciously to create the most positive experience of her life and her circumstances—maintaining her love for herself and realizing that she is worthy of love. She is able to put herself in their place (with their backgrounds, beliefs, and life experiences) and thereby realizes that they are doing the best that they are capable of under the circumstances. She continues to love them and remains open to them changing their attitudes, knowing that she is all right whether or not they acknowledge that.

Now that I have indicated some of the ways in which functioning powerfully is different from functioning power-lessly, I must point out that these are not the only two options for how to be. There are many other states of consciousness from which one can operate—and a powerful person includes them all. To be powerful you must be conscious of what you do and how you do it. You will be willing to do the work that it takes to establish and maintain a powerful way of viewing life and to accept that you are responsible for your life each and every day.

What I am about to present conceptually as a way to consciously enhance your power in life is a synthesis of the work of many people and is filtered through my own experience and perception. I particularly want to acknowledge Vern Black, a friend and colleague who died of AIDS in 1989, for bringing the core of this material into my life as a tool with which I have been able to work—and a context within which I have been able to expand my own life. I offer it to you with love, as it was offered to me.

HOW TO BECOME MORE POWERFUL

In this section you will be given a sense of what steps you go through to become more powerful in your life. We will be working through a scale of consciousness—describing several states of consciousness between being powerless or depressed, and being powerful and simultaneously empowering to those around you. In the next chapter, How to Come Out Powerfully, I will apply these concepts directly to the process of coming out. Some of this material is complex and may be difficult to master in one reading. It might be helpful if you allow yourself to think about this material in reference to any particular circumstance that you are dealing with in your life at this time. You may choose to focus on a health issue, a relationship, a car accident or a theft, breaking up with a spouse or lover, dealing with a friend's death, or anything else that is appropriate to your own life.

    Becoming more conscious means you can continually integrate more aspects of any situation until you get the entire picture—including your role in it—and are thereby able to function in a more powerful manner. Most of the time, many of us get so caught up in the situations in our lives and our problems that we are unable to see them in perspective. In this chapter we will look at how to step back from a situation in order to see it in a broader context. Please keep in mind that the steps I will discuss are those that people generally go through. This is meant to be a tool that you can use—not a rigid rule book to adhere to.

Similar to the process of coming out described in Chapter 3, the process of becoming more powerful is an inclusive one. As you become more conscious and more powerful you keep including more states of consciousness along the way. When you are powerful and empowering you haven't eliminated other states of consciousness but, rather, have included them as part of your experience. I conceptualize this holographically, as a series of concentric spheres, with the experience of being powerless and depressed at the core, surrounded by each other state until one is able to include all the rest.

Each of the states of consciousness includes emotions, attitudes, and ways of experiencing life situations that are characteristic of that state. Each of the states of consciousness consequently leads to different types of actions and reactions in regard to life situations. Again, the situations may be the same—yet how we experience and function in the situation varies depending on our state of consciousness in relationship to it at a given point in time. Each of us has the capacity of changing our state of consciousness every moment. In order to do this we must:

- Be aware of what our state of consciousness is in regard to a given situation.
- Be willing to expand our power
- Be willing to inhibit any reactions that produce results we do not want;
- Be willing to take the steps that are necessary in order to function more powerfully.

If you want to function powerfully, then you must be willing to include a broad range of feelings and attitudes in yourself and in others. To get there you must also incorporate all of the steps that will be enumerated as "tools to become more powerful." I will describe each state of consciousness and the tools that can allow you to step from that state toward a more powerful way of being. You may not, at this point, choose to take these steps, but I offer this ma-

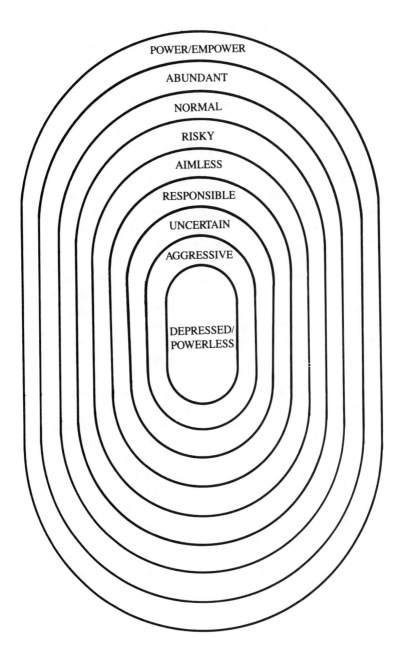

POWER/EMPOWER

ABUNDANT

NORMAL

RISKY

AIMLESS

RESPONSIBLE

UNCERTAIN

AGGRESSIVE

DEPRESSED/
POWERLESS

terial to provide you with options. You may feel one way about this material at this moment and quite differently about it if you choose to come back to it and apply it to your life at some other point.

It is my sense that we all started our lives from a state of being powerful—it is our natural state of being. From a spiritual basis we are all one and all powerful. When we enter this life, coming into our bodies as infants, we rapidly begin to experience our separation, isolation, and dependency. We feel like victims and experience being dependent on others to survive. We are trained, from birth, to feel powerless. We are trained not to express all we know, "to be seen and not heard," to be like everyone else.

As we begin to grow up we intuitively know a great deal more than we are expected to know for our early age and stature. We learn that it is unwise, however, to express what we know. It seems to make more sense to play the game as we are supposed to—to let the grown ups be the authorities. Often, as we have previously discussed, we get to adulthood without ever having allowed ourselves to be the authorities in our own lives, and we keep looking for approval from others. Our experience of our power has been trained out of us, if you will. Using the tools to become more powerful is a process of reeducation. It is a process of remembering what you already know.

For each of the states of consciousness, I will first describe what that experience feels like and then describe the tools to use, or steps to take, to become more powerful. Remember, as we add new tools we don't stop using the ones that came before. You may even notice that along the way there are some steps that may not appeal to you. Unfortunately, we don't get to pick only those we like. If you notice yourself resisting doing what it takes to move from one state of consciousness to a more powerful state, it may be because you don't like the tools that are being suggested.

Powerless/Depressed

You feel powerless, like a victim, you don't trust yourself. You have resisted making agreements with others, and even with yourself, because you so often don't do what you say you will. You probably don't feel like you really make a difference. You are holding yourself back and pressing down your feelings as you withhold the truth from yourself and others. You may experience yourself as depressed or fearful. You feel trapped, threatened, or overwhelmed.

Tools to become more powerful

- Make a decision to trust yourself.
- Tell the truth about your experience.
- Make agreements with yourself as to what you are going to do and how you are going to function. Don't make any agreements you are unwilling or unable to keep, and by all means keep the agreements you make.

Since you made the decision not to trust yourself a very long time ago, probably as a child or adolescent, make a new decision today as an adult. This is what we discussed in Chapter 2. Unless you make a decision to trust yourself you won't be willing to tell the truth. Then make agreements with yourself or with others that are based on truth— agreements that you are actually willing to make and keep. If you then don't keep these agreements you will stay powerless, since you will have proved to yourself once more that you are not trustworthy. If you tell the truth and keep your agreements you will be taking a stand, and that will allow you to feel more powerful.

Since most of us feel some anger, often a great deal, as a result of holding ourselves back, part of the truth you must tell may involve expressing anger and perhaps rage.

You probably learned as a child that you shouldn't express your anger. Not to express your anger may have been a wise decision at that time, but that decision must be re-examined today as an adult. As a child, it may have looked like your survival was at stake if you expressed your anger and took a strong position in life. As an adult, the quality of your life (and perhaps even your life itself) is at stake if you remain silent or turn your anger inward.

When you take a strong stand—declaring what you believe is true no matter what the consequences might be— you are moving into an Aggressive state of consciousness.

Aggressive

You feel angry, antagonistic, hostile, defensive. Your attitude is one of arrogance, contempt, vindictiveness, defiance, or outrage. You anticipate being attacked or insulted and see others as the enemy. *When you take a strong and aggressive stand you most likely generate opposition.* You expect others to be your enemy, and they will generally mirror this back to you.

Tool to become more powerful

> • Step back from the situation enough to observe whether you are actually being yourself, or whether you are taking an extreme position.

Notice what results you wanted to produce. If the position you are taking is getting in the way of those results, recognize how you are creating opposition to what you want. Tell the truth about the payoff you are getting by being aggressive. You may be right, and your positions may still be getting in the way of achieving the results you want. When you notice this, allow yourself to choose another approach. Go for the results you want. Being right may be nice, but if it isn't producing the results you wanted it is the booby prize. You may not know precisely what to do next, and you may even have a difficult time letting yourself back off of the approach you have been taking, but when you do you will probably notice that there are lots of options. You will probably be uncertain which one to choose, and the state of consciousness you are moving into is an Uncertain one.

Uncertain

You are willing to take another approach to the situation. You know there are lots of options but don't know which path will lead to your goal. You may wait indefinitely rather than make a choice. This will move you back to being Powerless. You may charge down one of the possible paths, being sure it is the right one. This will take you back to Agressive. When you are Uncertain you may feel bored, annoyed, exasperated. The situation you are in may seem insolvable, and others may appear to be evading the issue or deflecting your efforts.

Tool to become more powerful

- Simply make a choice. Do something new. Take your best shot at approaching the situation in a manner that may work.

When you are in a state of uncertainty you are not sure what path to follow. Realize that whatever path you take will lead to the results that are at the end of that path. *When you make your choice you are also responsible for the results you produce as a result of that choice.* Your awareness that you made the choice of what path to follow moves you to a state of being Responsible.

Responsible

You chose a path and followed it. It may not have produced the results you wanted, and you may feel guilty, disappointed, reluctant to try again, or self-conscious. While perhaps feeling obligated to try again, you may also feel that this will really be an effort. You are striving to find a way to produce results. You may sometimes feel powerless, aggressive, and uncertain about what to do, but you know that you will continue to "go for it." You've come this far and you're not willing to go back.

Tool to become more powerful

- Assess the situation and clean up any damage you created.

If the path you chose to follow produced poor results, or damage, make amends. Acknowledge your own ability to trust yourself. Acknowledge your trustworthiness. Be satisfied that at least you are making progress and keep going for results. You are likely to keep trying new possibilities, yet you may feel somewhat aimless in the process.

Aimless

You are accepting your responsibility for the results you produce in your life. You are still going for positive results, but not really sure how to achieve them. You are continually making choices, following through, and doing what it takes to clean up any damage you may create along the way. Life begins to feel bland and unimpressive. You are hopeful that you will achieve your goals, but as of now have not done so. Since you know you are responsible for the results you generate, other people's actions may seem somewhat unimportant.

Tools to become more powerful

- Make it a goal to provide support for others.
- Create a vision.

Instead of focusing only on your goals, begin to look at the experience of others, and at the world around you. You may choose to support an individual, an organization, or an idea. Discover what is needed and wanted in order to provide support and then start doing it. You still get to apply all of the tools that got you to this state in the first place. *When you start to look at how you can make a contribution to others you will discover more of your power.* You may, however, also discover that in order to do what it takes to provide a service (and take your attention away from your goals exclusively), you will have to take a risk. If you are willing to start doing this, you enter the state of consciousness called Risky.

Risky

You are willing to provide support and to provide a service. You're curious about what the result will be and may be testing the situation. You may have some anxiety or concern about what will happen. You perceive others as mentors. You may even take a big risk and experience it as a challenge. This may be amusing and satisfying to you. Others may even be seen as your partners in discovery.

Tools to become more powerful

- Recognize any detrimental elements that may come along and handle them.
- Keep your options open.
- Pay attention to the details of the situations that present themselves.

As you notice any detrimental elements or potential problems that arise, make sure you take care of them in an appropriate manner. You will have the ability to choose, so keep making choices that are truthful for you. Stiffen your integrity as you continue to use all the tools that got you here. Keep trusting yourself and keep telling the truth about your experience. These steps will move you to a Normal state of consciousness.

Normal

It is normal to have both highs and lows in life. Life is like a roller coaster, with goods and bads, ups and downs, highs and lows. It is not normal to move along without any bumps. When you are in this Normal state of consciousness, you understand and appreciate the ebb and flow of life. As you experience the good and the bad you are confident, enthusiastic, and cheerful. You see each situation as an opportunity. You are taking risks, and each one is an opportunity for growth and expansion. Others are aligned with you as you move through your life.

Tool to become more powerful

- As you notice positive and negative results, strengthen those things that cause the up trends—make fine adjustments as you see downward trends develop.

You are simply paying attention to what produces the most positive results and then focusing on attaining those results. As you strengthen the positive and adjust for the negative you move into Abundance.

Abundance

You are exhilarated and grateful, for your experience of life is on an upward trend. You can pay attention to the fine points in life and appreciate and respond to beauty. *You see each situation as providing you with an opportunity for expansion.* You understand and are willing to apply the principles and tools of living powerfully. Others are providers, even when you are serving and supporting them.

Tool to become more powerful

- As you are now producing fabulous results, don't allow yourself to get frivolous and squander your abundance. Learn what produces the very best results and do even more of that.

This will move you into a Powerful and simultaneously Empowering state.

Power/Empower

You are playful, compassionate, serene, ecstatic, joyful, and generous. You welcome each situation that comes along. You view other people you encounter as inspirers, supporters, and friends. All you have to give and to receive is love. Others reflect this back to you. You feel powerful and you

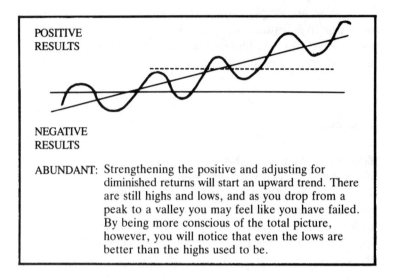

POSITIVE
RESULTS

NEGATIVE
RESULTS

ABUNDANT: Strengthening the positive and adjusting for
diminished returns will start an upward trend. There
are still highs and lows, and as you drop from a
peak to a valley you may feel like you have failed.
By being more conscious of the total picture,
however, you will notice that even the lows are
better than the highs used to be.

see power in others—thereby empowering them to be open
and loving. Your energy continually builds as you notice
that you are much bigger than you had ever conceived of
being. *You are no longer limited by the concepts you had
previously formed about yourself.* You are now part of a
larger whole, and you are able to draw on an energy greater
than yourself. You are radiant energy!

Tools to maintain your power

- Continue to use all of the tools that got you here.
- Expand your responsibility even further.

Increase your integrity, discipline, and love. Allow
yourself to be supported. Letting yourself be supported by
others is a means of supporting them to experience their
power. In turn you will mutually empower each other.

In being powerful in life it is important that we remember to include in ourselves, and in others, a full range

of emotions and attitudes—as well as all of the possible ways of responding to a situation. In reality, in order to function powerfully we must tell the truth about who we are and recognize others for who they are. The truth is that

SOMETIMES WE FEEL POWERLESS AND DE-PRESSED.

SOMETIMES WE ARE ANGRY AND PISSED OFF.

SOMETIMES WE ARE UNCERTAIN ABOUT HOW TO PROCEED WITH OUR LIVES.

SOMETIMES WE FEEL GUILTY BECAUSE WE MADE A MISTAKE, EVEN IF IT SEEMED LIKE A GOOD IDEA AT THE TIME.

SOMETIMES WE LOSE SIGHT OF WHAT LIFE IS ABOUT AND WE FEEL AIMLESS.

SOMETIMES WE GET BEYOND OUR PETTINESS AND TAKE THE RISK OF SERVING OTHERS.

SOMETIMES WE FEEL CONFIDENT, ENTHUSI-ASTIC, AND CHEERFUL.

SOMETIMES THINGS ARE WORKING AMAZ-INGLY WELL AND WE ARE GRATEFUL.

And throughout all of this, no matter how much we may try to cover it up, all any of us really wants is to love and be loved. We are all in this together, and we are all one!

I hope that as you read the above descriptions you were able to apply them to your own life. In the next chapter we will look at how to apply these tools to being more powerful to the issue of coming out. While I will discuss coming out as gay, I remind you that what coming out is really about is telling the truth. It is possible to come out from any of the states of consciousness—and the state of consciousness from which you are functioning will have a direct impact on how you approach coming out and how others respond to you.

Bernard, to His Nephew

Dear Allen,
 I heard from your sister, Sandy, that you hate faggots, and that the fags in Oregon drive you crazy—well, you little fucker, I'm a faggot, and if you hate me, please let me know by return mail, because I'll write you out of my fucking will.
 I enjoyed seeing you when my play was produced. You looked handsome getting on the plane, and you didn't look like a Fa'Coctah hippie, but a good-looking young man.
 Al, I don't want you to hate anyone—not only me, but anyone who is straight or gay. I expect much more from you than that.
 I came out to Sandy and now I'm coming out to you from the same position of love. I do love you, and you are the only nephew I have.
 I want to know you better, and love you more.
                              Your uncle,
                              Bernard

11

HOW TO COME OUT POWERFULLY

Having now discussed various states of consciousness, how each state feels and what tools you can apply in order to be more powerful in life, let's apply this concept to the process of coming out. There are many different options for how to come out. For example, you may talk with someone face-to-face or on the telephone, write a letter, talk openly about what you did on the weekend and with whom, put your lover's picture on your desk at work, march in a parade, write a letter to your congressman, bring a same-sex date to a party or family gathering, be discovered by someone else. The list of possibilities is endless, and the choice is yours. Regardless of how you choose to come out, the state of consciousness you are in at the time will greatly affect not only your choice of method but the impact that it will have on those around you and on you personally.

In this chapter let's look at what coming out might be like, depending on what your state of consciousness is. We will then look at how you might apply the tools to becoming more powerful to the process of coming out and feeling better about yourself as a lesbian or gay man. This could lead to coming out in a loving and powerful manner while being able to empower those to whom you come out so that they too are able to love and accept you as you are.

Powerless/Depressed

Remember, in this state of consciousness you don't trust yourself, you are fearful of losses and worried about your survival. You are likely to deny most of your feelings and to be somewhat of a "drama queen"—addicted to creating dramas in your life (frequently tragedies) in order to perpetuate the experience of being a victim, rescuer, or persecutor. You may not even be able to see this for yourself in spite of the fact that people around you are probably trying to point this out to you.

If you are functioning in this manner, you probably experience being gay as overwhelming or a burden. You are probably keeping it as a very private segment of your life, not well integrated into the rest of your life. You are likely to feel that it should be kept absolutely secret and that if the truth were known about you it would feel like a threat or a trap. Among the worst aspects of being in a depressed state regarding being gay is that you fear some form of major loss—rejection, illness, or other bodily harm, loss of job, loss of loved ones, excommunication from your church, and possibly even suicide. You may genuinely feel that your survival is at stake if you come out.

Because the opportunities for support in coming out are far greater now than they were years ago we might like to think that very few gay people are functioning in a powerless/depressed manner. Unfortunately the vast proportion of people who are lesbian or gay are still in hiding.

They are in small towns everywhere; in the bars of major cities with large gay populations; in careers in government, corporate America, and the media. They are hiding out in their homes, alone or with a partner. They are attending family and other social functions with an "opposite sex appliance" on their arms in order to pass for being straight. They are actively denying who they really are and may even be adding to antigay sentiment by laughing at "gay jokes," participating in gay bashing verbally or physically, or voting against the gay community on issues of relevance to lesbians and gays.

On the other extreme they may be presenting themselves as gay through a caricaturish victim role—bemoaning their fate of being forever a second-class citizen who will never be accepted, appreciated, or loved. They are generally not happy with their lives and may blame this on their being gay or on others who won't accept them because they are gay. If they come out while in this state of consciousness, they will want others to either reject them or possibly embrace them to make everything seem better. They are powerless because how they feel about themselves is dependent on how others respond to them. They are everywhere, and you may be one of them.

If you find yourself in the group of people I just described know that you are not alone and that I, for one, feel a great deal of compassion for you. Added to the difficulties already discussed about being depressed about being gay is that you often generate anger from others, even from other gays. Those who have moved beyond their depression about being gay may be angry with you for remaining stuck, and those that have not may collude with you to keep you stuck. This further plays into your feeling that you are a victim, and when others are sympathetic or show "pity" for your condition this perpetuates your poor self-image. There is a way out of this sense of hopelessness and despair, but it requires you to take some action in your own life. You must decide that you want things to be different, that you want to be happier and more powerful, that you want to enjoy life more.

How to become less depressed about being gay

If you have been in a state of depression about being gay it is time to do some work on yourself. Some of your feelings are because of your own beliefs about homosexuality and decisions you've already made about what it means to be gay. Start to re-examine these decisions. It is possible to be lesbian or gay and still be successful and happy. It is also likely that you made some decisions about your self-worth and your ability to trust yourself when you were a child or an adolescent. The exercise in Chapter 2 may have been helpful in sorting some of this out.

If you want your life to be happier, make a decision to trust yourself to tell the truth and to cope effectively with consequences that arise from it. At least acknowledge to yourself that you are gay and that you have been using this as a way to hold yourself back and create a great deal of discomfort for yourself. If you want to continue being uncomfortable keep doing what you are doing—it is working. If you want to change things, make some agreements with yourself and keep them. Some examples of the type of agreements you might start with are:

- I will no longer participate in gay bashing, verbally or physically.
- I will seek positive support for working through my personal feelings about being gay.
- I will speak up if I am in the presence of someone making a "gay joke."
- I will let my legislatures know that I want them to support such issues as a Gay Rights Bill and increased AIDS funding.
- I will affirm that I am a worthwhile individual.
- I will come out to some people in my life.
- I will express more of my feelings.
- I will treat myself and other people who are gay with more respect.

There are probably many more such agreements that you could make with yourself that would begin to enhance your self-esteem. It is important that you only make those agreements that you are willing to keep, and that you then keep those agreements that you make. Saying you'll do something and then not doing it will just reinforce your bad feelings about yourself and will keep you stuck.

As you decide to tell more of the truth you might discover that you become somewhat adamant about speaking up no matter what. You may even discover yourself becoming somewhat aggressive. Once you decide to stand up for yourself, it is quite likely that you will find yourself getting angry. Some of this anger may be directed toward yourself for not having spoken up sooner, but much of it is likely to be directed outward. You are likely to experience anger to those who you feel have kept you down—perhaps to your parents for not having taught you to love yourself as you are, perhaps to other gays who you feel poorly represent you, perhaps toward those you believe are bigots, perhaps toward government agencies, and perhaps toward society in general. Keep in mind that as you begin to take a stand for yourself you may discover some opposition and face some confrontations. This too may generate anger.

If you have been taught not to express your anger, and you still believe that it is bad to do so, you may not be willing to stand up for yourself. This will keep you stuck in a powerless and depressed state. If this is the case it is time to re-examine whether or not expressing anger would be preferable to denying your feelings. If you choose to take a stand by coming out as gay or by taking any of the types of steps mentioned above, you may notice that you are becoming aggressive.

Aggressive

Doing any of the things you agreed to do for yourself, no matter what, is likely to generate some opposition. For example: if you are with a group of people and they start to abuse someone gay, and you refuse to participate, you may be in opposition to the group. If you seek positive support for working through your personal feelings about being gay you might find it difficult (depending on where you live) to find such support, and in the process discover some opposition. If you write your elected officials to ask them to support issues important to the gay community you may find that they resist this. If you affirm that you are a worthwhile individual you may find opposition, even from your own mind, telling you that you are not. It doesn't matter what stand you take in life, the firmer you hold on to it the more you will discover the opposition (sometimes where you expected it and sometimes where you least expected it). You always have the option of retreating. This is an option many people take, which is why so many people function in a powerless/depressed manner. If you hold firm to your position, however, you may find yourself getting stuck in an aggressive state of consciousness.

If you come out aggressively, you may experience others as the enemy, or anticipate that they will be and thereby treat them as if they are. You may be hostile, antagonistic, and confrontational. You may even do things to provoke a confrontation and prove that you were right all along. Some of the stereotypic, or caricaturish, ways of being gay may actually come from this state of consciousness. The reasoning goes like this: I am gay. My parents don't like gay people. I'm furious with my parents for being so bigoted. I'll show them. I'll tell them I'm gay and too bad if they don't accept me.

Based on this type of reasoning you are likely to come out with a huge chip on your shoulder. In addition to giving your parents your sexuality to deal with, you are giving them your rage. Their response will be influenced by this yet also depends in part on their own state of consciousness. If they are depressed in life they may back away and be unwilling to engage with you at all. They will feel persecuted by your coming out and feel as if they are your victims. These are the parents who say, *"How could you do this to us?"* or *"I don't want to hear about it, it's just a phase you're going through,"* or *"Don't tell your father, it would kill him."* You can buy right into this, which will take you back to being depressed yourself. If, however, you remain in an aggressive state, you'll be furious with them. That will serve to validate their feeling of being victimized, and your anger will drive a wedge into your relationship with them.

If your parents are themselves aggressive, knowing exactly what's right (and that is not being gay), they will become your enemy, and you can fight and argue forever with neither of you being willing to budge a bit. You'll tell them you're gay and they'll say, *"No you're not . . . it's just a phase."* You'll say you can't do anything about it, it's just the way you are, and they'll say, *"You can to do something about it . . . abstain, get yourself to a psychiatrist, repent."* You'll argue religion, you'll argue mental health, you'll argue whether or not you love each other—but you won't resolve anything. Eventually, you'll move away and won't want to be at family functions, or they'll disown you and won't accept you at family functions.

I realize that neither of these are particularly pleasant scenarios. Unfortunately, since most people are used to functioning either in a depressed or an aggressive manner, such dramas may develop. If you are functioning in a depressed or an aggressive manner yourself, you will get hooked by these types of dramas and won't see a way out. You'll give up or you'll hold on to the belief that you are right and they are wrong.

It is, of course, possible that you can come out aggressively and that those you come out to are functioning from a higher state of consciousness and will let you know that they love you anyway. Unfortunately, if you are aggressive, anticipating that they will be the enemy, you may misinterpret their communications of love and support. For example: you come out in a hostile way and your parents respond, "We love you. What can we do to support you? If you'd like to see a therapist, we'll pay for it." If you're aggressive they just said the wrong thing. How dare they think you need therapy. See, you always knew they thought being gay was sick. The problem here is that if you are aggressive you won't be open to receiving support when it is given. It's a bit like being an adolescent and fighting for your autonomy. There is little or nothing that someone can say to you that isn't the "wrong" thing to say. Again, there are other options, but *it is up to you to change yourself and how you are functioning—not to change them.* The more conscious you become, the more room you will have to hear, understand, and accept others.

How to generate less opposition to being gay and coming out

Let's start by acknowledging that by feeling anger and aggressiveness you are definitely making progress from the hiding that you were doing before. Your anger may even be absolutely appropriate and justifiable. Everything you stand for and everything you believe and say may be absolutely right. Nevertheless, you are angry and fighting all the time and find this frustrating and debilitating. The positions you are taking, no matter how right they are, may result in battles and conflict. If this is the result you want, stay aggressive—it is working. If you want some other result, step back from the situation enough to see exactly what is happening and what role you are playing in it. It is crazy to keep doing the same thing and to expect different results.

As you distance yourself from the situation, a bit like a witness or observer, you will have a better vantage point from which to notice your position as well as the position of those you are engaged with. Let yourself be aware of the payoff of the positions you are taking. It is very likely that the payoff you are observing is that you get to be right and perhaps even self-righteous. You are also getting to do what you said you would do to move yourself, no matter what, out of being depressed. Continue to trust yourself to tell the truth. The difference now is that you need to look for what result you want to produce. For example: do you want to be fighting with people or do you want to accomplish something else? Do you want to change their position? Do you want to feel good about yourself regardless of their position? Do you want to improve your communication with them? Do you want to improve the quality of your relationship?

Sticking to your position, no matter what, is likely to assure that they will stick to theirs just as stridently. It will look like whoever changes their position is the loser, and nobody wants to be a loser. *You cannot change their position since that is completely up to them.* That is why aggressive games sometimes become "fights to the death," like war or family feuds. They are very reasonable when looking at them from within. It is when you observe them from the outside that they look a bit absurd and futile.

If you want to move beyond the battle, to where you can communicate and improve the quality of your relationships, stop doing what you are doing. Don't stop telling the truth but look for another method of communicating it. For example: when you're angry with someone and blow up at them they generally fight back (aggressive) or recoil from your anger (depressed). Sometimes a person is powerful enough to be able to accept your blow up as *your* expression of anger and doesn't become engaged by it, though this is less common. Another approach is for you to communicate your anger clearly and directly, yet without ranting and raving. The person you are addressing is far more likely to be able to hear you—mostly because they are listening. You have gotten their attention instead of pushing them away. You may see how this works in terms of effectively communicating your anger. If the goal of communicating your anger is merely to get it out, to dump it, you can achieve this by ranting and raving—yet other than dumping your anger very little else may be effectively altered. If your goal is to be treated differently, to clear up a misunderstanding, or rectify an insult and be treated with respect, you might look at communicating your anger differently.

The most effective way to communicate your anger and your rage is to deal with it in a larger context. For example: *"I am outraged with your lack of support because you truly mean a lot to me"* or *"I am furious about your behavior toward me because I love you, and consequently I take what you say very seriously.''* Your ability to operate in a larger context is directly related to how powerfully you are functioning. Furthermore, unless you are willing to acknowledge your hurt and your anger, you may block yourself from experiencing those feelings that are larger than that hurt and anger. You may, for example, block yourself from experiencing your joy, gratitude, and love. (You can see many examples of this dynamic in the letters throughout this book, and the exercise in Chapter 4 may have broadened your personal perspective on what there is to communicate.)

Similarly, with communicating that you are gay, if you want this to become an issue over which you fight in your relationship with others you can present it in an angry and hostile manner. If, however, you genuinely want to improve your relationships with others you might find another way to express yourself. Bear in mind, I believe it is preferable to let people know you are gay, even if this creates a battle, than to remain in a state of denial. Coming out, no matter how you do it, is preferable to being in the closet. Your first attempts at coming out may be done aggressively, very likely out of your own sense of defensiveness, but there are many other options. You needn't and won't remain defensive, or aggressive, forever. The better you feel about yourself, and the more secure you are in your own life, the more options will appear to you. If you are willing to let go of your position—to let go of the "right" way for you to be gay or to come out—you become free to pursue the results that you want. You might ask, appropriately, "What do I do now?"

Uncertain

Once you are willing to look for alternate ways of presenting yourself you will be able to see many. Nevertheless, you are uncertain as to what results will be produced by each alternative. You may have some good ideas yet cannot, with certainty, foresee the outcome. You must remain true to yourself and also be true to the results you want. It is being truer to yourself to go for the results that you want than to hang on to some decision you may have made as to how you were going to achieve them, especially if that method has not worked.

In terms of coming out, when you told your parents you were gay you wanted them to accept you. You also insisted that you were going to bring your current lover to family functions and that if they didn't like it "too bad." This may have generated a fight, and you may no longer be welcome at family functions. Other alternatives would have been to let them know you are gay and that you want to support them to become comfortable with that, would like them to get to know your lover, and that you love them and ultimately want to be able to function as you are within your family. There are these and obviously many more possibilities.

Rather than being defensive from the start, the options mentioned above involve a recognition that your parents will also have a process to go through, and a recognition that they have the right to go through that process. While you still ultimately want to bring your lover to family functions, you have opted not to make this the battleground but rather to love them and give them time to be comfortable with this new information. What you are recognizing is that prior to even talking to them about your homosexuality, you took time (possibly years) to get to the point of being comfortable with this reality yourself.

You may also want to look at when and how you'll tell someone you're gay. Let's say you decided that you were no longer going to tolerate gay jokes. You are absolutely going to take a stand on this. Then your boss makes a gay joke during a business meeting that you are attending. You may choose to get angry about it right there in the meeting and express that anger. Chances are your boss will not take kindly to this and will see you as undermining his authority. If what you want to achieve is raising your boss's consciousness so that he is aware that such jokes are damaging to you and others, you might handle this in a variety of other ways.

- You could wait until you calm down and then set up a meeting with your boss. You might let him know that you are gay and that the joke he made was at your expense and that you were hurt by it and quite angry. You would appreciate it if he would look at why he makes such jokes and really would like him to stop making them.
- You could write a letter to your boss and explain exactly how you feel.
- You could let your boss know that you were stunned by his joke, and while you would have liked to confront him in front of others you did not want to undermine his image in front of the rest of the staff.

Obviously you can never really know the exact impact of any of these choices. The more you observe the situation, and the better you know the player, the more likely you are to choose the action that will produce the best results. Nevertheless, the results of your choices are still uncertain.

Take responsibility for your actions and their results

To remove your uncertainty you must make a choice. You are certain of the results of staying in the closet (depressed/powerless). You are certain of the results produced by the positions you took when you were angry and aggressive. You are, however, uncertain of the results that your other options will produce because you haven't yet taken action. The way to discover, with certainty, what results a given action will produce is to choose an option and take it. The way to know, with certainty, what is at the end of a path is to follow that path to the end.

What is essential here is to know that how you approached the situation—the option, action, path, that you chose in coming out—led to the result you produced. You are the one responsible for choosing that approach and you are the one responsible for the results it produced. You can now see why this is a way of functioning that many people don't allow themselves. If you aren't willing to trust yourself, you will feel safer staying in the closet. If you insist on being self-righteous, you will want to blame someone else for hindering your advancement. Their bigotry has been keeping you in the closet or is getting in the way of their understanding and accepting you. Once you know that you have options, that you can make choices, and that you are responsible for the results produced by your choices, you must also be willing to acknowledge that you might make mistakes. You may actually have presented your sexuality in a way that was causing others to reject you.

Responsible

Knowing that the way you handle a situation leads to the results you produce puts you in a responsible state of consciousness. The way you come out to your family, your friends, or your boss may damage your relationship with them. For example: if you wrote to your boss and called him an asshole for having made a gay joke, you are responsible for not making it easier for him to hear you and for his getting defensive. If you meet with him and tell him you're quitting because you were furious with the joke he told, you are responsible for being out of work. If you do nothing, you are responsible (along with him) for his continuing to tell such jokes.

How to take responsibility without beating yourself up

Acknowledge to yourself that you did the best you could at the time. Every mistake seemed like a good idea at the time, and everyone makes mistakes sometimes. Although you may feel some guilt, remember that where you are now is far better than being closeted. You are an active participant in your life and are in the process of learning and growing. Continue to trust yourself and be willing to look for ways to repair any damage you may have created.

This may be where an apology is in order. It won't work to apologize for telling your parents you are gay or for calling your boss on the gay joke he told. It is probably more important to apologize for the manner in which you chose to communicate with them. After all, since you probably wanted a different reaction than what you got, indeed you are sorry for how you approached the situation. For example: you may tell your parents that it is important to you that they know you're gay and that you are able to be who you are at family functions. Nevertheless, you're sorry for having confronted them with all of this so abruptly that they didn't have any opportunity to deal with this new information. *"I'm sorry that I got so angry with you for reacting the way you did, and I'd like us to be able to relate to each other better."* In terms of the situation with your boss, you might want to let him know that it was difficult for you to confront him and you realize you were pretty hostile in your approach. *"I'm sorry for calling you an asshole and realize that in doing so I made it more difficult for you to hear what I was saying about gay jokes."*

Even when you make your best attempt at apologizing or cleaning up any damage you might have created, you may discover that the damage has already been done and there is little or no way to undo it. Once an action is taken it is not possible to erase it—only to move on. When you apologize, the other person has the right to accept your apology or reject it. This will depend on them, and there may be nothing you can do about it. What is important is that you take responsibility for your actions and do your best to rectify the situation.

Aimless

Once you're taking responsibility for being gay, and for your own process of coming out, you may feel somewhat aimless. You're telling the truth about being gay, you've been cleaning up any damage that may have been produced by the manner in which you have come out, yet you still don't feel really good about yourself or the situations you've been creating around you. You know there is more you could be doing, but don't know what that is.

Create a vision and support others

Again, applying the tools discussed in the previous chapter, *turn your attention away from yourself and focus on a larger vision.* Instead of focusing on the immediate dramas you may be in, create a vision for your life and for your world. If you do not have a job where it is all right to be gay, you might create a vision of one where you can be open about who you are. If you are at odds with your family about your sexuality, you might create a vision of a family where you can openly give and receive love. If you live in a community where it isn't all right to be gay, you might create a vision of a community where it is absolutely fine to be gay. Next, discover what it would take to manifest that vision and start doing that. *By supporting others, and working toward a vision, you will be discovering more of what you have to offer and more about the powerful person that you are.*

Risky

Creating a vision takes you out of aimlessness, for you now have some direction. Yet moving toward a vision generally involves taking some risks. You must look at what is required to support yourself and others to manifest the vision you are going for. The risk lies in doing what is required. You may very well notice that what it will take to manifest your vision might not be comfortable for you. It might not be something you really wanted to do, or it might be something that creates a great deal of anxiety, since it may require you to function in ways that go beyond what you have done in the past.

To follow the situations we've been looking at up to now:

- You might discover that in order to support your parents to accept your homosexuality and include your lover in family functions, you must have a lot of patience with them, and perhaps even increase your dialogue with them. This may be risky if you have spent years distancing yourself and don't know whether you want to take the risk of being vulnerable with them again.

- You might discover that your parents are unwilling to budge (staying aggressive and holding on to their position) and that in order to support them you must let go of trying to change them. The way to move toward your vision may be to choose a new "family," where you are able to give and receive love freely as yourself. This may, however, also give your parents the confrontation they need in order to change their position. Faced with losing their child, they may choose you over their position that homosexuality is bad. This is risky, since you actually must be willing to move on and leave the family. You are also running the risk of discovering whether they value you more or less than they value their beliefs about homosexuals.

- When you pursue a workplace in which it is all right to be gay you may discover that your current place of work isn't it. This is risky because to manifest your vision you might have to look for an-

- other job and approach your interviews as someone who is openly lesbian or gay.
- If you discover that your boss is willing to support you and will stop telling gay jokes, you may decide that you will stay at the company and support the kind of changes that will make it an even better work environment for someone who is gay. This is risky because you will now be functioning in a more open manner, and you may have to confront similar situations with other employees, or they may begin to ask you questions about homosexuality that you would just as soon not be asked. If things improve significantly in your place of employment so that you can be yourself, you may now find yourself included at more social functions, where the risk might be showing up with a date, thus taking an even further step out of the closet.

It is not possible to become more powerful with your sexuality, with coming out or with anything else in life, without taking risks. If you envision yourself as a really powerful skier you discover what it takes to go down a challenging run, and then you take the risk of going down that run. If you envision yourself as a highly successful business person, you must discover what it would take to expand your career, and then take the risks involved in meeting that challenge. It is no different with being gay and coming out. As you go through these risky encounters you will feel tested and challenged, and will probably be anxious and also curious about the results you are producing.

How to create more enthusiasm about the risks you are taking

Recognize that you are growing and expanding and that you are no longer functioning out of fear, anger, or guilt but are now well along the way to manifesting a vision. You are investing in your future and not being held back by your past. Since you are curious as to what will happen, pay careful attention to the details. Here are some examples, following the previous scenarios:

- Your parents may be stuck between the positions they hold about homosexuality and their love and respect for you. If you're paying attention to the details you'll see their conflict and perhaps be able to clarify it for them. For example, they'll make a negative comment that hurts you and you may say, *"I know you've always thought homosexuals were sick and not capable of success, but you can clearly see that I am emotionally healthy and very successful."*

- Your parents may be refusing to include your lover at family functions. If you're paying attention to the details you may discover that they are most worried about particular family functions. They might, for example, not want you to come with your lover to a function where children will be present because they are afraid that if you and your lover are present you'll hold hands and make the event uncomfortable for the other people there.

- Other people at work might be distant toward you, which could be the result of either their unwillingness to deal with your being gay or their awkwardness over knowing how to approach you. These are very different attitudes, even though they may be manifested in similar ways. To discover why they are responding as they are you might choose to ask them or make the first approach toward them.

When you pay attention to the details you will be in a much better position to recognize the detrimental elements in the situations described, and to handle them. The more clearly and specifically you can address the real situation the more effective you will be. In the second situation above, for example, you might state that you know the comfort of others is important and that you have no intention of doing anything to make anyone else uncomfortable. It is also important to remember to be ethical in your dealings with yourself and others. This means always allowing you and them to choose freely. Your parents may accept you at some family functions and not at others. The people with whom you work may be comfortable with you being gay and may choose not to discuss it. You may find that handling your co-workers' feelings about homosexuality is going perfectly fine, yet you still may choose to leave the company and find one where your sexuality is not an issue at all. As you continue to function in a manner in which you are handling the specific details of each situation, you will notice that the way you handle these situations becomes quite natural and normal for you.

Normal

It is normal to have highs and lows. This is so with just about everything in life once you have been willing to take risks. When skiing down a hill that is more challenging than one you've been on before, you are likely to have some successes and some failures. You may not have fallen for a long time, but you have opened yourself back up to that possibility. All advancement is like this . . . and you can approach such challenges with enthusiasm by knowing that they are opportunities for growth.

When you are paying attention to the details of your coming out to others and allowing for free choice as you handle any detrimental situations, you are likely to have some very positive experiences. You can only have achieved these positive experiences by also having taken the risks of having negative experiences, and these too may occur. *All of your experience—the positive and the negative—provides equal opportunities for growth and expansion if you allow it to.*

How to create more positive experiences

You are paying attention to details and can now look at what caused the positive experiences and do more of those things. You can also observe what caused the negative results and do fewer of those things.

- If you notice that agreeing not to take your lover to family functions where children are present opens the door for you to attend them alone and for you to attend adult-only functions as a couple, you might go to those functions willingly and pleasantly. You may notice that once you have done this for a while your parents may become more comfortable with you and your lover as a couple and alter their position about functions involving children.

- If you notice that your fighting to bring your lover to family functions where there are children not only doesn't succeed but makes you unable to keep communication open with your parents, you might choose to make this less of an issue.

It is also valuable for you to start noticing those people who you see as living integrated lives. They can be used as models—particularly when you are willing to pay attention to the details of what it is that they are doing to produce positive results for themselves.

As you begin to flow with this, strengthening the positive results and adjusting for the negative results, you will probably begin to notice that you produce more and more positive results for yourself. You are actually in the process of creating abundance. Being gay is becoming less of an issue to you and to those around you, and is just one more aspect of who you are.

Abundance

*You will still have highs and lows, but you'll begin to experi-
ence that even the negative things are better than the positive
use to be.*

- You now are able to comfortably bring your lover
  to family functions, even those with children. This
  is a very long way from where you started, and
  you can really see the positive results you've created and how much more powerfully you function now than in the past. There is dancing at
  this function, and since you feel so comfortable, you and your lover begin to dance together.
  This was done out of love and your intention
  was not to make others uncomfortable, yet that
  is the result. From your positive results you
  have now generated some negative ones.

You may get depressed, angry, or aggressive after
this experience, which will put you back to the beginning of
the process. Remember all of the tools you already learned
and do more of what produced the positive results in the
first place. The following steps will help you.

- Acknowledge that this situation makes you angry
  and ask what you might have done differently.
- Though it didn't seem like it at the time realize that
  you may have made an error in judgment.
- Clarify your vision and point out how it includes
  being able to dance together, yet leave open the
  option of dancing or not dancing at the next function and accept that others may make a different
  choice than you.
- Continue to go to functions with your lover as you
  did before and ultimately you will be able to
  dance together at them.

- To move on to a truly powerful/empowering way of functioning, express your gratitude and love.
- Being in the position of dealing with this situation (dancing with your lover at a family function) is something to express gratitude about to yourself and to your family—for you've all come a very long way.

I am aware, as I write this, that you may feel that such gratitude should never have to be expressed, that you have the right to do this anyway and that it should just be accepted. Sometimes I feel that way as well. Yet let's be honest about the circumstances we are in and recognize that being able to function in a totally open way in society as lesbians and gays is a vision we are in the process of attaining—we are not there yet. When we realize we are moving toward it we can empower ourselves and others by expressing our gratitude and joy each step of the way. Too often we focus on the vision not yet attained and are upset, rather than focusing on the steps involved in manifestation.

Power/Empower

By doing more of what caused your abundance in the first place—including all of the tools you employed to achieve it and expressing your gratitude and joy in the process—you are empowering yourself and others. Being powerful means being able to freely give and receive love.

Being powerful is about being totally free to be all of who you are and who you can be. Being gay is naturally included into the rest of your life, and all the other aspects of who you are can be included into your world as a lesbian or a gay man. You are integrated and whole. You are a real human being. You allow yourself to be all you are and to continue to learn and grow. You allow others to be all they are and to continue to learn and grow. You remember that you are radiant energy and that all you—or any of the people you encounter moment by moment—really have to give and receive is love.

Keep in mind that as you function more and more powerfully you are not abandoning all of the other states of consciousness but are including them. A person who functions powerfully in terms of being gay and coming out has a full awareness of all the other possibilities—since they are a part of his or her experience. When faced with an incident of bigotry or rejection, a powerful person may feel hurt (depressed), angry (aggressive), confused about what to do (uncertain), guilty (responsible), that there is more work to be done (aimless), willing to do what it takes to change the situation (risky), enthusiastic about doing it (normal), focus on the opportunity for growth (abundant), or continue to give love even to those who are rejecting (power/empower). A person who is functioning powerfully has the option of operating from any of these states of consciousness and may choose to be aggressive at those times when it looks like the most appropriate thing to do. For a powerful person, becoming aggressive is an option, a choice. For an aggressive person it is an act of habit, or possibly a conscious choice not to be depressed, but other options are not as apparent. Being more powerful and more conscious increases the options that are available for you in any situation.

I also want to address a frequently raised question, and one that you may be asking at this point: does this mean that to be powerful I have to love a bigot? No. I am not saying that in order to function powerfully you have to love a bigot—it's much more complex than that. When you are functioning powerfully you will love yourself even when confronted by a bigot. Likewise, you will be aware that the bigot is expressing an aspect of yourself—of each of us— that is scared, defensive, ignorant, self-righteous, and petty. If you let yourself observe a bigot, you will be able to see the child and adolescent that was raised with the beliefs now being expressed. You will see a person who most likely is not very happy or satisfied with his or her own life, and is taking this out on others. You will have a full range of feelings toward this bigot, including compassion and love. This will open a context large enough to allow the bigot to change if he or she so desires. If you operate out of a depressed mode you will shrink away, hide, and the bigot gets his way. If you function from an aggressive state you are a perfect mirror for the bigot—for you are just as arrogant, rude, and self-righteous as the bigot you oppose. This is one of the most difficult concepts to get across, because your willingness and ability to grasp this depends on your state of consciousness at the moment.

If this material was difficult for you, as it may have been, I encourage you to read and reread it at different times, and in different moods. It will be easiest to hear when you are in a particularly positive and loving frame of mind (and heart). *The ability to be powerful, the ability to be more conscious, and the ability to love yourself and others is yours now and at every moment!* Manifesting that ability is up to you.

12

COMING OUT TO FAMILY, FRIENDS, AND BUSINESS ASSOCIATES

Having already looked at how to come out powerfully, let's briefly examine some of the particular issues that might be involved in coming out to parents, spouses, children, friends, business associates, and employers. Paradoxically, while it is most liberating when we are able to be open and truthful with these people, they are also the people whose love and support we most fear losing. If you are not open with these people, take some time to clarify for yourself what you are withholding and why you have chosen to do so. Notice whether this is still an appropriate decision, and if you decide that it would be better to come out to them, commit yourself to following through on this.

EXERCISE

Take a sheet of paper and put the name of someone significant in your life with whom you are not being fully open. Then write down what you are withholding from that person. Place a line down the center of the page and label one side: What I might lose by being open and honest. And the other side: What I might gain by being open and honest.

Do this with each significant person with whom you are withholding being gay (or anything else). Allow yourself to write down all the things that occur to you in each column, without censoring what you put down (this is for your use). Once you have completed this, look over what you have to lose and what you have to gain by being more open. As you compare the issues with different people, see whether there are any common elements. Having examined the issues with each person, let yourself decide whether or not to be more open with that person. If you decide to be more open with them, write down how and when you are going to come out to them. Make an agreement with yourself to follow through by completing the communication with them.

PARENTS

With parents, in particular, there is often a fear that they will not approve and will withdraw their love. This was discussed more fully in Part I of this book. If you are afraid of losing your parents' approval, it is important to realize that you are probably setting them up as the authority figures in your life. This may be very appropriate if you are still dependent on them. Adolescents and young adults often are dependent on their parents for housing and financial support. This escalates the risks involved in coming out to them.

I very frequently, however, encounter adults in their thirties, forties, and even fifties who are still afraid of losing their parents' approval, even though they are no longer dependent on them in any material way. Most people have a very strong bond not only to their parents but also to their own role in their family. If you are in this position, I encourage you to examine your role carefully. It may be interfering not only in your coming out but also in your blossoming into a powerful adult in your own right.

I also frequently hear adults say that they don't want to hurt their parents. In my experience, when you withhold your sexuality from your parents you usually create a major barrier to communicating openly with them. Now that you are familiar with how to come out powerfully, see if you can develop an open and honest relationship with your parents that includes not only honesty about being gay but also honesty about your love and concern for them as well.

EXERCISE: WRITING A LETTER

When we approach authority figures, as parents often are no matter what our age, it is not uncommon to hold back part of what there is to communicate as we sense their reactions. You may hold back in a conversation or even be cut off midsentence or midthought. For this reason I believe it works far better to write a letter where you say everything you've ever wanted to say. What comes out the first time, uncensored, is usually appropriate. It may contain statements from all states of consciousness—including hurt, pain, anger, confusion, enthusiasm, joy, and love. Once you get out all of your feelings, what you have generally been covering up through your withholding was how much you love your parents, even if they've done lots of stupid and lousy things over the years.

The letters included in this book give a sense of what people have to say once they open themselves to communicating in a free and uncensored manner. They were written as part of a workshop after the participants had done a number of self-exploration exercises to enable them to communicate the breadth of their feelings. If you have done all of the exercises in this book, you may be in a good position to write such a letter yourself, and you may choose to do so now or as a final exercise for yourself after you complete your reading.

Once you've written a letter you may choose to mail it in its original form or to rewrite it and then mail it. You may choose to call your parents and read it to them, or you may choose to wait until you see them and let them read it in your presence. The advantage of a letter is that you are less likely to hold back, and they will have it to reread, thus minimizing the possibility that they will distort what you actually said. Another advantage of sending a letter is that it gives the receiver time to absorb the information before they respond so that the response isn't just impulsive but something thought out.

You will undoubtedly have your own feelings on the appropriate means for you to use in communicating with your parents. I encourage you to follow through on communicating what you need and want to say. You may try to figure out the right time to tell them. It is important that you consider them and the circumstances. For example: you may prefer to talk with them in private rather than tell them all you've ever wanted them to know about you when twenty relatives are over for a holiday dinner. If, however, you struggle to find the right time and discover that it never seems to come, it may be because there is really no right time. This doesn't mean not to communicate—it means take a deep breath and do it now.

Once you have moved beyond the barrier of communicating honestly with your parents, you will not only be freer in your own life but you will actually be in a better position to be available to your parents if and when they need you. Over and over again people tell me that delivering the letters written during The Experience actually gives them back their families. People who couldn't find a right time to relate openly with their parents, and whose parents died while they were waiting to find the right time, usually feel very incomplete. For this reason I strongly encourage you to communicate openly and honestly with your parents while they are living, no matter how old they may be.

If your parents are already dead, it often works effectively to set some time aside to bring them clearly into your consciousness and then write to them. Some people find it effective just to complete their letter, others perform a ritual such as burning the letter or taking it to their parents' grave and leaving it there or reading it to them. Often I am told that, *They're dead and there's nothing left to say.* I encourage you to write to them anyway. Sometimes there are residual feelings that need to be communicated and are only discovered once you are willing to engage in the process and see what comes out. If your relationship with them is truly complete, all that is left to say may be an acknowledgment and an expression of love. This too is valuable to express.

People who communicate openly with their parents, and then willingly and lovingly complete the process that their parents have to go through to deal with any new information, are able to be there for their parents when they need them. There is a vast difference between being sure your parents know but *"It's something we never actually talk about"* and having everything out in the open with them. Once all is said, you are free to truly express love.

Tommy, to His Father

Dear Papa,
    I want to start by telling you that I love you!
    We have had a terrible loss when Mama died, I miss her very much.
    The pain of her death has been something that I've had great difficulty accepting. I tried to reach out to you, but I understand your rejection because you are also having a great deal of pain.

Throughout my life I've been reaching out to you and Mama but somehow you were both always busy with something else and I guess I felt that what I was feeling couldn't possibly be as important.

My self-worth seemed to be pushed aside, and I feel that most of my youth was spent in the shadows of all the things that you were involved in, like your six other children, most of whom were adults and having their own children by then, your grandchildren, your social life, which left me alone so many times when I needed to be with people.

I was born to old parents who didn't quite know what to do with me, so you very much ignored the fact that I was there.

When I think about it at this moment I can only feel sorry for you for missing out on some pretty wonderful things. I had and still have a wonderful fantasy life with clever thoughts and ideas, you and Mama truly missed out on experiencing your seventh child!

When I started this letter I thought I was saving the hardest part for last, but now I realize that it's going to be the easiest.

I'm a homosexual! I know that comes as no great shock to you except that you may not want to hear it!

I know that you all have been aware of it long before I knew what the word meant. I have to tell you that being gay has not been an easy thing for me. I'm very comfortable with it now, but it took many years of guilt, pain, and secrecy to get to where I am now. I want you to fully understand that two men can truly love each other and live together involved in a meaningful and productive relationship, and the image of queer that you have does not exist in my world.

In my thirty-four years I've never reached out for you as I've been recently and I am right now.

It seems to me that you have two choices at this point: 1. continue to totally reject it; or, 2. begin to experience your son.

I do love you,
Tommy

SPOUSES

If you are married and gay, and your spouse doesn't know, it is very likely that your marriage is not a particularly happy one. There are usually problems in communication that manifest themselves in a wide variety of ways, including sexually. Frequently marriages falter because of a lack of trust in the love that exists between the partners. Marriages, like other romantic relationships, are often based on being "in love" rather than on truly loving each other. Let's look for a moment at the distinction.

When we truly love someone we accept them as they are and want them to be all of who they are and who they are capable of being. In order to do this, the truth must be known, and in order to experience being loved in this way the truth must be told. This can be referred to as unconditional love, as was discussed in Chapter 8. When you love you do not need to get married, set up house together, or live together forever and ever. The form of the relationship you develop can be one that works well for both of you based on the truth.

If you know you are gay and still want to get married and have children, the most loving thing to do is to discuss this openly prior to marriage. This is an act of love and respect for your intended spouse, since it gives that person clear choices in terms of the form of the relationship. If the person you want to marry chooses not to "tie the knot," this does not mean that he or she doesn't love you unconditionally, but that they have conditions for who they are willing to marry. Not discussing one's sexual orientation before marriage, like withholding any other information that you feel may lead the other person away from a commitment, is a manipulation. When this is the case, and somewhere into the marriage the other person finds out, it is no wonder that they generally feel manipulated or used. It is easy to misinterpret the anger that may subsequently be expressed as being about the nature of the disclosure. More likely, however, it is about feeling foolish, duped, and manipulated. *Openness is an expression of love—manipulation is not.*

When someone is "in love" they usually experience an overwhelming need for the object of their love. A person who is "in love" tends to give a tremendous amount of their power away to the person with whom they are in love and feels a need to possess or have that person. When you are in love, whether you feel good or bad is largely dependent on how the object of your love responds to you. Consequently you are likely to feel somewhat powerless. In order to create the illusion of control in such a situation, people often manipulate. It is not uncommon to say what you think the other person wants to hear and present yourself in a manner that you think the other person will respond to. People who are in love often withhold a great deal and are not even willing to see the person with whom they are in love in a truly honest and objective manner. If you have been in a relationship like this, as most of us are or have been, you are probably familiar with this dynamic. Manipulation is often an expression of being in love—openness is an expression of love.

When two people are in a marriage (or other form of relationship) based on being in love, they may collude to stay somewhat mysterious to each other by keeping some things hidden. It is no wonder that as more and more information comes out the experience of being in love may wane, and whether the people love each other begins to be put to the test. If two people get married because they are in love and later are afraid that the truth about them will destroy the marriage, they may continue to withhold from each other, thus becoming progressively more distant. Ultimately they may continue to cohabitate, though often with tremendous distance and friction between them. They remain in the relationship because of how much they have invested in it, generally at the expense of being happy and fulfilled.

You might ask why I am discussing this here, since we are talking about coming out as gay to one's spouse. I am focusing on this because a large number of lesbians and gay men are, or have been, married. Some of these marriages were based on love and intimacy, and the reality of one partner's homosexuality did not become known (even to that person) until well into the marriage. Other times someone who is gay gets married because they are in love with a member of the opposite sex, because they are in love with the idea of marriage, because they believe that if they get married their homosexuality (or inclinations toward it) will be cured, because they have a strong desire to have children, or because they feel they need to live up to society's expectations in order to "fit in" and be a success in life. Most of us were brought up to equate marriage and family with happiness. To some extent this is an equation in the process of changing, though many people still hold on to it tenaciously.

If you are in an opposite-sex marriage and are gay, the first step is to be clear within yourself about your sexual identity. It is important to be honest with yourself about when you first knew you were gay. Was it before or after getting married? Why did you get married when you did and how has and does your homosexuality affect your spouse and the quality of your marriage? Once you are clear on this, the next step is to be open with your mate. I realize that this is likely to generate great anxiety, for there is a genuine risk involved. Taking this risk, however, opens you up not only to potential negative consequences but also to positive ones as well. You may truly enhance the quality of your relationship with your spouse if you follow the tools laid out in the previous chapters. As you open up, remember to pay attention to the details, handle detrimental elements, and keep your options and your partner's options open.

It may happen that your marriage ends, or the form of it changes significantly. Nevertheless, from people who have come out to their spouses in an honest and loving way, I often hear magnificent stories about the tremendous support they have received and how much better the relationship has become. If your mate thought that the sexual problems between you was "their fault" then it might even be a relief to have some explanation as to why there has been a lack of sexual passion and perhaps even a lack of intimacy. I have also heard many stories of men and women who have had bitter divorces and "lost a great deal" in the process. Virtually every time I ask, however, whether or not they would come out again or go back into the closet if that were possible, the answer is a resounding "I'd do it again." Once the dust settles, as it inevitably will, the freedom resulting from finally being honest usually outweights the losses.

Paul, to His Former Wife

To my dear wife,

Prior to our marriage, while I was "courting you, I shared with you the part of my life that I was gay. At the time you accepted me for what I was and agreed to marry me.

I have never understood your reasons for accepting me, knowing that I was gay. You have stated that you love me as the reason, and over the years I got the impression you felt I had "gotten over the problem."

I have already told you that I married you to satisfy the desires and wishes for me by my parents. The church also continued to tell me to get married and that homosexuality was sinful and deliberate on my part and that the only salvation for my soul was to confess my sins and to have sexual relationships only with women.

Society, also through our concepts of law and order, directed me to toe the line and to maintain a heterosexual life or suffer the dire consequences of the law for participation in gay life.

Therefore, with all this admonition about how I should live my life as a heterosexual man, I consciously made a decision to live a type of life that would be acceptable to my parents, the church, and society. Thereby I would win their love and not be rejected or have their love withheld from me.

Therefore, I set out to find a woman to marry me. Our friendship at church led me to ask you to join me in this plan for me to be accepted. This is why I shared my homosexuality with you prior to our marriage.

I feel that over the years I tried to be a good husband and eventually a good father to our sons. During this whole period of time, we never discussed any of my gayness, and I would hide my feelings by having a few drinks.

This worked so well with alcohol that every time I felt bad about my gay feelings or to cover up those feelings from you, I would escape from the pain by drinking more.

As time progressed, I not only was using lying to cover up my gay feelings but also to cover up my alcohol consumption and drinking problem. Each time I did this, the more I gave in to your need to control my life because I was unable to make proper decisions because of the effect of alcohol on me. The more I drank, the easier it was to let you take care of me and to treat me as a child. You not only mothered our three sons but also treated me as just another of your children.

As my drinking continued I allowed more and more for you to take over my personal responsibilities, and I got worse and worse as I lost the ability to function and control my own life in making personal, husbandly and fatherly decisions.

In order to continue the family tradition of church attendance, we maintained very close ties with the church—which continued to condemn my homosexuality and validate our marriage and to indoctrinate our sons to believe in homosexuality as sin.

As I became sicker from alcohol and lost all capabilities of physical and mental control, I finally did something about my life to stop drinking and begin to establish a new order of values and priorities for my continuing life. I could no longer live my life as it was.

This change also meant that I wanted to regain for

myself the ability to make decisions I should be making
as a person, husband, and father.

It was at this point that you did not understand my
need to reestablish my personal needs, that you would
have to give up control of my life. As you well know, this
did not work out. Even the marriage counseling and the
spiritual counseling with our pastor did not bring us to a
resolve on this major issue in our lives.

As it stood, the bottom line in the contract I agreed
to with the marriage counselor was that if we got through
all the crap, we would have to discuss my homosexuality
and our marriage.

As you know, we never got that far, and in one of
your parting threats as I was physically moving out of the
house, you demanded that I not tell our sons about my being
gay. My response was that if they were to find out, the
responsibility would be on your shoulders—as I would not
tell them.

My dear, more than a year has passed since I moved
out, and I have come very much into contact with my own
self. Many old value systems of marriage, family, church,
and society that I upheld in the past have now changed.

With our pending interlocutory dissolving our close-
to-twenty-five-year marriage, I wish to be truthful to our
three sons and to share with them the fact that their father
is gay.

These three sons of ours are the greatest reward I
have in life, and I no longer feel I should lie to them.
Our sons should have the opportunity to understand and
share their love with their father for what he is as a person, and not a living lie.

If we can look upon one another with love, then all
of man's ideas about God and sin are put to shame as a sham.

For as God created me and you and allowed us to
have three sons, then he loves all for whatever each one of
us is.

Being gay is not sinful, for it is something that has
always been a part of me and not something I did to separate me from my children, wife, parents, and God.

My dear, I love all of you. However, due to my alcohol addiction and to being gay, I must live my life anew,
expressing my love in new ways for a new life as a whole
and beautiful person.

Love, Paul

CHILDREN

When coming out to your children, about being gay or
about any other aspect of your life, it is important to address them in a respectful manner. Just as you may put your
own parents into the role of an authority figure, so may
your children cast you in that role. You may even resist
sharing yourself openly with your children, even those who
are already adults, in order to maintain the role of the
authority figure in their lives.

Telling the truth to your children is a step toward
releasing them from your shadow by allowing them to begin
to see you as you really are. When you open up to them you
are granting them the respect they deserve and trusting
them to love you. If you have been a good parent the
chances increase that they will respond favorably. If you
have consistently put them down, your coming out to them
may give them some ammunition that they can use against
you, or may be seen as one more thing that you are doing to
hurt and inflict emotional pain. Again, what you will be
doing by being open and honest with them creates the
possibility for you and your children to become more powerful and adult.

When opening up to one's children it is important to
provide that information which your child is capable of grasp-
ing. As you may recall from Gerald's letter on page 246,
with young children a metaphor may work better than using
words that are meaningless to the child. This sets the stage
for future conversations rather than for future hiding. In
Bob's letter to his eight-year-old, which follows, he uses the
word *gay* and explains same-sex relationships, without actu-

ally discussing sex, by making comparisons to opposite-sex relationships in a manner that an eight-year-old can relate to. He also reassures his son about his love for him and that his son still has a father.

Bob, to His Eight-Year-Old Son

Dear Daniel,

 I love you, Daniel, and I want to share something that feels quite important to me right now. Months have passed and I've been living with the need to explain what the word *gay* means and tell you that I am gay.

 You know how Mom likes to sleep with George and make love with him. Most people prefer to sleep and make love with people of the opposite sex, but some like people of the same sex. I'm one of them. I like to be lovers with a man—like Paul. Do you remember Paul? I loved him the way Mom loves George.

 Unfortunately, some people in the world are uncomfortable with gay people and feel the need to attack them. You may hear some attacks in school. Please don't take them personally. I am healthy and powerful—the same man I've always been, the same father who will support you in your growing up.

 I'm absolutely certain about my love for both you and your mother. She and I lived together for eight years, and my leaving was a mark of the love and respect we have for each other.

 Sometimes life doesn't turn out to be the thing we ordered. No, it's more difficult than that and definitely more interesting. I'm here to support you in handling whatever comes up in this. Thanks for being my son.

Love,
Dad

When your children are adults it may still be difficult to come out to them for fear that they will judge your behavior negatively. Adult children have a great capacity to reject their parents. If they are looking for reasons to separate from you, they will find them. Giving them your love and respect may actually improve the relationship rather than damage it. In Fred's letter to his adult sons and his daughter-in-law (Chapter 6, p. 74) he clearly states his desire to have his children know him better as he really is. Fred not only states that he is homosexual but also expresses some of the values by which he is living as well.

Many gay men and lesbians are parents, and there are currently many same-sex couples raising children. Sometimes these are their natural children and sometimes they are adopted children. There is a trend toward acceptance of gay parenting. Many people still fear that someone gay will bring up a gay child, though the evidence in this regard is overwhelmingly to the contrary. Most gay children are raised by heterosexual parents and most homosexual parents raise heterosexual children. There is no evidence that the sexual orientation of the parents is transmitted to the child. Once again, sexual orientation seems far more compelling than mere modeling of parental behavior.

In my experience, knowing many lesbian and gay male parents, when children are brought up with love and respect the sexual orientation of the parent does not lead the child to reject the parent. Rather, when parents are able to be honest with their children I notice that the children grow up far more willing to open up to their parents and to have a clear sense of their own identity and high self-esteem.

FRIENDS

You may have said, or heard someone else say, about someone you are in a nonromantic relationship with that he or she is "just a friend." This phrase has always eluded me, since friends so often outlast romantic relationships and even marriages. You probably genuinely love your friends, though you may not be "in love" with them. When you withhold from your friends, you are cutting your friendship short of the true intimacy that can exist between you. You may have to hide or distort what you do on the weekends, how you live your life, and what you value. If someone is, indeed, a friend they will ultimately stay in a relationship with you as they go through their own process of learning how to deal with your disclosure to them. As Ken's letter to his friend Bobbi (Chapter 4, p. 52) illustrates, to be honest is a way to validate your friend and the significance of his or her role in your life.

BUSINESS ASSOCIATES AND EMPLOYERS

Many people resist opening up at their place of employment for fear of losing their jobs or diminishing their standing in the eyes of their fellow workers. This feeling makes you vulnerable. If you are hiding in your career you are furthering the impression that being gay is something to be ashamed of.

As much as I would like to see things be different, when one comes out at work there may be a real threat of losing a job or losing the respect of co-workers. This will undoubtedly change as more and more people come out, but you may choose not to be a martyr when it comes to your career. Some states have antidiscrimination legislation, and it is valuable to know the laws (or absense thereof) protecting you on your job. Nevertheless, most people would prefer not to have to resort to legal measures to keep their jobs if they are being discriminated against.

If you are in the closet at work I strongly urge you to assess this situation carefully. You probably spend more time a week at work than doing anything else. If you have to hide during that significant part of your life, what is the cost to you at a physical and an emotional level? I would suggest that there are probably many places where you can find employment that will allow you to be free to be yourself in your work environment. If you lose a job because you are gay, and only because you are gay, you will probably gain in the long run by seeking employment in a healthier atmosphere. I do not say this cavalierly, for I know the risks involved, but with strong conviction that you will change your work environment to a healthier one when you are using your energy efficiently by applying it to your career rather than to hiding who you are.

It is truly a shame that the sexual orientation of so many gays in the workplace has only become known as a result of AIDS, and that many companies that now have policies protecting gays on the basis of discrimination have only instituted them as a result of a health crisis. There is still much progress to be made in the workplace, and you can be a part of creating positive change for yourself and others.

13

AIDS AND COMING OUT: IMPACT AND IMPLICATIONS

Coming out as a gay man to one you love, and who loves you, during the past decade has also meant having to address AIDS as an issue. The AIDS epidemic was present throughout the 1980s, yet there are still many people who are just beginning to pay attention to it. The willingness to be aware of and acknowledge that there was a major health crisis was slow in coming. Perhaps the resistance to acknowledging this epidemic was in large part the result of society's avoidance of such "unpleasant" topics as homosexuality, intravenous drug use, and sex in general. Since these were topics to be kept in the closet, even by the media, it was difficult to deal with them in an open and enlightened manner. This is one more extension, even reaching to government and the health care system, of how difficult it is to function effectively when *"some things are better left unsaid."*

172

Now, a decade later, more people have died of AIDS than died in the Vietnam War. Because gays were not openly integrated into mainstream America, the gay community was left to fight the AIDS battle pretty much on its own. While this has been a devastating war, and one fought with far too few resources, many people have grown as a result, and the gay community has been rapidly coming into maturity in many ways.

I have often heard it said that AIDS is pushing people back into the closet. I, as well as many others, perceive that this is not the case. To begin with, people who are already out of the closet don't go back in. Furthermore, AIDS, and the manner in which it has been dealt with, has caused many lesbians and gay men to become more aware of the need to contribute to the gay community as well as to align support from others. AIDS has brought many people out of the closet in terms of acknowledging their own homosexuality and/or their love for and support of their family and friends who are gay. Sex in general, and homosexuality in particular, have become more commonly discussed topics as we recognize the need to talk openly in order to educate the public, prevent the further spread of the Human Immunodeficiency Virus (HIV), and care for those who are sick.

The impact and implications of AIDS on the process of coming out are many. For a number of people, having friends who are living with AIDS or friends who have died of AIDS has sped up their willingness to come out. When someone is in the closet about being gay, and his or her friends are ill, the need to tell the truth in order to share oneself with others becomes more important. If you have a friend who has died of AIDS and you are unable or unwilling to share this with those around you for fear of rejection, this both damages your integrity and demeans the love you shared with your friend. Many people become angry with others when they feel they must refrain from telling the truth, and that anger may become a catalyst for movement through their coming-out process.

For someone who has been diagnosed with AIDS, the need and desire to tell the truth is often intensified.

Being diagnosed as HIV infected (antibody positive) or with ARC (AIDS related complex) or AIDS has for many demonstrated the importance of being honest in order to allow loved ones to provide support, both physical and emotional. The stress associated with continuing to hide requires energy that could be put to far better use in healing. Coming out, in itself, is a part of that healing process.

When someone has AIDS and is still hiding their homosexuality, they must become more and more distant from the people to whom they are not out. Over time it becomes progressively more difficult to hide one's illness, and consequently more and more difficult to stay in the closet. Coming out as gay as a result of developing AIDS is a frequent occurrence. Often family and friends respond in an extremely supportive manner. There are, of course, times when support is not present. This is most likely to occur when considerable distance was present even before an AIDS diagnosis.

If, as you discuss both your sexuality and AIDS with others, you discover that they don't want to talk about it, remember what your initial reaction was when you first heard about AIDS. You probably paid little attention to it until you knew someone personally who was sick or had died. Even then you may have reacted as if it couldn't happen to you. During the first few years of the epidemic AIDS was happening to "them"—to those gay men who were going to bathhouses every night, using drugs and participating in a variety of bizarre sex practices. It wasn't happening to "us." For years I heard myself and others explain why we were at "low risk" for being infected. Over time it has turned out that we were wrong, and that we too were at risk. I use to ask, *"How close does AIDS have to get before you realize that it is your problem too?"* This question is still in order.

Far fewer people are now able to pretend that AIDS is happening to someone else, since in most large cities people either know someone directly, or know of someone, who has AIDS or has died of it. If everyone were aware of the fact they know and love a gay man and that that person is at high risk of contracting AIDS, the way the epidemic has been and is being dealt with would change dramatically.

From a sociopolitical standpoint, therefore, it is important to address this issue of AIDS while coming out. Especially if you are a gay man, it is also wise to be aware that AIDS may raise a number of considerations for those to whom you come out. Those who know little about AIDS may be concerned that they might be exposed to it. Those who know that AIDS is not casually transmitted may still have concerns about you and your health and well-being. Be prepared to deal with such questions if they arise, for they are now a part of the coming-out process. *Coming out is not only a process of self-disclosure but of education as well!*

In Laurence's letter to his parents (p. 86) he raised the subject of AIDS in a way that was intended to put his parents' concerns to rest, as well as indicating his willingness to discuss it further with them. He has subsequently told me that while his parents have been learning to cope with his disclosure about being gay, sometimes having some difficulty talking about it, they have been sending him articles about AIDS and are still concerned for his safety. Rather than reacting negatively to receiving these articles, Laurence has taken them as an indication of his parents' love and concern for him and as an opportunity to keep dialogue open with them and further their understanding of him and his life-style.

Other letters in this book address AIDS from different perspectives. Michael (p. 233) is "pissed" at his parents' ignorance and feels that this is contributing to his friends dying. Gerardo expresses his unwillingness to continue to hide his sexuality and his relationship with his lover who is HIV infected. In his words:

> When you say "Please don't tell anyone about your life" you don't realize that you're asking me to deny all of the love and the pain that surrounds me and pretend I'm someone else.
>
> —Gerardo, to his mother; p. 205

Jeff, a physician, expresses his judgments and shame for allowing himself to become HIV infected as well as some of his concerns about his role as a doctor:

I honestly do not know whether I will be one of the long-term survivors of this AIDS epidemic. I hope I am. I do want to continue to serve my fellow man in a humane and just manner. I realize now that this can only be done when I think of myself as spiritual and as an extension of God, and not just a body or title like "doctor."
—Jeff, to his parents; p. 240

And Nick discusses the impact of his own AIDS diagnosis and of his lover being close to death from AIDS and lets his mother know how important her support is at this particular time:

Reid developed AIDS first, and our relationship had to change. Boy did it. We became even closer and when my diagnosis hit me he was there to pick up the pieces. When my family turned their backs on me he helped me and felt my pain with me. I need you to understand that each day he gets sicker, and as he gets closer to death part of me dies with him. The other half of my soul is dying and I am in agony. When you reject him you are rejecting me. He and I are one. When you don't stand up for us you help to kill our beauty. When you attempt to invalidate our love and commitment you are helping us Die. Mom, I am dying . . . I need you to fight for me and for Reid. I need you to get a spine and tell my brothers and sisters that I am good. That I am a person and equally your son. That my lover is equal to their spouses. That our disease is not leprosy. I need you to protect us. I need you to love me unconditionally—now. I need you to see the home Reid and I have made for ourselves. I need you to bear witness to our love so that when we are gone you can remember our dignity and our pride. I need you to fight for us.
—Nick, to his mother; p. 209

In the opening letter of this book (p. xvii) my dear friend Scott expresses his frustration over fighting for his life, losing his lover Peter, and feeling that society just doesn't care. Having been close to the AIDS epidemic both personally and politically from its beginning, he wasn't sure where else to turn and just wanted to get some release. He wrote to Dear Abby in early 1989 because, as he said, *"I am simply compelled to write you and get this off my chest!"* His letter so beautifully speaks to the relationship between coming out and AIDS and to our need to *"heal our lives and the planet by telling the truth."*

In the following letter, from Doug to his parents, AIDS is dealt with on many levels. Doug's parents already know that he is gay, and he had a gay brother who died of AIDS. Doug had not, however, told his parents that he too had been exposed to the AIDS virus because he didn't want to hurt or scare them. In an attempt to include them more honestly in his life he chose to disclose this information to them.

Doug provided the following information to make it easier to follow his letter. Doug is thirty-two years old and is vice president of a small business in San Francisco. These are the relationships to Doug of the people referred to in the letter:

WILL: Doug's younger brother, who died of AIDS at twenty-four
TIM: Doug's older brother, who is also gay
RICH: Doug's lover of eight years
JACKIE: Doug's grandmother
JOAN SMITH: Doug's therapist

Doug, to His Parents

Dear Mom and Dad,

I love you both so much, and at times I feel that my phone conversations with you don't express that strongly enough. I've thought so much recently about our relationship—

—how good it is now that we're all adults and how much closer I feel to you since Will's death.

That event brought us (Tim, too) so close together—albeit tragically. You lost a son and we lost a brother. In his illness, Will taught me that it's OK to take risks in family relationships: he trusted that I could care for him here in SF; you and Tim trusted me in caring for him and many of his needs through Rich's and Jackie's good graces; you supported me with your presence here when I needed you, and you were here at the end.

I saw Will change, and his love for you, Tim, and me grow stronger and stronger. How wonderful it would be now if we had been able to remove the tragic qualities from those renewed and inspired relationships and been left with all the "goodies" we helped create.

That's what I want for us to continue to do. There are so many things about my life I want to share with you—more "goodies"—but I withhold most of them from you because they are connected to my sexual orientation. As a gay man in a large San Francisco gay community, there are many things to do to be of service, and I do them. Rich and I also have a lot of remarkable friends we have great times with.

I've been on the board of directors of the Intrepid Foundation, a community foundation that funds worthy projects and organizations around the Bay Area. I volunteered time to the Names Project, the AIDS Memorial Quilt, which traveled across country this summer. I've given money to various human rights and political causes that seek to ensure that gay men and lesbians are not discriminated against in housing, insurance, and employment. You know of my commitment to the church's feeding programs, the search committee, and the organ committee; but you may not know that the majority of the parish's members, leaders, and financial supporters are gay.

I know it may be hard for you to understand, but I consider my sexual orientation an asset, an opportunity, and a challenge—a facet of my identity that has produced

extraordinary results for me and my friends, gay and
"straight."

From those challenges, particularly health issues in
our community, came a need to assess with more scru-
tiny my own health. What I found out nearly two years ago
is that I have been exposed to the AIDS virus. This fact
does not mean that I have AIDS or that I will necessarily
go on to develop AIDS. I took that AIDS antibody test
(the test they use to determine exposure) when it became
apparent that new therapies, namely a drug called AZT,
were shown to have beneficial effects in prolonging resistance to debilitating infections. (I have had no such infections.) Since my antibody status was/is "positive" (HIV +),
I wanted to begin as a healthy man to take steps to improve any chances of keeping the virus at bay. I chose to
begin taking AZT sometime later (you recall my beeper
in Houston), and my health remains stable. I see Joan Smith,
exercise, travel, take vitamins, "eat healthy," and generally focus on the positive things in my life and my relationship with God to stay healthy in addition to taking the drug.
I will begin taking another drug called pentamidine in an
aerosol form to ward off any problems or involvement with
my lungs. Let me say again that these are preventive
methods.

I tell you all of this now not because I want you to
worry, although I know you will. I tell you not because I
need your help financially or otherwise—even though I know
you will offer it. I tell you not because I need you to find
out medical information for me, although I encourage you
to make suggestions and ask me questions about what
you've read or don't understand.

I do tell you because I want to share more of my life
with you, its good and not-so-good parts. I trust you to
do the same with me. Needless to say, the question of
whether to tell you or not has been troubling me for some
time. My decision to speak now came after the realizations
that I would want to know anything about your health
that was out of the ordinary, and I would want to have the
opportunity to offer my support in any way possible.

By the way, Tim has known of my HIV+ status since shortly after the test results came back. He has been of tremendous support beyond words, and he supports my writing you this letter. You should know, too, that Tim took the HIV test in December of last year: his test results were negative. Rich also tests negative.

There may come a time, along into the future, when I do need specific support from you, and I feel that giving you the facts now will equip you to respond. What you can do is to keep loving me, talking to me, praying for me and supporting me in all the ways you always have in the past. That will allow the love between us to grow and mature even more. I want us to continue to deal with one another as adults, co-equals, and friends—as well as parents and son. I have found that there is so much life out there to live and share, and that keeping things from you, no matter how painful they may be, will keep me from achieving my goal of becoming ever closer to my family.

The months preceding Will's death, our trips to Jamaica and Hawaii, and two Christmases in Houston are among the most priceless and cherished times I have experienced. I want more. I want to visit you at home more often, and when you're ready, you're always welcome to visit me out here. How I would welcome that!

God has blessed my life with the very best parents, brothers and love than any man could ask for.

I love you so much! Call or write me anytime you're ready.

Love,
Doug

Once again, all of the principles outlined previously in this book also apply to coming out in this age of AIDS. You may not even know your own HIV status, since many people still resist testing. Just as coming out is a process, functioning openly about AIDS is also a process. It begins with a willingness to stop denying it's existence and to deal with it at a personal level. Then to begin talking about it privately with people and ultimately to bring it out into the public arena so that it can be dealt with in a more honest and enlightened manner.

14

COMING OUT AS A COMMUNITY

"We are everywhere" is not just a catchy slogan, it is the truth! By most estimates roughly 10 percent of the population is homosexual. In the United States this translates to over twenty-five million men and women. Whether this figure should be higher or lower is unimportant to me. What is significant is that lesbians and gay men are present in virtually every extended family, friendship circle, ethnic group, religion, organization, field of employment, political party, economic strata, town, city, state, and country. *In spite of this most people don't think that they know anyone who's gay because we are so effective at hiding.*

The fact that lesbians and gays must declare who we are in order to be noticed is proof, in itself, of the fact that we are more similar to heterosexuals than we are different. The vast majority of people who are homosexual are "passing" on a daily basis for being heterosexual. Nevertheless, stereotypes persist, and fear and hatred of homosexuals (homophobia) is commonplace. Homosexuals are often treated as second-class citizens, though frequently paying a disproportionately high amount of taxes and being in many positions of power and respect in society.

Ironically, with a dearth of positive gay role models presented by the media, many media moguls are themselves homosexual—often afraid to come out for fear of losing their power, influence, and affluence. Even more paradoxical is the fact that many of our male and female idols and role models in theater, film, television, and music are also gay—rarely coming out for fear that it will destroy their image and subsequently their careers. What an odd situation, to have so much potential power and to function in such a powerless manner.

It seems that everyone is waiting for someone else to come out in order to make it safe for all of us. If this were to continue it would ultimately be safe for none of us, but fortunately things are changing and have been for several decades. Since the Stonewall uprising in Greenwich Village in 1969, homosexuals have been more willing to stand up and be counted, and openness about homosexuality has increased in most major metropolitan areas. There is a long way to go and many ways to proceed.

The discussion of *how to come out powerfully* in Chapter 11 applies to coming out powerfully as a community as well. When referring to a gay community I mean the collective efforts of lesbians and gays. We are not one united community, any more than there is a single heterosexual community, yet we do have some basic goals that would be to all of our advantages to achieve. Among these are to end homophobia and to secure those rights and freedoms that are granted naturally to heterosoexuals. *We do not need to be treated specially, only treated equally.* Many of the pressing issues we must address day by day are short-range goals resulting from the fact that we are frequently feared, hated, and treated as second-class citizens.

In terms of these immediate issues (such as quality AIDS education, funding for AIDS research and treatment, domestic partnership legislation, hate crimes legislation, etc.) we will be most successful at achieving our goals the more visible we become and the more willing we are to take a stand for ourselves. This is almost impossible to do until we come out. The long-range goal of equality is absolutely contingent on our willingness to come out individually and collectively. It will only be achieved when people are disabused of their stereotypic image of lesbians and gays and of their fear of the potential damage we can cause to values they hold dear.

I am always struck by the strong belief held by many people that homosexuality can or will destroy families. Families are strengthened when love and understanding is furthered. A family that loves and accepts its gay members in a natural way is a much stronger family than one that struggles to change or tries to disassociate or disown those family members who don't conform. Lesbians and gay men do not want to destroy their families, rather they want to be included in them. To quote from an article in a newsletter from the Lesbian and Gay Public Awareness Project, "It is homophobia that destroys families, *not* homosexuality."

It seems to me that the primary goal of the gay community ought to be liberation, and this means ultimately making being gay no longer be an issue. Until this is achieved we are not making homosexuality an issue, it already is. The vision I hold, and many others hold as well, is a vision of unity—a society in which we are all functioning together with compassion, love, and understanding.

Returning to how to come out powerfully, it is clear that we will never achieve freedom and liberation if the gay community functions in a depressed manner. If people continue to hide and are willing to settle for second-class status, then second-class status is all that can be expected. If we remain hidden we will remain powerless.

Functioning aggressively is far preferable to staying depressed, for it means taking a stand. Nevertheless, remember that being aggressive generates opposition and tends to create a win-lose scenario. This is certainly an unwise approach if one doesn't have the strength and support to win in such a game. The activities of ACT UP (The AIDS Coalition to Unleash Power) and Gay Pride parades frequently fall into this category. While taking a stand they often backfire. Sometimes they are a way of venting anger or breaking out of the closet, though they don't always create a positive image of lesbians and gays. Many gay men and lesbians attempt to disassociate themselves from these groups and use these activities as an excuse not to participate in the gay community or not to support community organizations. Just as described for nuclear families above, we will be stronger as a community when we love and accept those in it rather than trying to disassociate or disown those in it who don't conform.

Whether you approve of Gay Pride parades or of groups such as ACT UP, they reflect an important step (and for many the next step) in the process of functioning powerfully as a community, and I applaud those who organize and participate in them. Rather than sitting on the sidelines lamenting the way things are, participants in these activities are often demonstrating their anger and outrage at how things are. While perhaps not the most effective way to align broad-based support for our issues, approaches such as these play a very productive role in the overall progress of the gay community and must not be silenced. Lesbians and gay men must do and say more, not less!

It is time to go back to basics. It's time to focus on coming out and doing so in a manner that shows who we really are as a community—the diversity that exists among lesbians and gays and also our fundamental commonality with heterosexuals. We are not all alike, and it is important that we validate the breadth of who we are. I do not propose that any of us return to the closet, go into hiding, or change our way of being. I am suggesting that all of us come out so that we can create a truer and clearer picture of what homosexuality is and is not. We may not all be proud of every aspect of the gay community, any more than all heterosexuals are proud of every aspect of the "heterosexual community." What is important is to tell the truth about who we are—with all of our diversity.

This will be accomplished most effectively as more and more people who have been hiding stop hiding. It can also be done when we organize to present ourselves to the world more effectively and accurately rather than relying on others to present us. On October 11, 1987, well over half a million people gathered in Washington, D.C., for the march on Washington for lesbian and gay rights. In spite of this being the largest turnout for any demonstration in the history of the United States, and being peaceful throughout, the march was largely ignored by the mainstream media and by the Reagan administration. It was at that march that I found myself wishing that each of those marching had come out to their families, or to ten, fifteen, or twenty people on a personal basis. Our power cannot depend on the press alone—it depends on ourselves and on the risks we are willing to take in our personal lives.

It is clear that gay-related issues will not be taken seriously, or given adequate consideration, until it is known who we are. We are not out of the mainstream, we are part of the mainstream. We are not obvious, but we "pass" every day as heterosexual. While some may see it as an asset, our ability to "pass" and to hide has perhaps been our greatest liability. More than anything else, the closet has kept us from being accepted and respected for who we actually are.

I made a commitment to myself to be more honest and open with people who are important in my life. That decision was easy enough to make and is not difficult to uphold. I want to be honest with you, because I'm sick to death of having to feel ashamed of something that I'm not ashamed about. At this point in my life it is important for me that I come out to you.

—Doug, to his brother; p. 256

In February 1988, when two hundred lesbian and gay leaders met in Virginia to consider the future agenda for the gay community it was obvious to all, and unanimously agreed on, that the time for a National Coming Out Day (NCOD) had arrived. October 11, commemorating the 1987 march on Washington, was selected as the date for this annual event, and Jean O'Leary and I volunteered to coordinate and co-chair NCOD with the support of our organizations, National Gay Rights Advocates and The Experience. NCOD's goal was, and is, to increase the visibility of lesbians and gay men through a grassroots effort to encourage people to take their next step in their coming-out process. With local efforts throughout the country, and national media coverage (particularly "The Oprah Winfrey Show"), the gay community is refocusing its attention on the importance of coming out. While every day is an opportunity to tell the truth, October 11 is a day for paying special attention to our progress in coming out—and for making a difference in the way homosexuality is viewed and experienced by all of us.

> *I have to say that I am a happy individual. You know what I'm like, and hopefully I don't fit into any stereotype you may or may not have of gay men. . . . It's a real drag being in the closet. I only wish I had the courage to have told you eight years ago.*
>
> —Doug, to his brother; p. 256

NCOD had been supported by organizations, large and small, throughout the country. Its success continues because these organizations are focusing on supporting people to come out socially, athletically, emotionally, artistically, professionally, and politically. While several of these organizations are listed in a Resource Directory in this book (p. 273), I want to call particular attention to two of the projects that are making it safer for lesbians and gay men to come out.

The Lesbian and Gay Public Awareness Project, a media project to end homophobia, has been producing marvelous advertisements, which are available for publication in print media. They clearly speak to the issues of coming out, and help to create a positive image of lesbians and gays. Some examples of these ads are included here.

PHOTO: Mary Whitlock

Do you believe in CIVIL RIGHTS?

During the 1960's Black Americans made many strides in attaining civil rights but for some the fight continues today. Many Black Americans are gay and lesbian, and they do not have their civil rights. I remember how my grandmother and aunt participated in the civil rights movement in Mississippi. Today, I find myself inspired by their courage. Now I'm working for civil rights for gays and lesbians. I want to take part in paving the way for future generations so that young gays and lesbians do not have to struggle so hard to feel proud of who they are. That's what the Lesbian and Gay Public Awareness Project is all about. One of the most important things that I learned from my grandmother and aunt is that truly no single person can be free until we are all free.

Xavier E. Hall

©1990 Lesbian & Gay Public Awareness Project

LGPAP

P.O. BOX 65603
LOS ANGELES, CA 90065
(213) 281-1946

People United To End Homophobia
I want to help LGPAP
increase understanding about homosexuality
Enclosed is my tax deductible contribution:

☐ **$35 (membership)** / ☐ **$50** / ☐ **$100** / ☐ **Other** _____

Name _____

Address _____

City/State/Zip _____ Phone ( ) _____

LGPAP • P.O. Box 65603 • Los Angeles, CA 90065 • (213) 281-1946

Photo: Valerie Snyder

(l. to r.) Lamonta Pierson, Lynn Shepodd and Honey Ward

I'm proud of my
LESBIAN DAUGHTER

It's been over a decade since we at home were responding to Lynn's "I'm gay" letter mailed from college. Reading it to the family, I suddenly knew I'd had a plan for Lynn, and this was off course. She had put miles between us before making her announcement and I was feeling her courage. How terrible for her to have worried: "Will they love me after they know . . . love me with restrictions . . . check me off?" The process of my adjustment wasn't instant or without fluctuation, but I asked myself, what of real importance had changed? Lynn was still my pretty and winsome daughter, still the young woman, a crusader, bent on correcting every social and political shortcoming. Surely, she was entitled to her own life.

Many busy years have passed and today Lynn has established — with a perfect companion — a remarkable, loving home full of trust and respect.

Yes, I not only love my daughter, I am filled with a sense of pride and completion as her life unfolds.

Lamonta Pierson

©**1990 Lesbian & Gay Public Awareness Project**

LGPAP

P.O. BOX 65603
LOS ANGELES, CA 90065
(213) 281-1946

People United To End Homophobia
I want to help LGPAP
increase understanding about homosexuality
Enclosed is my tax deductible contribution:

☐ **$35 (membership)** / ☐ **$50** / ☐ **$100** / ☐ **Other** _____

Name _____

Address _____

City/State/Zip _____ Phone ( ) _____

LGPAP • P.O. Box 65603 • Los Angeles, CA 90065 • (213) 281-1946

June 24, 1963 - Aug. 27, 1983

Are you abusing your child without knowing it?

 Bobby Griffith committed suicide at the age of 20. This is an excerpt from Bobby's diary written when he was 16. Correct education about homosexuality could have prevented this tragedy.

"I can't ever let anyone find out that I'm not straight. It would be so humiliating. My friends would hate me, I just know it. They might even want to beat me up. And my family? I've overheard them lots of times talking about gay people. They've said they hate gays, and even God hates gays, too. Gays are bad, and God sends bad people to hell. It's really hell. It really scares me now, when I hear my family talk that way, because now, they are talking about me. I guess I'm no good to anyone . . . not even God. Life is so cruel, and unfair. Sometimes I feel like disappearing from the face of this earth . . . "

No one chooses their sexual identity. If you are teaching your child to hate homosexual people, you might be teaching them to hate themselves. That isn't right. That is a form of emotional child abuse. **ARE YOU ABUSING YOUR CHILD WITHOUT KNOWING IT?**

REMEMBER: 1 in every 10 Children is Homosexual

©1990 Lesbian & Gay Public Awareness Project

LGPAP

P.O. BOX 65603
LOS ANGELES, CA 90065
(213) 281-1946

People United To End Homophobia
I want to help LGPAP
increase understanding about homosexuality
Enclosed is my tax deductible contribution:

☐ **$35 (membership)** / ☐ **$50** / ☐ **$100** / ☐ **Other** _____

Name _____

Address _____

City/State/Zip _____ Phone ( ) _____

LGPAP • P.O. Box 65603 • Los Angeles, CA 90065 • (213) 281-1946

Photo: Robert Daroff

How would you feel if your son were GAY?

I have to admit, having your son grow up to be Executive Director of the National Gay and Lesbian Task Force — well, it's not exactly every father's dream. It took me a while to accept — not just tolerate but really accept — that Jeff is gay.

I came to this country from Germany in 1937 where most of my family was killed in the Holocaust. The Holocaust taught us two paradoxical truths. The first is that people who are perceived as different cannot pretend to be otherwise. The second truth is that people who are perceived to be different cannot withdraw into isolation and think that they can build a world separate from the larger one in which they live. They must always remain vigilant, ready to defend themselves against injustice.

I am proud that Jeff is guided by these truths in his work. In a way, isn't Jeff's and the Task Force's work part of a larger dream, part of a vision of the future that we all share?

Max Levi

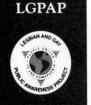

LGPAP

P.O. BOX 65603
LOS ANGELES, CA 90065
(213) 281-1946

People United To End Homophobia
I want to help LGPAP
increase understanding about homosexuality
Enclosed is my tax deductible contribution:

☐ $35 (membership) / ☐ $50 / ☐ $100 / ☐ Other _____

Name _____

Address _____

City/State/Zip _____ Phone ( ) _____

LGPAP • P.O. Box 65603 • Los Angeles, CA 90065 • (213) 281-1946

The Human Rights Campaign Fund, the national lobby and political action committee working for lesbian and gay rights and AIDS issues, sponsors Speak Out—a constituent mail program. Both gay and nongay people are a part of Speak Out, and it is an excellent means for you to come out to your congressional representative, generating vital grassroots mail to back up the gay community's lobbying efforts on life-and-death AIDS and gay/lesbian issues. Even for those who are unwilling to come out to their own family or friends, coming out politically can and does make a major difference.

Coming out, and doing so in a loving and powerful way, must be a major focus for the gay community on a local and national level. Whether supporting people emotionally, spiritually, legally, or politically, gay organizations play a major role in furthering our progress in coming out as a community. It is time to support each other, to stand up for the truth, and to come out with a vision of unity and love!

15

YOUR NEXT STEP

Whether you are homosexual or heterosexual, I hope this book supports you to understand more about the process of coming out and about how you can take *your next step in being open about yourself* in the most effective and loving manner. What you do from here is up to you.

> **Whatever you can do or dream you can do, begin it. Boldness has genius and power and magic in it. Begin it now!**
>
> —Goethe

Fundamental to living powerfully—as individuals, as communities and as a society—is our willingness to trust ourselves to tell the truth. Sometimes the truth makes us uncomfortable, yet it is the pathway to freedom and liberation for us all. It has not been my intention in this book, or in any of my other work, to make you more comfortable—it is always my intention to support us all to be more powerful and loving.

Being gay is only one of the things we withhold from others. When we hold back any part of who we are we hold back a great deal more at the same time. This is always difficult for us to believe until we have already "come out" fully as ourselves.

My gayness has been a powerful catalyst for me to become a person of much greater love, truth, and integrity.
                                        —Nicholas, to his mother; p. 19

Coming out is an act of love. It is an expression of self-worth, self-esteem, and self-love while simultaneously being an expression of trust and love for those to whom you come out. Relationships find a natural form and flow when people allow one another to be all of who they are, and all of who they can be. This is truly what love is about.

Remember that I love you and that I realize the difficulty of doing what I ask. I don't want to die knowing my mother and my brothers and sisters didn't love me enough to accept me as I am, didn't love me enough to see the adult I have become, didn't really love me at all.
                                        —Nick, to his mother; p. 210

I have used the term sexual orientation in this book when referring to homosexuality. This is the "politically correct" term and also seems to capture most persons' experience of being gay. As a sexual orientation, homosexuality is just the way one is, it is not considered a choice. That homosexuality is not a choice is frequently used as evidence that lesbians and gays should be accepted by society.

The positive part of this lack of choice is that it may eventually lead to external (social/political/legal) acceptance of homosexuality. It may do little, however, to alter negative feelings about homosexuality, and if anyone ever discovers that sexual orientation can be altered, there may be pressure on gay people to change. As I envision freedom it means that people are free to choose to be who they are and to choose to do what they do.

Each of us—homosexual and heterosexual, individually and collectively—has the power to create freedom for us all. As all of us come out more publicly, I expect that the perception of what it is to be gay will become far more positive. This will lead to more acceptance, more understanding, more love, and ultimately to more freedom, and what it means to be gay may change significantly. As we go through the process of coming out together, I expect families and communities to become closer and to function with more honesty, acceptance, and love. *Liberation means freedom of choice!*

Again, I cannot make this or anything right or wrong for you. My intention has been to share more of me . . . all of me . . . so that we learn to live together with dignity, compassion, pride, and full expression in all parts of our lives.

—Bud's reply; p. 109

An Open Letter—From Arlene's Daughter Linda

To Children of Gay Parents and Parents of Gay Children:
My mother is gay, and I would like to share with you some of my thoughts and encourage you to attend The Experience—the impact of which enriched immeasurably not only my relationship with my mother but also opened up new dimensions in my relationship with my husband, who attended with me.

First a word to children of gay parents. It is unfortunate that most children (of any age) do not think of their parents as being "people." I only recently realized that my mother was a person—with a heart that breaks, and a soul that changes and grows and she wants to be loved—not in spite of this or that, but she wants to be perceived, to be acknowledged, to be loved unconditionally and in total. I was surprised to find out that she was more than a bottle of milk—more than a provider of my education. More correctly, I was startled to realize that I had held such a narrow view. This startling realization lead to the discovery of one of the best friends I have—my mother.

Please look at your parents as people. Growing, changing, dynamic people. Listen to them. Get to know them—everything about them—what makes them cry, what makes them happy, what kinds of lives they live. If you do, you'll find a wonderful friend who will always love and support you.

And my message to parents of gay children is the other side of the same coin. Parents forget to see their children as people too. Too often they are only seen as our children— they are never allowed to grow up to be people. As parents we feel the responsibility to shape and teach our children— but too often we carry it too far—because we love them and want the best for them. But we forget that we can't choose what is best for them—only they can. And if they choose something other than we would, we will be far more enriched and rewarded if we see them as people, get to know them as they really are, and love them unconditionally as they are.

If someone in your family is gay, please don't say "okay, but let's ignore it." That's like saying that you don't understand and you don't want to—that's rejection. Talk it over. Understand it. Sweep away the myths—your loved one is far more important than myths. You'll find someone very wonderful that wants to love you very much.

One of the most inspiring, enlightening, rewarding, and wonderful ways to learn to know and understand and love a gay person near you is to take The Experience. It will do far, far more even than that—it will give you the one thing we all want more than anything else—unconditional, free-flowing, magnificently warm love—enough to last a lifetime and more.

With warm affection,
Linda

PART III

I AM GAY AND I LOVE YOU: ADDITIONAL LETTERS FROM THE CLOSET

Many of the letters included in this part of the book have been quoted in Parts I and II. They are presented here to provide more breadth to this book by sharing varied personal experiences. I have grouped the letters based on whom they are addressing: mothers, fathers, parents (including a letter to a grandmother), children, brothers, and some special letters (to a high school, to the Catholic Church, and to a bishop in the church).

LETTERS TO MOTHERS

Brad, to His Mother

Dear Mother,

I'm writing to you today to tell you some very important things. These matters concern who and what I am and pertain to you and to me and our emotional relationship.

First, I will thank you for a job well done. You were the best mother for which any child could ask. You always did more than was necessary, and I know you did it out of love for me and love for the role of nurturer and provider.

Second, thank you for all of the times you've helped me financially. I could never have had the interesting life I've led and had the opportunities I've had if you had not been willing to be my friend when I needed it and to trust me when that was needed too.

Third, my life has for the most part been lived separate and apart from yours since I was eighteen and started

college. Perhaps it has seemed mysterious and not so clear
or well understood, but my reasons for hiding my life from
you were my own and were never because of anything you
have ever done or said. I have remained apart from you
because I didn't want to hurt you or offend you. I wanted
only your good opinion and approval. I never wanted to
risk losing your affection or love. For those reasons I've always been silent about who I am.

I knew after I received my 4-F classification from my
army draft physical in 1969 that you knew that I am gay.
I knew you knew after our conversation just prior to my
moving to New Orleans in 1978, that you knew the course
my life was taking, that I am homosexual, that my affec-
tional requirements could be met only by men. I knew
that you knew that my relationship with Rod was more than
"just roommates."

I knew that you might have wanted to discuss this
with me from the beginning, but I told you flatly that it
was not your concern, that it was for me to deal with, and
that I did not wish to discuss it. One of my intentions in
writing to you at this time is to let you know I am open
to discussion about myself now if you need to talk to me
or need to know what my life is like.

I will tell you my life has not been easy, but it has
been no more difficult than any human existence and certainly a lot less difficult than a great many. I have found
satisfactions and happinesses probably as easily as anyone, and they are more dear to me because they seem harder
won and to a greater degree self-created than the usual
ones people get by on.

This means that I am proud of myself, that I know
who I am and what my qualities are, and what I can expect of myself and this lifetime. My values, of course, to a
great degree are your values. I prize honesty above all
things and being true to my heart. I love beautiful things
and cleanliness. I love to see happy children. I love to
see men working together for things that are good for everyone, and women being free and open and comfortable
with who they are.

In this time in our lives, there are now, of course, larger considerations than mere personal happiness. I intend that my writing to you now in this way should allay some fears for my health and happiness that you might have. I want to speak of AIDS, which, as I told you a few years ago, had claimed as its victim a very close friend of mine. Now, in 1988, I have lost five very close friends, and other men who are close to me are battling this strange malady.

I recognized after my October, 1980, trip to Vermont and New York City that there was bad, bad trouble ahead for this nation and all of the gay men I knew. I learned this from my friend, a doctor in New York, who was on the staff in Greenwich Village of what then was called the Gay Men's Health Clinic. He related to me how concerned and worried he was about what was happening to the patients he was seeing and the things he was learning from other medical people in the city. I'm not sure that you know this, but it was not until over a year later that the first alarms were sounded in the media. I saw then clearly that I must gird myself for the coming storm, and a raging disaster it has certainly been.

Thanks to your genetic input, I am and have always been a very healthy person, but thanks in abundance to your attitude toward doctors I believe I have a greater chance of surviving all of this in better than excellent health.

Remember how you've always mistrusted doctors and said, "You don't need to run to a doctor every time you don't feel well," and other things that communicated your self-reliance on your ability to get well and get on with your duties and responsibilities no matter how you felt physically? Believe me, "it took." I paid attention. And now I've learned in spades what I know to be essential to my own continued good health: "Health is a function of participation." I know what happens to people who turn their health over to an authority outside themselves. They die. I've seen it again and again.

The medical professionals don't know what AIDS is, and they are so locked into their belief systems about the

efficacy of modern medical science that they cannot admit
that they don't know. I have seen them kill five close
friends by means of medical blunders, and, without the cloak
of medical authority, they would be indicted for murder.

The only people I know who have died of AIDS are
the ones who have received this death sentence from doctors, called a diagnosis of AIDS, and have stayed in the care
of those doctors. The only ones I know who have survived and are surviving in good health have been those who
removed themselves from the "care" of their physicians
and have invented, created by themselves, their own continuing good health. I have not been to a doctor for stan-
dard medical attention since 1981, and I will be found dead
in a ditch before I will ever consult another one or have
anything to do with any of them.

You know, you always wanted me to be a doctor,
and I will admit I considered it as a career before I began college, but something inside told me not to make that
choice. Now, in retrospect, I see when and why.

Do you remember Sandy who died when I was at Em-
ory? That was 1970. I knew Sandy pretty well. I knew
that he at that time was confronting the fact of his homosexuality, and how frightened he was of his parents'
—particularly his father—finding out and being disappointed
about the truth of his homosexuality.

Mother, he died within three weeks of his coming
down with pneumonia. He died, I contend, of the same
symptoms so many of my friends have died of in the 1980s.
The signs, symptoms, and complications, are identical.

AIDS as a diagnosis did not come into existence until about 1981 or 1982, and, yet, I knew what was going
on inside Sandy, and that was a full ten years before the
present crisis. I see now that he died of hypocrisy, shame,
inability to confront his own truth, and fear of disappointing his parents.

I will not, and I absolutely, catgorically refuse, to be
a victim of such unnecessary insanity. I saw Sandy's death
as an unnecessary failure of modern medical science, and I
disdained even then any involvement with such a system.

That is a part of the complicated and convoluted reasoning behind my telling you that I am homosexual at this time. It is not to hurt you. It is not to upset you. It is purely and simply, on my part, survival, and survival with good health and a clear head.

So what is AIDS for me now? It has made me into a caring, supportive person of those who are not going to survive this gay Auschwitz of my generation. I fervently believe that AIDS is a gift generated by the mass psyche of the gay men of my time and all people of the world to confront in a life-and-death scenario the fact of personal responsibility for individual health; and, at the same time, the overall, overarching fact that every human being must look to the care of every other human being on this planet. This is an enormous yet specifically personal challenge.

You survived the Depression and World War II. You know the difficulties and triumphs of your experience, and you know no one would have survived those hard, hard times had they not been honest and accepting of things as they were, and had they not committed themselves to what worked.

The same workable principles apply to my generation and what is happening today. We must depend on the willing cooperation of each other if we are to survive with any dignity, any hope, and any real ability to make the human experience worthwhile.

This is the real purpose of this letter, to let you know your love and affection are terribly important to me. I know deep in my heart that, no matter what I am or what I do, you need my love and affection, too. You know you have it.

Now, please, if you need to talk to me, please pick up the phone and call. Don't make a big drama of this, because we both know you knew the truth about me long ago. I am strong and healthy and a formidable warrior. You are an adult, and I am an adult, and I intend to be an honest, effective adult with an abundance of integrity, the same as my father and my mother showed me how to be.

I love you. I miss seeing you. I wish we could be comfortably closer. I wish Daddy were alive so you wouldn't have to be alone. I hope you're not disappointed in me. I need your love.

Love,
Brad

Gerardo, to His Mother, in Argentina

Dear Mom,

Somehow until today I had thought our communication was pretty good. You know I'm gay and you love Chris, and I love you for the acceptance and love you showed us when you visited us.

But I just realized that things don't stop there. You recently wrote me a letter asking me to hide my homosexuality at home in Argentina. And because of the way you've insisted on this, home doesn't feel like home to me anymore. I don't feel like going back because I don't want to have to face my uncles and aunts and your friends and pretend that I'm straight, or that I'm alone here in the U.S.

I have a lover that I love more than anything in my life. I am proud of him and of my love for him, and of his love for me. I cannot go to Argentina and pretend this doesn't exist or feel ashamed of it.

Mom, you don't know that for the last fifteen months Chris and I have lived with the fact that he's HIV positive. This means that maybe some day soon I could lose the one person that I have loved most in my life to AIDS. Every day people that I know or know of die of this terrible disease, and I see the pain of parents, lovers, and friends around them. When I see this I support them and do what I can to reinforce that support system by working with AIDS organizations or with gay people and helping them deal with it.

When you say "Please don't tell anyone about your life" you don't realize that you're asking me to deny all of the love and the pain that surrounds me and pretend I'm someone else, so that the uncles I haven't heard from in ten years and the "friends" who couldn't care less about who I am will not criticize me or you.

I know this is hard for you. It took me thirty-three years to get here and, believe me, I know it's hard to face the world with the truth. But please think that since you started telling me not to talk about my life, I have been considering never returning to Argentina again. In fact, it got so bad that I came to think I hated the country and the people, and every time I saw an Argentinian I immediately shunned him or her.

Now I realize that I don't want to lose my roots. I want the freedom to go back whenever I want to, to visit you there as you visit me here, and be who I am without fear that you will be embarrassed by me, or sad for me, or afraid of what I might say.

If something happened to Chris, I would never be able to keep my mouth shut about any of it. That would be as if you had been asked not to talk about Dad's death when he passed on.

I have a question for you, Mom. What would you do if I died of AIDS? Would you lie to your friends? Would you invent a different cause of death? Or would you tell them I'm still alive and pretend you hear from me?

I love you and I know you love many of the things I am or have. I want you to start loving me unconditionally for all my things and all of me. This doesn't mean that you have to go around saying I'm gay. But it does mean that I want you to defend me if someone hurts me or anyone else for being gay.

For many years, when I was growing up, you watched Dad hurt me and did nothing about it but make me feel that it was my own fault or that I should accept him as he was. Well, you're asking me to do the same thing now, but this time I won't because I know I'm right and those who insult me or are afraid of me are not.

One day I will go back to Argentina and see the people you so protect. When this happens, if they ask me what I am, I will tell them I'm gay. I don't know what you're hiding from them now, but I do think you should perhaps start preparing those you care about because, as you well know, lies don't go very far.

The option may be for me never to go back, and if I do, to see you secretly and away from your friends and relatives. You tell me what you think about this.

I love you, as always, enormously,

Gerardo

John, to His Mother

Dear Mother,

I would like to have you come to California to live either with or near me. I realize it has been too long since I made the invitation originally and haven't asked since, but I really do want you to do it and I'm finally clear on why I didn't insist earlier. It's because I wasn't complete in representing where I was on that score and many others.

I want you to know that I'm gay. In the odd case that you don't know what that means, it means I'm homosexual. I told Lucy when she was here last fall and she said not to tell you—that it would only worry you unnecessarily, but actually I do want you to know. And not to worry. I am happier now than I've ever been in my life. Stronger and more full. Of life. Of love. I guess I always wanted you and Dad to know. So that I could share more of my life with you. And it's true that I left a lot of myself out of our lives, which may not have been fair to any of us.

I love you a great deal and want to share my life with you . . . honestly and completely. It's true that we're all down on our scuppers a bit—at least relative to where we've been in the past. But we have a great deal of vitality, wit,

warmth, intelligence, and plain old spunk. We'll all get better if we make it happen and I want to try . . . with you
to share if you'd like. I don't have the money I once did,
but I will again I think. And once I'm through paying child
support and spousal support, I'll truly be a free man again.
In the meanwhile, I'm anything but starving. I'm living
well and am truly the happiest I've ever been.

I'm sending a copy of this to Bobby and Florence and
to Lucy. I really think we've harmed each other too much
and unnecessarily so by protecting each other from truths
in the fear we'd stir up too much or only cause pain. It
has caused me too much pain the other way and no more—
ever again—if I can help it.

I love you and I love Bobby and Florence and
Lucy and I hope you will be able to share with your
friends someday that someone you love is gay without feeling apologetic about it. That would make me the happiest
of all.

More later. I love you all.

John

P.S. A friend of mine asked me why I was writing to you
about this and I said I hoped you loved me and it was
painful to be loved as an illusion rather than what I am.
He said that was worth writing and I had presumed it but
left it unsaid—I love your reality. Please love mine.

Nick, to His Mother

Dear Mom,

I need to let you know a few things. A few things
about you and few things about me. When I was growing
up I don't remember seeing you much. I felt as if I were
some evil child that only Dad could love. You were a complete blank except once when I was four. I remember being
spanked. I also remember it was for a good reason. After that I can't recall you. That's when my nightmares be-

gan. There was something evil trying to get me and I couldn't find you to help me.

When Dad broke Ritz's nose, you miraculously appeared. Before then I knew you were around the house, mainly in your room, but it wasn't real. It was like you were some faceless person who was not reachable. When you came to life and put Dad in jail, I was the one who had to suffer with him. I felt unloved and even hated, by you and my brothers and sisters. So I tried to fit in, I began to hate Dad. When he came out of jail it was the most horrible experience of my life. For years I had nightmares about him breaking into the house.

After you and he reconciled you changed once again. I felt only dislike from you when I was nine until I was fifteen. I tried to be a good son—I only wanted your love.

When I decided to go away to school you were very supportive. I will always remember the time you went with me to San Diego to take my entrance exams. I felt only love and support from you. It may sound silly and I don't even know if you remember. After I aced my exams we took the bus back to downtown San Diego. We were on the wrong bus and ended up miles from downtown. We didn't have any change, just a ten-dollar bill. The bus driver got a little snotty and you out-bitched him. I was so proud and, funny enough, I felt protected by you.

Later that same year, Dad's cancer was worse. I'm sorry that I wouldn't come up to see him. I didn't have the courage to watch him die. I didn't have the ability to love him because of all the things he did. That's not entirely true. I was taught by you and my sisters to hate him, and I couldn't overcome it. So he died without knowing I truly loved him and I stayed a hundred miles away. This is over and done with and I don't blame you or anyone.

The next few years of my life were aimless and unproductive. I tried to figure out what was missing in my life. I didn't seem to fit in anywhere. I was twenty years old before I acknowledged my gay identity. This realization started me on the road to spiritual completeness. I met Steve, and to be real honest with you, it was a mistake. I married the first man who asked me. It didn't work out and I went back to single living. I had a lot of fun but it was an empty existence.

A few years later I met Reid, and suddenly I felt like a whole, complete, loved person. Reid loved me more than I thought I had a right to be. He made me feel clean and pure and good. We made a life together. We took life by the horns and lived it. A love like this comes once in a lifetime and I thank God I had the opportunity and didn't waste it. We had our ups and downs but it was *life*!

Reid developed AIDS first, and our relationship had to change. Boy did it. We became even closer and when my diagnosis hit me he was there to pick up the pieces. When my family turned their backs on me he helped me and felt my pain with me. I need you to understand that each day he gets sicker, and as he gets closer to death part of me dies with him. The other half of my soul is dying and I am in agony. When you reject him you are rejecting me. He and I are one. When you don't stand up for us you help to kill our beauty. When you attempt to invalidate our love and commitment you are helping us Die. Mom, I am dying. Half of me is dying with Reid and I won't be too far behind. I need you. I need you to fight for me and for Reid. I need you to get a spine and tell my brothers and sisters that I am good. That I am a person and equally your son. That my lover is equal to their spouses. That our disease is not leprosy. I need you to protect us. I need you to love me unconditionally—now. I need you to see the home Reid and I have made for ourselves. I need you to bear witness to our love so that when we are gone you can remember our dignity and our pride. I need you to fight for us. When Reid dies I'm going to need you to help me keep living for as long as I can. I need you to be with me and love me and let me die peacefully. I need you to pull our family together while I am still healthy enough to look like me. I need you to pierce through Martha's hypocritical self-righteousness and tell her that maybe God put me in this family so that they may learn to look past their pettiness and learn to truly love. I need you to do this for

me or let me go. I don't want to find new parents and
new brothers and sisters but I can.

Remember that I love you and that I realize the difficulty of doing what I ask. I don't want to die knowing
my mother and my brothers and sisters didn't love me
enough to accept me as I am, didn't love me enough to
see the adult I have become, didn't really love me at all. I
am losing everything that ever really mattered to me—my
lover, my home, my family, my life. Mama, I need you.

Love,
Nick

Note: Nick wrote this letter to his mother in August 1988.
Reid died in January 1989.

LETTERS TO FATHERS

Jim, to His Father

Dear Dad,

This letter is incredibly difficult for me to write. I'm not at all sure how to express to you what it is I have to say. It would be so much easier to leave it unsaid, and I want to tell you. You're the only one left I haven't told.

I haven't for a lot of reasons. I remember all too vividly a day when I was marched into the office in the garage and beaten so badly by an enraged man that I lost the hearing in my left ear for at least a day and a half. The reason was I had in my possession a pornographic book that detailed explicit homosexual scenes. I used every excuse in the book to get out of admitting the real reason for having it—I liked it. It made me sexually aroused. It triggered all the fantasies of puberty and awakening sexuality.

211

Only, they weren't with women, Dad; they never have been and never will be. And I knew it. I've known since the kid down the block used to babysit and I'd ask him to take off his shirt so I could lie on his chest, because it felt good. I didn't know what it meant, of course, and I knew I liked it—and more importantly—wanted to do it again and again and again.

I had that book because I liked it, and I knew I liked it. And, what I got from you was a beating—the *only* one I remember getting from you—and the remark, "If you're going to be one of *those* you can pack your things right now and move out. You're no son of mine!" I didn't understand what the whole thing was—I was who I was and for that I got a beating and threatened with disinheritance. So for the next fifteen years, I hid from you; I shut you out, more and more, little by little—I caused a rift to happen between us so that I could remain your son without being who I am. I "knew" you'd never "understand."

Mother, I thought, would "understand." She didn't. I thought John would—he didn't either. Now, however, I've come to realize that "understanding" is the booby prize of life. It isn't necessary for you, or them, or anyone else to "understand."

I choose not to hide any longer. I choose to stop making decisions for you and other people about whether or not you'll play the game of life with me because I'm gay. I choose to take the risk, you will not play and for the first time in my life, it's OK. It's OK for my whole family to say "nix," because for the first time in my life I'm in charge of it—I'm taking responsibility for it. I choose to no longer allow the little voices and images from the past and the reactions I assume people will have to manipulate me.

I want you to know, I'm gay; if you choose not to play the game of life with me, I love you. And, if you choose to play, I love you.

I am gay, and it's something we both know and have known for a long time. It's something that has to be dealt with, and however that happens, please get that it's OK.

I'm doing this for one reason and one reason only, Dad. I choose to leave home and I cannot leave home and be in charge of my life as long as that home is not completed. I thought by telling John, then by telling Mother it would be. It cannot until everyone in that home knows.

I only apologize for not saying all of this sooner. I'm very sorry I made you the very last to know, and you were the hardest to tell.

Love,
Jim

Ray, to His Father

Dear Dad,

For a long time now, I have wanted to discuss with you the fact that I am gay. I feel that you already know this, and that we have both been avoiding it for years.

In one sense I do feel very accepted by you (for which I am very grateful) but I feel somehow very dishonest, and incomplete, and not free.

I want to be honest with you while we are both still alive. I feel that we do have much in common that we can build a satisfying relationship around. I would like to do things with you (alone)—fishing, walking in the woods, but especially talking. I want to share more of your world than I have for many years. I miss you.

I don't want to be only polite and discreet around you—I want to be serious and meaningful

I feel that you will understand. I expect that you may not accept a lot of the details of my life-style, but that is probably true of every other human being that you know as well.

What I am asking for is recognition rather than acceptance. I want you to know who I really am. I don't want any longer to pretend to be different in your presence, nor do I want you to pretend that I am not something that you know I am.

I am not an evil person.

I love you,

Ray

Stioux, to His Father

Dear Dad,

Boy, do I have a lot to clean up with you!

You fucker! You shithead! You schmuck!

You fucked me over so well, I'm still playing victim over it!

Well—I'm ending that! Let's clean it up. And if WE can't clean it up, at least I will.

Let me tell you how you fucked me over. How you weren't there when I wanted you. How you laughed at me when I fell down, how you laughed when I dropped a ball—*at three years old*! How you called me "five by five" and laughed again each time, especially with other people— even strangers! How you let those people (the Elephants?) tie me to a tree and laugh at me again, and told that story laughing again, and again and again. How the only affection you showed me was slapping me with those big hands of yours. How you'd come home from work and pick on Mother and Melvin and me! How 98s on tests were never good enough. How coming in second in a race wasn't good enough—for you!

What race did you ever come in first?

You had a lousy marriage, you hated your job, your children hated you, the whole neighborhood laughed at you. You were thought of as a schnorrer. You had no friends, you never appreciated anything you had. You never encouraged us. All you ever did was yell and slap and complain. Your message was "LOSE! LOSE! LOSE! The world's against everybody! NO ONE EVER WINS!"

I heard enough stories about: "if only you were rich." Well, get over it! You are! You have me, you schmuck! And much else!

How crushed I was when you discovered my gayness. I wanted you to react positively—or even negatively—but at least react. Instead, it didn't seem to mean anything, just like everything else. So what, Stioux is just another burden.

How many times I reached out to you—Love me . . . please? Now let me try to get the other side of that.

I pulled away from you. If I couldn't be the perfect son you wanted—well, I wanted you to be the perfect Daddy. Well, perfect wasn't it—but you didn't even come close. So, when I reached out so many years and got worse than nowhere, I finally told you how nonnourishing you were and I wouldn't talk to you. I want to tell you how much I loved you and needed you and still want to love you. I don't know how to tell you that now except to say it.

I'm sorry I never was whatever you wanted me to be, and I'm sorry your life is so rotten for you. I wish we could talk like this—at least you could share with me—whatever . . .

And I could have you as—as least the shitty father you are.

Stioux

Bob, to His Dead Father

Dear Daddy,

I love you. I have never wanted to hurt you. But all my life I have sensed that you have disapproved of me. I was not the strong son that you wanted. Oh, how I wanted to be and I did try. I wanted your love more than my life. Just a touch or a hug, I can't ever remember one.

I feel you removed yourself from me. You chose not to experience me because you sensed a difference in me

and I know that you knew what it was. You knew that it
had a name and you knew the name. You knew what I
was and you were unable to deal with it. What I got from
this action of yours was that you were ashamed of me. I
have learned this from you and use it in my life today so I
know how much it must have hurt you. I know you are a
sensitive and gentle man and just as afraid of dealing with
shit as I am. Now for the purpose of this letter, I am a
homosexual who chooses to live a gay life-style. At the moment your relationship with me colors every relationship
I have had and may ever have. It hurts me, Daddy, that
something so distant to me now as your inability to communicate love to me hurts me still now. I do not blame you,
but have become you in all of my relationships. I perceived this was the way to be a man. To become acceptable to you I had to become you. I also know that you
did not handle other family relationships this way but rather
lavished your affection on Becky. I think it is ironic that
the one you could show love to is also gay. I wish that there
were some way that we could be writing this letter together with the same hand because I know her pain. And
that pain has made us separate even though we share the
same type of love.

   Communication for me today is lousy because of that
feeling so many years ago.

   I wish I could deliver this letter to you because you
should know that I feel responsible for your death. Even
though on an intellectual level I know it is not so, I still
carry this with me and pray it isn't so. I know you were
aware of me when our bodies met, even though you did not
participate in a demonstrative way and I know you were
at the level of fear, hate, or love.

   I hide in the memory of that afternoon, push it down
and have allowed it to ruin physical and emotional sex
with the only beings on this planet that I want to play with.
No fair. I became a drunk and a very unhappy (most of
the time) person because I feared approaching you when
you appeared unapproachable. Daddy, I feel hurt. I am
your hurt. I bleed with you. We did it together. I don't know

if I want your love now, I just want you to know that I am and will continue to be a part of you forever and always. Death did not change it for me. I feel your presence.

Don't let what I do with my body ruin a love that we both should have and enjoy. I am a worthy person that behaves in unworthy ways because I feel I must be punished for not being what I perceive that you wanted in a son.

We are one and I think we both lose. Let me love you!

Your loving and forever devoted son, Bob

P.S. I wish it were possible for you to answer this letter because I really want and need to know what you think and feel, whatever that may be even though it may not be what I think you should think or feel on this subject. I am willing to be open and caring with you. I am tired of the cold in my life and desire whatever to fill its space. You are very real to me. I lost you at birth, not at death. I am relieved at this opportunity to write to you and intend on mailing this letter to your last known address.

Love,
Bob

LETTERS TO PARENTS

George, to His Parents

Dear Ma and Pa:

This is a letter that will contain real words and feelings that I should have shared with you years and years ago. I am thankful that one of you is alive and can read my words, and I know that the one who is dead will get them too.

The bottom line of everything I want to say is I love you. I have lived a long life, many years, many years convinced of the opposite—convinced that I didn't love you. Convinced that I didn't care very much—in the case of Ma—and convinced that I hated you, Pa. I felt that life had given me a raw deal by allowing me to be born into a poor family, when I should have been born into a rich one so that I could have had all the things my greedy self

wanted. I felt that I was born into a family where there was
no love at all, for I certainly didn't feel any. I was so busy
with my own feelings of hatred and selfishness, I couldn't
see anything else. I convinced myself neither of you loved
me, that you didn't love any of us kids. And, believing this,
I withdrew and withdrew and withdrew from you both. I
wouldn't give you a single drop of love. So I grew up with
this big gulf between us—this big hole.

And I knew this hole was there and I felt guilty about
it and rather than place the blame where it was—with
me—I put the blame on you and made you wrong. You,
then, became the bad guys. I was the real bad guy and
couldn't admit it, so I put it on you. And I rejected, really
rejected any attempts you made to give your love to me.

I went into hiding, not letting you see my feelings,
and I even removed my body from the house as much as
I could so I wouldn't have to face the problem I had created by telling you how much I loved you then.

I resented you, and I showed this feeling all the time.
But the real truth was, and is, I loved you. Loved you
very much.

To further complicate the problem—or maybe it was
the one and only reason for the problem—was the matter of the thing I was trying to hide so desperately—my
sexuality—afraid that if you knew about it you wouldn't
be able to love me. I don't know at what point in my young
life I became aware that I was "different." Maybe four
or five, or earlier, yet I didn't acknowledge it until years
later. The truth was and is that I am homosexual, or gay
as they say today. As a young kid I was different—shy, withdrawn, not into the things other kids my age were into. I
wasn't *made* that way, I was *born* that way. But I didn't
understand it and couldn't communicate about it and so I
hid it and felt guilty and ashamed. And I was terrified you
wouldn't love me if you found out about it, that you would
take your love away. And I wanted your love and I needed
your love.

And because the mind is such a monster thing and
was clever, I listened to my mind when it said to me:

"They're going to find out, they're not going to love you when they find out, so what you better do is stop loving them *first*, before they stop loving you, because if you don't love them then it won't hurt when they stop loving you."

So I withdrew my love and rejected yours and went into hiding about being gay.

So I committed the greatest crime there is in this world—a crime far greater than war or murder. I denied love. I denied myself the joy of receiving your love for me and I denied you both the joy of receiving my love for you. This is a great wrong. A very great wrong. Now that I am aware of all of this I must communicate it to you so that the wrong will end.

I asked you to forgive me. And I know you will because you love me.

It's no big thing that I am gay, yet I have made a mountain out of it all my life and have allowed it to damage half a century of living. I plan to do more living and I don't want to do any more damage. So, I can't live with any more lies. Lies are horrible, horrible, horrible—they destroy life. This I've discovered

So I want you to know the truth—which you probably have always known—but I want to be sure that you hear the truth from me, and not a lie from me.

I have nothing to hide from you anymore, and if you are interested in knowing about gay life and what it is to be gay and to prefer members of your own sex, then I'll be happy to write you and tell you about it. Just let me know, or ask me questions.

I have suffered a lot by not telling you all of this before. And I have made you suffer too. The suffering is over now and all that is left—all that there ever really was—is, I love you. And I know you love me.

Your son,
George

Chuck, to His Parents

Dear Mom and Dad,
          This is probably the most difficult letter that I've ever had to write. You see I've taken a workshop that is helping me to resolve some problems I've been having for quite some time now and these problems are affecting my everyday decisions, relationships, and interactions with others and with myself. I'd like to talk to each of you separately and then together. I wish that I could do this face-to-face not over the phone or through the mail, but we can never seem to talk about anything serious without one of us misunderstanding and getting hurt or just shutting down or off. So I'm doing this this way and if you'd feel more comfortable replying the same way, then please do. This is something I must do right now and not let it wait until we see each other again because God only knows when that will happen. I wish we weren't separated by the entire continental U.S., but unfortunately we are, and in more ways than one. I hope you don't take this letter as my way of starting a fight because it's not meant that way and I'm so tired of fighting—to keep my job, to get my medication, to keep my apartment, FOR MY LIFE. Sometimes it really gets to be too much, and in fact in the five months since my AIDS diagnosis I've almost ended it all twice. I have everything I need to do the trick, in the house, just in case it gets to the point where I can't handle it anymore. I've done all the necessary research to be successful and not by some miscalculation end up as a vegetable. You see, it is not my desire or intention to become a burden to anyone. Mom, you and I talked about this when Michael killed himself. The difference between him and me is that he didn't even try to deal with his diagnosis, he was still in the closet with his family, which fortunately, I am not. I have always been open and honest with you about my life-style and you know from our discussions about Michael's decision and my own diagnosis that suicide, as an option, is and will be my last resort.

I can't help but feel hurt by your reluctance to have me home. I know the people at home are ignorant, but remember when I came out to you and you said "What can change? You're my son." Well, Mom, many things change and I'm disheartened to find that *you* are now in the "closet" because you're afraid that your friends and neighbors will "find out." Isn't it strange that now you are where I was fourteen years ago? Well, I came out of that closet and became honest and accepting of who I am, and believe me it hurt to lose some friends but the ones who stick around and love you anyway are far more precious and important than those who sit in judgment. I hope you realize how important your love and support are to me. By the way, next October 11 is National Coming Out Day. I'd like to send you some info about this and maybe I can help you and Dad come out and be proud and supportive, without fear of abandonment, of someone who loves you very much. No one is saying this is going to be easy for you but it's not as difficult as you might think. Finally, I'm sorry we had to go through that tough time twelve years ago. You know the one I mean. What an unfortunate coincidence.

Well, I've gotten that off my chest and I hope I've cleared the air some. I'll speak with you some more after I talk with Dad.

Dad—

This is tough. How do you talk to someone you don't know? I have to say this because it has bothered me for months since Mom told me about it. She told me you cried when I called from the hospital and told you that one of my worst fears had materialized and that nagging cough that I had was indeed pneumocystis. Dad, that is real difficult for me to visualize, the emotion I mean, because I never actually remember you as anything but someone to fear. Someone who was called from some mysterious place called "the plant" when there was punishment to be meted out or on holidays or graduations. Do you know that I have no memory of you ever holding me? And now I find out that you're holding yourself responsible for everything that's hap-

pened to me. It must be tough to know that you'll out-
live at least one of your children. Dad, I'm sorry, but I just
can't handle that guilt. That's something that you're going
to have to look at. Who's to say that if there was a strong
male presence in my youth and adolescence that I wouldn't
be gay. I know I can't say that. Maybe it was you that I
was looking for in all those men I slept with just to be
held in someone's arms. The fact is that I don't know who
you are and I resent the fact that there always seemed to
be time to teach Edward how to play ball. Where was I?
Was I that frail as a child that I would break?

It's unfortunate that you weren't around to witness
firsthand the situations that passed between Mom and me
before I was informed that it was time for me to find a place
of my own. Picture this—she was going through meno-
pause and I was coming out. Hot flashes and hot tempers.
I'll let your imagination take care of the rest, talk about
raging hormones. I'm not trying to make you feel bad, but
that was then and this is now and what I'd like to offer
and explore with you is friendship. I hope this works for
both of us because if what Ed, Jane, and Barbara Jean
say is true you must be a wonderful person that I'd be proud
to call my friend.

Together, rest assured that I'm taking care of myself
as best as I'm able. I have wonderful friends who look
out for and support me. I'm grateful to you both for my
education, which has enabled me to make it out here on
my own. I hope you realize and accept that I am happy with
what and who I am and that I wouldn't change a single
thing, AIDS included, even if I could, because to do so
would mean that I might have missed out on one of the
other parts of my life that I hold so dear. You know what?
I turned out just fine!

All my love,
Chuck

Richard, to His Parents

Dear Mom and Dad:
         This is no doubt going to be the most difficult letter
I've ever written or will ever write. I want you to know
something very important about me because without knowing all about me, you can't know anything about me. I
am gay and probably have been gay since I was born. For
many years I've wanted to tell you—and, in fact, I've re-
hearsed a speech many times. Somehow, whenever I felt
the time would be appropriate, it never was when I faced
you. I never felt that it was kind to write and tell you because it wasn't fair not to be able to face you.
         I don't know what your feelings are about gay people
and I know that it is a situation that you probably know
very little about.
         I first began to notice that I had strong feelings for
men when I was about seven or eight and we were still
living in the Bronx. I always thought that I was the only
person in the world like "that," and was terribly ashamed.
After being bar mitzvah, I used to pray for forgiveness
and hoped I could change, although I knew that it wasn't
possible. I even thought that by going out with girls I would
magically be "normal." Of course that couldn't be. I remember trying to play stickball with the rest of the guys or
joining the Boy Scouts or going on overnight hikes, thinking that by doing that "manly" thing, I would be all right.
Nothing really changed—I just didn't like doing those
things and they didn't have anything to do with me, as a
person. All I really wanted to do was to be what you
wanted me to be. I blamed myself, I blamed you, I blamed
domineering mother, absent father, etc., and none of it
really meant anything. What it means now is that I am gay
and I enjoy what I am and what I do. You've met many
of my gay friends over the years and it seemed to me that
you liked them as people. It makes no difference to me
what you are—you are my parents and I love you both. You

did the very best you could with what you could and I
am happy with the results, and I hope you are, too. You've
taught me the important things about life and living. I live
the way that you showed me it was appropriate to live. I
wanted to take this opportunity to thank you for all your
assistance in my becoming a very happy and satisfied person.

I have a sense of you, based upon many supportive
years, that you will join me in celebrating my awareness and
well-being, rather than assigning blame or becoming upset.

All that is left to say is that I love both of you very
much and I want you to know that I know that you love
me very much, too.

I'll be speaking with you and seeing you very soon.

XXX Richard

A Follow-up Note from Richard

A few days after I sent it I flew home to visit with
them, and nothing was mentioned about the letter until it
was time for me to leave. My mother handed me the letter and said, "I wanted you to have the letter back so you
would know we received it. Your father and I have known
about this for years and it has never affected us. We love
you very much."

Ron, to His Parents

Dear Mom and Dad,

This is just a short note to let you know how much I
love you, and how much your support has meant to me
this past year. This has been the second most difficult year
of my adult life—the first being when I divorced and left
my children and their mother.

You were absolutely wonderful the night I told you I was gay, and I will treasure that memory forever.

I was most fearful, Dad, of losing your love and respect. I should have been more trusting, but after tragically losing your daughter, and then your eldest son, who had caused you so much pain, how could you possibly handle your only surviving child being a faggot? I love you so much right now, Dad—so very much.

Yes, there was a lot of shit in my youth, but none of it—absolutely none of it—contributed to making me gay. And even if it did, then I thank you for it, for I like who I am and what I am. Your immediate and steady support when I told you the most difficult thing I've ever told anybody in my life has contributed to my finally entering the real world.

The process is not complete. I still have headaches and too many colds—all induced by the everyday stresses and experience in simply living and being gay in a straight world. But, I'm actively working on these difficulties, and they are minor compared to the distance I've come this past year.

Right now, this moment, I'm enrolled in a two-day therapeutic process called The Advocate Experience. Its purpose is "to transform the experience of being gay into richer contexts wherein the gay person can live his/her life in ways that are truly self-enhancing and contribute to all of society."

We're halfway through our second day, and it's been a beautiful experience. Right now there are 118 other gay men and women around me writing letters to their parents or other important people in their lives. There has been and is a lot of crying going on during the letter writing. I'm one of them. It's very touching, and in a way beautiful to witness my gay brothers and sisters getting in touch with their feelings about their families and their gayness. I'm feeling a great deal of love for all of them. We share a bond—we all know the pain of hiding.

Many in the room now are writing to tell their parents that they are gay. I pray for each of them that their parents are as accepting and supportive of them as you have been of me. They need that love.

Again, I love both of you very much. Thanks for being just who you are, and thanks for letting me be just who I am.

Love,
Ron

Joe, to His Parents

Mom and Dad,

I can't believe its the middle of 1988, I'm nearly thirty-four years old, and I am just now able, I honestly believe, to confront, or rather discuss, a lot of what is me and my relationship to both of you.

I wasn't sure, really sure, if my love for both of you was true, beyond the fact that you were my parents of birth, but now I know that I do love both of you very much. *I love you!*

I have been hurt by "things" you have done in the past, but to dwell on the past is not positive. I will only mention that perhaps I thought you, at times, abandoned me, criticized me beyond what was necessary and maybe didn't gives me the attention and love that I thought I needed and deserved. But maybe you didn't know any better. No one gives you any tools or guidelines to go by to be a parent. And sometimes you just do the best you know.

And I'm sure that I have hurt you at times and in different ways. In either case, I would rather not discuss individual incidents—I want to just let go, drop, such incidents.

I am an adult now, not Joey, and you are Mom and Dad, not Mommy and Daddy. I'm not the sensitive child, nor the moody, uncommunicative adolescent. I know about myself suddenly deeper than I ever thought I was going to. Deeper than maybe I've ever really wanted to.

And because of this I must communicate like an adult.

Not like a child or adolescent—afraid of what might be
said or done—for fear of my survival. I love both of you!

So let's not mince words. What I am about to say
you may already have "feared"—though I would rather
you didn't see it in that light. What I am about to say is
not meant to shock you, or make you hate me, or turn
you away, or make you feel ashamed—although these may
be emotions you may experience. And I want you to feel
your emotions—they are your right and they are healthy.

Mom and Dad, I am gay. I am not sure why I am
but I am and I have been fighting it for years and I realize that it is nothing that either one of you did—not at all—
because I feel that I have been this way since birth. To
explain in a nutshell would be ridiculous and ludicrous. I
have been through therapy and because of this therapy I
have realized my true self. Whether it is because of my chemical make-up, a gene, or something else—no one knows.
What I do know is that it is. And I don't expect someone
who is not gay to understand fully. Nor do I expect you
to understand all at once, overnight. Since it took me
years to come to this point I don't expect you to come
to terms immediately and act as if the boat has not been
rocked.

But after all the years I have agonized I don't know
of any other way to approach this. And I will reiterate
that *I love you* and I am not doing this, I would not do this
or anything, to hurt you.

You are my parents and I will always be your son.

I will hope and pray that you will not abandon me
now, and that you will love me still. I will hope and pray
that you will understand me eventually and that our lives
will be much closer—not further apart.

I know the two of you have gone through much in
your lives and that much of this has been with your
children—I hope you have the capacity to go through more.
I don't wish, would never have wished, for you to go
through this, another big event in your lives. I hope God
gives you the capacity to handle this much more.

I will try to close here now, because I understand

much has been said for you to ponder, to be angry about, and to be sorry about. I don't know what more I could say. Please love me, and know that I love you.

Your son,
Joe

Billy, to His Parents

Dear Mom and Dad,

Boy, it has been a while since my last letter. I hope things find you well. I have been a little hesitant to write for quite some time, as a matter of fact three years now. I was expecting a reply from you to my last letter. I heard from Debbie and Sarah that you were offended by my last attempt at communication, isn't it funny how things can be perceived in such different ways. I thought my last letter was such an expression of love.

I've worked on forgiving you for a long time now. I think I have finally gotten to the point I can forgive you for rejecting me, but better yet, I am finally beginning to forgive myself. I forgive you for being who you are and where you are. I never gave a lot of thought to the fact that maybe you don't think or feel the same as I do, or maybe you do not have the same resources and experiences to rely on. Looking at the whole picture, you were not as fortunate as I was. I was given many more tools to build my concepts and ideas. I am realizing you have done the best you can, given the knowledge you've been given. We are all victims of victims.

Reflecting on the past, how could you have been expected to deal with my sexuality when you were never given the tools to support and deal with your own. Mom, your own mother didn't even explain marriage or sex to you prior to your marriage to Dad. I heard the story from Debbie about your honeymoon. You should thank God that Dad is as supportive as he is.

I recognize you're doing the best you can. In forgiving I have allowed a new awareness of love to enter into my perspective of our relationship. You are beautiful people and I love you. I guess that is what has always been the important issue and the one I want you to understand the most.

I no longer need you to love me, but I'd prefer it. The fact you didn't answer my last letter, the fact you asked me to no longer call your house in Spring Hall, the fact you made reference to me having AIDS in the hospital three years ago (as if it were wished upon me, or I deserved the pain) was only your way of handling a confusing and painful experience. Well, fact of the matter is I have been diagnosed with exposure to the AIDS virus. The struggle I am currently handling is much greater than that hospital bout.

You are bigger than the hate and disappointment you feel. I know those are your tools in handling this issue. It's OK for you to love me. I love you too. This is all so silly— why are we doing this? I had two choices when you asked me if I were gay: 1) to lie; 2) to tell the truth. I did what was right. I'd make that choice all over again. By rejecting me you gave me the opportunity to heal, to stop groveling for acceptance and be my own man. I think I deserve the same love and acceptance as the rest of your children.

I want to be happy, joyous and free . . . I also want that for you!

I love you with all of my heart.

Billy

Doug, to His Parents

Dearest Mom and Dad,

I love you both so very much. I know that you know that, but it is important that I write it to you as well.

I've just had an incredible experience. For the first time we've really become a single entity, whole, power-

ful, experienced, and above all, loving. I know that I am
part of you both. Not only physical components but emotional parts as well. This was achieved through a process in
the workshop I've been doing this weekend. By visualization we were instructed to see our parents, and the experience and life they created, and its impact on us. My
first sensation was a peculiar one. I felt tingly all over and
your love pouring over me. It was great.

I want you also to know that I am very proud to be
your son and that I am proud of you both as well.

Your unending support of me and my life-style means
more than you'll ever know. I don't know what life would
be like without you both in it. We've gotten through a lot
together. When I came out you didn't turn me away. We
talked and dealt with it. I know it wasn't particularly easy
for you to learn that you had a gay son. But I admire
your sensitivity, and that a sensibility such as being gay didn't
cloud over your vision or your ability to love me and respect me for who I am.

We have a really powerful relationship. There are
some things though that could make it even better than
it is.

I would like us to be even more open. I believe there
are more closet doors that need to be flung wide open.

First, I hope that you don't feel closeted about being
parents of a gay child. If you choose to stay uncommunicative about that I think it is unhealthy and actually a denial of who I am. I know that you are proud of me. Please
be proud of all of me, not only the aspects that please you.

I too am tired of feeling closeted and have written a
letter to Ron and to Stu coming out to them. I am sure
they know, but I want it to be perfectly clear. I will not
live a half life because of their reaction. If they can't deal
with it, so what. I will have already dealt with it.

There is no issue that comes up that our family cannot handle, but we must all work together, being supportive of each other.

Going back to the visualization process, one part gathered up all of my emotions from deep within, as if Nep-

tune had reached deep into the ocean to create a colossal tidal wave. We were to picture each of our parents as adults, holding hands with their child and adolescent respectively. Meaning each of you at age six, fourteen, and as you are now. And then, floating toward me, becoming very small, the three of you coming right into my heart.

As I write this I am starting to cry again. This was a very powerful image for me. Because I do carry you both in my heart. I always have and I always will.

I must say that I intend for whatever time we have left together to be really wonderful. It is difficult for me to look at your mortality. I guess I assumed that you'll always be here with me. I suppose you always will be, it just will not be in the same way that it is now.

Thank you for expressing yourselves in a loving sexual way and creating me. Even if I was a surprise package. Or, if I was a little angel on a cloud hovering around and I actually chose you, as you have told me, I have to admire my good judgment.

You're the best. All throughout my life you've been an active part—giving and receiving, loving.

I love you both with all my heart!

Doug

Michael, to His Parents

Dear Mom and Dad,

This is the letter that you didn't want to get and the letter that I didn't want to write. What I am about to say has been with me and affecting me for too long. You have made your feelings and thoughts clear to me and I feel I deserve equal time.

I attended a workshop this weekend to perhaps find out why I act and re-act the way I do in different situations. I wanted to find out if I could have done things differently, and thus had different results. Among the exercises was a visualization where I was encouraged to have a conversation with you both. To ask you questions about my life. To tell you things I may have never said. To let out feelings I may have repressed. After that we were to write you a letter. My letter was over twelve pages and I wasn't able to finish it because I ran out of time.

This is that letter. It is typewritten because I kept crying on the handwritten one and my writing became almost illegible. Here goes . . .

Dear Mom and Dad,

Our last conversation in December was rather emotional. Mom, you said "you could never forgive me for the things I did to Dad." Often during our previous conversations you would refer to a certain phone call and say, "your father was sick and you couldn't care less." Well, if we all were crucified for an incident of insensitivity, we would all be dead. So I have to believe that you were instead referring to my being gay. Well, I didn't do that to him. I was destined to be gay by a combination of yours and his genes and chromosomes. Realize that I can choose to act gay, I cannot choose to be gay!

I feel you are masking your self-imposed guilt when you say the reason you have disowned me was for my inconsideration. I can't see ignoring thirty years of love, accomplishments, successes, and failures because of one incident. Dad, I feel that your reaction is also due to your questioning your role in my being gay. You are probably (and understandably so) saying, "What did I do wrong?" Well, there are a shitload of things you could have done different or better, but you did the best you knew how. You didn't take a class in child rearing prior to my arrival, or for that matter, anytime in the last thirty years. But to allow those decisions to affect today's decisions is a mistake.

I promised myself that I would tell you how pissed I am at you, just as you have told me for thirty years how I've disappointed you. Your inability to verbalize the words I LOVE YOU was deafening. You never told me, I love you. Mom always wrote, "We love you, Mom and Dad."

You never said to me "I'm happy that you are smart."
Maybe you were resentful that as a child I could back you
into a corner with words. Guilty of letting your anger and
fists battle my words. maybe you were sorry that you hit
me, beat me, drew blood from my face, pulled hair from
my head, left bruises from hitting me with tools or lumber,
created mental scars from your tirades in public and private. But you never said, "I'm sorry." You never said to
my face, "I'm proud of you." You ridiculed my efforts
to make our community a better place to live. You insulted
my desires to be more than an aquaintance to people. You
wouldn't even let Mom have any long-term friendships because of your inability to have any friendships yourself.
The fact that your real father left you so early in life affected your trust in others and ultimately affected all of
us. The only person to show you love was Mom, and you
weren't willing to share it with anybody else. To this day
you resent our being so close, even after I moved out. You
were determined to use my being gay as the best reason for
her to hate me and "love you more." And you never held
me. I guess the thought of two men loving or helping each
other was upsetting even among family. For that I am pissed.

All this is not meant to say you were wrong or that
you were such a failure because, as I said at the first, you
did the best you knew how. I want to tell you both how all
of this has affected me and still is affecting me.

Dana and I weren't allowed to be children, we were
small adults. You expected it, you treated us like it and
we acted it. We were conditioned to get love or acceptance
by our successes. There were always strings attached. By
attaining our goals, Dad, our affection from you was either earned or given as purchased gifts. So I spend the
rest of my years trying to earn love by being successful or
buying it. I have been on a constant search for that love,
from lover to lover, man to man, one-nighter to one-nighter.
Looking for someone to say I love you. Looking for someone to say that I'm worthy of being loved. And many have
tried. And I won't believe that someone can love me, for
me, no strings attached. No conditions.

I fight off the words you used to tell me: you're lazy, you're a flash in the pan, you want everything handed to you, you're like a nigger—make ten bucks and spend twenty. I ended up believing you are right. I go buy a trucking company, you tell me it's the biggest mistake of my life. I make hundreds of thousands of dollars and you don't say you're proud. And what do I do? Try and tell you I love you by taking you to dinners in limousines. Buying you the most expensive champagne for special occasions. Reward you the same way you rewarded me. Hoping you would tell me something. For that I am pissed.

You could have offered me some encouragement when I lost everything I owned. You could have told me "even though I don't understand it, I am sorry the most important person in your life is gone after five years." But you didn't. You could have offered me a bed when I had nowhere to sleep. You could have offered me a few dollars when I couldn't afford to eat. But you didn't. And remember the only two times I borrowed money, you were paid in full, with 12 percent and 13½ percent interest each time. I guess I wasn't a good risk. Or was it because I was gay and not worthy of a hand. You could have tried to help when I tried to commit suicide, but you were busy hiding behind your own feelings. I could have died and you would have been relieved. I would have been done embarrassing you.

When your friends tried to convince you that I was still your son and you should talk to me, you told them to mind their own business. What a proud father figure.

On that night in December you told me that I should go off with all my faggot friends and die. But I look past that and realize that is your way of saying "I love you so much and I hurt even more." I know it's a strange way to say it, but you weren't so good with words anyway.

Why I am really pissed is that I am forced again to look for parental love and affection from strangers. Family dinners are at Jerry and Diana's. You remember, Scott's parents. Hell, we broke up over two years ago and his parents still are considering me their second son, welcome

at the table, welcome to sleep, welcome to share their love.
No strings. Christmas is spent going from house to house,
watching people open gifts, kiss and hug and laugh. Birthdays. (Yes I know I forgot yours that one year, but according to Mom, it was to hurt you again.) Birthdays are spent
with friends, each one taking me here and there for dinner
and such. My bosses taking me shopping for clothes, shoes,
and car tires. It really hurts when my boss has to be my
father or mother. Any special occasion or event, spent
with strangers. Strangers who show more love than you can
even imagine.

I am pissed that you've taken Dana away from me.
We were rebuilding a relationship when you poisoned her
mind. After your phone call, she didn't even call or write
to say thanks for the Christmas gifts I sent up to her and
Chuck and Brittany. You said, "Don't come around my
grandbaby, I don't want her to get AIDS." What an ignorant asshole. First, I don't have AIDS, but thank you for
asking or caring if I did. Second, I have no desire or need
to share my bodily fluids, or used needles, with her. Thank
you for knowing what you are talking about. And heaven
forbid anyone squeeze between her and you buying her love!
Yes, I understand there is a closet of clothes and toys to
make most stores envious. Insure that she will love you, yet
you can't find it in your heart to make a phone call or
write a letter to your own son. What special parents. What
terrific role models for Dana and Chuck. I pray that
Brittany doesn't develop a fondness for softball.

And I am pissed that your stupidity is helping to let
my friends and lovers die! I read this morning where
Donna was brutally murdered. I imagine you were upset.
Would you have tried to save her if you were there?
Would you have spent a hundred dollars to save her life?
Given a thousand dollars for a chance that she may live?
Well, just imagine how I feel. In the last year and a half,
Jerry died, he was eighteen. Les was murdered, he was
twenty-one. Billy died, twenty something. Jimmy died. Matt
died. Paul died. John died at twenty-three. Sylvester died.
Dan died. Maxine died. They were all friends of mine. And

I did spend hundreds of dollars on the slim chance that they might live. Wait. At least fifty more of my friends are looking at death. They have between a few weeks to a few years to live. And I will continue to do what I can to save them. And you and your kind don't give a fuck, you don't care. You hope they will die. And for that I hate you. For that I don't want to be your son. For that I don't want to be your genes, your cells, your anything. I never want to be so hateful, so wicked, that I feel better than any human life.

I want you to understand my anger. Not to accept it. Not to say tough shit. Not to say so what. I want you to understand. Because you were only doing the best you knew how and I am only doing the best I know how.

Love,
Michael

Well, that was the letter, cut short by the time limit, but the general tone and thought is there. I'm sending a copy to Dana so that she might understand a little more and realize that even though it wasn't said much, you both love us the only way you knew how to. I am sending a copy to Scott. Our entire relationship was clouded by your actions. My actions were conditioned and structured because of how I was raised and the decisions I made as a child and as an adolescent. He deserves to know why. And he deserves an apology from me—with an explanation, I was doing the best I knew how.

This letter demands nothing from you, other than reading it twice. Both of you. If you care to respond, that's fine. If you choose to ignore it, well that's fine too. I've had my equal time and that's all I asked.

Honestly,
Love, Michael

Jeff, to His Parents

Dear Mother and Dad,

There is so much to say. First of all, never doubt that I love you, As a child, I never felt as if I got the love and attention I needed. As a result, I felt isolated and alienated from you and from your love. I so much wanted to feel loved by you. Later in life I came to hate you for abandoning me—at least in my own mind. Now I realize that you were only victims of your own parents and thus carried into my life all of your own values and judgments.

Because I wanted acceptance, I sought it through schoolwork and academic achievements. Dad, it wasn't until my graduation from high school as valedictorian that you said for the first time—"I love you." You will never know how shocked I was to hear those words and how happy (and sad at the same time) I was to realize their meaning.

There were times that I received mixed messages from you. When I was a young boy at the time of puberty, I remember both of you saying how "unclean" and "bad" girls were because they wore miniskirts at that young age. So like a good boy, I stayed away from them. Later on I heard you say I should marry them. I was so confused. I just wanted acceptance. Now I know that this mixed message did not make me gay.

How I wish our religion had not kept us so far apart. Both of you, especially you, Dad, have always been so religious; but I saw the hypocrisy through it all, which made me see your weakness which scared me. And I was mad at you for not being the strong man I thought you were.

When I came out to both of you as being gay, all I was looking for was acceptance of what I was, since I could not love myself. All I got was silence, and it hurt so bad; I felt so alone. I felt so abandoned again and unloved. Why couldn't you have loved me? I needed it so badly. And yet now I realize that you were only doing the best you could, coming from where you came and knowing what you knew at that time. And yet the kid in me was looking for two strong persons that I was a physical part of to unconditionally love me. How could you when I could not unconditionally love myself?

Mother, thanks for being there for me in your own way when my lover Tim left me. If you only knew how good that telephone call felt at that time. With Tim gone and my job going down the tubes, my whole world in Houston collapsed around me. I was so very desperate for human love that I had unprotected anonymous sex. I have felt so guilty about not having safe sex, especially since I'm a doctor. It's been so hard to forgive myself and release all of this into the past.

Between you and me, I knew that I had been infected with the AIDS virus as early as September 1985, the first time I got my T-cell count in Houston, even though the full meaning of these tests was not understood for some years to come. When I found out, I wanted so much to have you hold me like you did when I was sick as a child. But I was so ashamed of being gay and of having let myself get infected. All that religious stuff about being sinful and not being good just overwhelmed me. All I wanted to do was to die and not have to face the future. Fortunately for me, I seemed to have enough good "genetic" stuff and belief in God to want to go on—so I moved to LA for help.

We are now some three thousand miles apart. I am doing my best to survive. I do my best when I keep my attention span in the present moment. I wish we could see each other more often. I do know how stressful this has all been for you. You never want to be stressed in your life. It hurts too much for you. But don't you realize that if we could just get through all this "bad" stuff together, we could be closer together in spirit. And isn't that what life is all about? Becoming of one spirit, of one God—who made all of us in his own image.

There is so much I wanted to say, most of it has been written. Some remains in my heart. No matter what I have said or done, I never, never meant to hurt you or anyone else. I did it as a human with all of the human characteristics a mortal does things with. Please forgive me for ever doubting your love for me. I was looking for a certain expression of love that I understood, and you were giving me the love you best knew to give. We just never seemed to connect fully.

I have so much to work on—but it's a start. I've got all of these judgment barriers up which I need to bring down, especially in my conception of what a doctor is, and what is expected of me as a human being on this planet. I honestly do not know whether I will be one of the long-term survivors of this AIDS epidemic. I hope I am. I do want to continue to serve my fellow man in a humane and just manner. I realize now that this can only be done when I think of myself as spiritual and as an extension of God, and not just as a body or title like "doctor."

I feel so much better for having had the opportunity to tell you all of these things about me. As I've told you before, I would rather have you know me for what I am rather than to love me for what I'm not. If some of this writing got somewhat illegible, it's because I wrote it through my tears—and you're reading it through your tears.

We have a blessed family, not because of what we have in money or material goods, but because of that common thread which binds us all together—the unconditional love of a family, and as created people of the universal God.

Love,
your son Jeff

Richard, to His Parents

Dearest Dad and Mom,

I'm writing this letter to clarify and complete some perceptions either I have of me or that I believe you may have of me.

You know I've been in therapy for quite a while, nearly five years if you can believe it. I told you that one of the key reasons was to deal with my mother's death. I also said that one facet that I was working on was my sexuality. That's where I stopped our talks. I want this letter to continue and complete that dialogue.

I won't spend a lot of time telling you how difficult this letter is for me to write, but rather attempt to be clear and concise.

I'm sure that you always suspected that I may be homosexual. The answer to that frequently unasked question is "yes." I don't even want to qualify my answer.

"What about Anne?" you may ask. That's the best part. What I've learned about me is that I love and am attracted to both women and men. It's taken a very long time over great resistance to believe that, but it's true. I have been in and actually still am in love with a wonderful man, a person I want to be very close to. Simultaneously Anne and I are strengthening our relationship. She's always known the bisexual me and has loved and supported me in dealing with who I am. And I love her. We're planning on a splendid old age together.

I remember, Dad, either on our wedding day or shortly thereafter you said to Anne, "Thank you for making a man of my son." I was incredibly hurt. I have never equated and still do not equate manhood and sexuality. They may line up with conventional norms most often, but I represent at least one exception.

One thing I want to share is that because I am attracted to men does not mean I'm flocking either to the bars or grammar schools. I do believe in recreational sex; that's one of the joys of marriage and being with people. I don't think it's like a prescription of daily vitamins. And Anne and I have a constantly improving sex life.

Over the past twenty years or so I've wrestled with the sexuality question. I managed to do a terrific job of suppression. I even spent no small effort in erecting a façade of the assured, heterosexual me. It was really tough. I was absolutely terrified of being thought a faggot by straights or some half-fish half-fowl by gays. I refused to focus on the question because I didn't want the answer; I didn't want to be responsible for who I am. All that's changed, and recently, too.

I've spent time in self-actualization workshops in addition to therapy. These condensed experiences provided a disciplined opportunity to explore these issues with other people who in their unique ways shared the same problems.

Now I don't think I'll have problems being who I am, but acting in accordance with that realization by discarding the façade is the challenge. Of course I don't expect to throw my sexuality up into someone's face, but I won't deny it either. I'm even leaving room for both our marriage and a relationship with a man.

One final point, I want you to know that you didn't go wrong, you aren't to blame or at fault. I don't think that's at all relevant. I'm satisfied with me and realize I am blessed with more than the usual capacity to love. You may have reasons to feel guilty or to feel the blame; those belong to you. I want to be close to you and love you more than ever, especially since I'm using this letter to shovel an obstacle out of your way.

If you want to tell the other kids, that's fine. I plan to write each of them today.

Anne and I both send you our love.

                                                                Richard

Jeremy, to His Grandmother

Dear Grandma,

I love you so much. I learned about dying from you.

Remember when Lisa and I found the dead scuba diver at the beach. I came home and said I realized that being dead was just not being in the body. You were sitting in an easy chair in the living room. You said how in the old days people used to have the coffin in the living room and the loved ones would sit with the body all night until day and say good-bye. You said the loved ones would realize that death was not unnatural. It was just that the one who died was gone from the body. That the body wasn't the person you loved. It was just what held the person you loved until they were gone from the body.

I loved you for telling me that. I knew it was true. I decided then that when your time came, I wanted to be with you.

I live a very exciting and rewarding life, Grandma. I love my job at the restaurant, and it will do fine until I start working as a performer again.

When I was little you used to hold me close when I cried, or needed a hug, or just needed to feel I belonged in this world.

Christmas at your house was always special to me. For a day or two none of us kids would fight. We would be too busy. While Mom was working, you would see that we made paper chains, always red and green. One red, one green, were pasted until it was long enough to go around the tree a couple of times, and you always said how pretty they were. Donna would make the paste and Gerry and I would cut and David would paste. Donna would "cook" the paste, water and flour, because it was better than store bought. Me and Gerry would cut with little bitty scissors and David would paste because he was the oldest and wouldn't make a mess and you would cook and cook and cook.

Getting ready for Christmas was always better than Christmas.

We would make long long strings of popcorn. They were pretty because they looked like snow. And Mom would come home from work and then help us decorate the tree.

And one year Gerry and I got creative and used old thread spools for Christmas ornaments. We would sprinkle gold and green glitter on them and tie a string thru the holes so as to hang them on limbs and you said they were pretty and last year I saw one on the Christmas tree you had.

You had eight children, I guess about thirty-six grandchildren, and eight great-grandchildren. Gerry has an-

other on the way. So does Bobbie Jo. We all love you
because you have loved us all so very well.

Oh, Grandma, I remember us living with you and
growing up in your house and Mom would come home
tired and we kids would be fighting and she'd say, "Now
why do you wait 'til I come home to fight. You're good
all day until I come home," and it took her until a few years
ago to realize you just didn't report our misdeeds to her.
"Oh, Elma," you'd say, "kids will be kids, they act just fine.
They're good kids, Elma."

But Mom was in charge when she came home. You
never argued with her on how to raise us.

I don't remember you ever yelling at us. You never
had to, except once.

When I was about five you had gone to the store. I
don't know where Gerry was, and David and Donna were
at school. I had snuck into your bedroom and found Aunt
Lete's graduation dress you told us about. It was so pretty
to me, Grandma. I didn't mean any ill respect. It was just
so pretty. I remember knowing I was bad, but I took it
off the hanger and laid it across the bed. It had long sleeves
with ruffles at the end. Little hooks to make the sleeves
close. It had lace around the neck, and it had two big ruffles at the bottom.

And I put it on. I was just playing, Grandma. It
reached to the floor and I pretended I was on a covered
wagon train going to California. I tiptoed to pretend I had
high heels.

I ran out of the bedroom and I sat on your easy chair.

And the front door opened. I became like stone. I
couldn't move and you came in. I saw your eyes, Grandma.
You said, "Take that off." It was like a loud whisper.

I ran back to your room and jerked it off. I had trouble with the hook on one sleeve. I was crying. I put it
back on the hanger as fast and as best as I could and hung
it up.

You never mentioned it again. I never did it again
and you loved me anyway. I think you made peanut but-
ter cookies that afternoon.

Grandma, I love you. You taught me how to love people just the way they are. You never gave advice to anyone unless they asked. You never interfered with your children's lives.

I've learned about living from you.

I don't know why I am the way I am.

All I know is I love you and that I am a homosexual. I am also a person, your grandson. I'm still your kin. I will love you always.

Your number five grandchild,
Jeremy

LETTERS TO
CHILDREN

Gerald, to His Four Small Children

Dear Kids,

When I came to this planet to live I brought many
gifts with me, but there was one gift that was quite separate from all the rest, a gift so special that it would take a
large part of my life to understand it, and then all the
rest of my life to completely give it away.

I was excited about this gift, because I knew that it
made me happy and it would make a lot of other people
happy too. But early in life, about the age that you are now,
I began to be aware that other people brought gifts also,
each one of them priceless, necessary, and filled with joy
and happiness. As I grew older, I realized that some peo-

246

ple considered their gifts to be better than others; in fact, some of them insisted with loud voices and angry faces that their gifts were right and good and that my gift was bad and evil. It wasn't long until I learned that some of them even hated me for my gift and if I tried to share it they would make things very unpleasant for me.

I began to be afraid, especially when I learned that some other people whose gifts were like mine had been killed, or put in prisons, or treated very meanly. It was then that I decided to hide my gift rather than face all the trouble.

But everyone was sharing their gifts and I wanted to share mine too. So I put together a phony gift, one that wasn't real. It only looked like the gifts that other people were sharing, and for a long time I smiled and shared my pretended gift and felt I was doing the right thing because it seemed to be making others happy.

So I kept my real gift hidden well within me and tried not to let anyone see that it was in there. Once in a while someone would look into my eyes with a wondering look and, being afraid that he would discover my gift, I would quickly push it farther within. Then I would look quickly away and get him to talk about my pretend gift instead. That always made me feel bad, because secretly I loved my real gift, I knew it was good, and whenever I would think about it I felt good inside.

About the time that I became what you call a grown-up person, I began to be really afraid of the angry people who hated my gift. So I pushed it even farther back inside of me, back away from the light, farther back into the shadows.

Every time I did that I felt worse and worse.

One day I heard the people at the church talking about the evil gifts that some people had, and I knew they were talking about my gift. And even though they were wrong, the more they talked the more afraid I became until one day a friend from the church looked into my eyes when I wasn't watching and suddenly he got a very surprised look on his face, and asked me, "Do you have *that* gift within you?"

I knew he had seen it and I didn't want to tell a lie. "Yes," I said apologetically. "I have *that* gift within me."

My friend didn't say anything. He just went quietly away and I never saw him again. After he left I went within myself and with a feeling of sadness I took the gift to a dark place within me where there was something like a cliff and I threw the gift over into a chasm of darkness and ran very quickly back out of myself and went quietly to church with my friends.

Soon an awful feeling began to grow inside of me. A feeling like cold lead.

Then a strange thing happened. One day I went to the place within me where I used to keep the gift, and was quite surprised to find it sitting right back in its place. I ran to pick it up and quickly took it back to the cliff and threw it over once again. And again to my surprise, a few days later, there it was back in its place. So once more I threw it over the cliff, and again it appeared. This went on and on. Every time I threw it over the cliff, it mysteriously appeared back in its place.

Now I was afraid more than ever that someone would look in my eyes and see the gift. And some of them did. No matter how hard I tried to hide it from them, some of them could see it anyway. Finally one day, a man in the church who reportedly talked a lot with God told me that I would be punished terribly for my gift. He told me what I had to do to get rid of it.

I went home and then within myself, and took my gift and with a trembling heart bashed it into thousands of pieces and hurtled it over the cliff for the last time. I told myself that I had done the right thing. And maybe I would have believed that from then on, but the strange feeling inside of me like cold lead not only came back but began to get bigger and bigger. It wasn't long until it filled up the whole inside of my body until suddenly I realized it wasn't cold lead at all, but was more like death, and that I was filled with it completely. I began to cry because I did not want to die, and I wished instead that I had my gift

back because even though it caused me trouble, I never
once felt like I was going to die when I had it.

But I didn't have it, and the death-like feeling inside
of me continued to get stronger.

After a while I decided to travel. I wandered to many
different lands, lived in different places, saw lots of different people. Finally I went to a special city, a city so wonderful that many people said it was magic. In that city I
met a young prince, and after we became friends he told
me that he had a gift for me. When he gave me the gift I
was very surprised because it was exactly like the gift I had
destroyed within myself a long, long time ago.

"That's my gift!" I cried.

"Yes," he said, "it is for you."

"No, you don't understand," I said. "It's exactly like
a gift I had a long time ago, but I lost it."

"Then do take this one," he said.

"But you will need it," I said.

"Oh, no," he smiled. "You can keep it. I have many
others like it, and every time I give one of them away
another one appears magically right in its place."

"You give them away," I gasped. "But you're supposed to hide them or you'll be in great danger."

"Oh," he said with a peaceful light in his eyes, "not
in this city. This is a magic city where everyone's gift is
considered a great and priceless treasure, no matter how different it may be."

Well, the moment he said that I had a sudden urge
to look inside of myself because that feeling like death
was suddenly beginning to melt. And when I looked I was
so surprised to discover my very own gift in the place
where it used to be. I ran and picked it up and hugged it
like an old friend, and immediately another one, just like
it, appeared right in its place, and exactly how that happened I'll never know, but as the prince and I exchanged
our gifts, and as I have shared gifts with many others in the
magic city, I have come to see that the more we give of
our gifts the more we have yet to give. And out of the
awareness of such great and endless abundance has come

a joy and a happiness that has melted completely that cold, lead feeling like death; and in its place is another feeling like living forever and ever, and every time I give my gift away, and every time someone shares theirs with me, that feeling gets stronger and stronger. And from that feeling I know now that there is a part of me, much bigger than I ever imagined that will live on and on and on.

My dear children, each of you came to this planet with gifts of your own also. Gifts of great price and value. I hope with all my heart that you will find out what your gifts are. Next I hope that you will share your gifts freely with joy and courage. And I hope that you will find the peace and understanding that comes from regarding the gifts of every person as being as wonderful as your own.

Love,
Dad

Bob, to His Children

Dear Bobby and Kari,

I am writing this letter, to you, to explain my position of being gay. I know that your mother has already told you that your father is a homosexual (gay). I do not know what she said or how she explained it to you, I can only speculate.

I do know that I am gay, not by choice, but because that was what I was meant to be. As a teenager I realized that I had attractions to people of my own sex. All of my learning of those feelings was that they were wrong, and having nothing else to compare my feelings to, I believed it to be wrong. I also felt, and believed, that when I married your mother, these feelings would disappear. For five years I tried to suppress these feelings. I was unsuccessful. One day I met a person I learned to respect and later found he was gay. At that time I knew I had to make a decision about my life and that decision would ultimately affect the lives of those closest to me. I made the decision to "come out" of my closet and live the life I knew was better for me, even though others would be hurt. I did know one thing, however, and that was that in order for me to be honest with myself, I had to be honest with your mother and my parents. I told them all why I was leaving. This, I know, hurt them deeply, but it was better than just letting them wonder why or blame themselves.

As I look back on my life, I know now that, had I been taught that my sexual preferences did not make me right or wrong, good or bad, I would not have gotten married nor would I still be battling with my own self-worth today. My sexual preferences did not change my validity as a person, except in the eyes of people too narrow-minded or bigoted to allow themselves to get to know me and to broaden their experiences.

Contrary to many beliefs, gay people are no different than heterosexual people. We have the same hurt, love, feelings, and needs as everyone else in the world.

My love for you is not lessened by the fact that I am gay. I am proud of you both and even though I have apprehensions about being with you for the first time in years, I really am looking forward to having you with me this summer so that we can learn and experience our lives together.

Love,
Dad

Paul, to His Son

To my second son, whom I love very dearly.

Your life in the family setting, when compared to your two brothers, appeared to be one of personal independence and rebellion against parental authority.

As your father, I was aware of these characteristics of yours; but for reasons of my own, I either did not inter-

fere or felt I should not either endorse or criticize them.
During your development, I was totally afraid of you, for
I felt so inferior with my own shortcomings that I did not
feel I had the right to interfere with your life. The times
that I did manage to intercede or to interfere were when I
was under the influence of alcohol—or just plain drunk.
Then I got carried away and overextended myself by in-
flicting physical pain and hardship upon you as well as
upon myself.

I beg of you to forgive me for the way I treated you
both physically and mentally. My reasons for escape from
the pain of living were multiple, and the release from all of
this was in the bottle. Soon the addiction to alcohol itself
was all I could think of and to satisfy. That is when my entire life collapsed about me, and I was hospitalized.

It was during the period of my hospitalization that
you stood by me and came with your mother to see me
and to participate in family counseling that was being offered.

After I stopped drinking and started the attempt to
put my life back together, I became aware my life could
not be as it was before, that changes would have to be made.
Many of these changes you and I are well aware of, including the major decision for me to dissolve the marriage
your mother and I shared. Your own pain coping with
the attitudes of your mother are known to both of us, and
I grieve deeply that this authoritarian control has been
attempted upon your life. I believe we both have handled
this with love and to the best of our abilities.

Our lives over the past year or so as we have lived
together have changed so greatly that I have come to respect and love you way beyond a degree I ever thought was
possible. It is because of this love I have for you that I
wish to share with you how I feel deep down and who and
what I am.

Every since I was a small boy, I can remember that
I had an attraction to persons of my own gender. As it
turns out, the statement is that your father is gay.

Your father's knowledge that he was a homosexual
was very real to him. As a "queer," his parents (your

grandparents) did not think well of him. Their attitude was
that there was something wrong with me, and that I was
sick. In order to satisfy them and to find acceptance from
them, I went out and married your mother and have tried
to live a straight life these twenty-five years.

All of this weighed so heavily I became an alcoholic
and almost died. Your father is alive again and will live
his life as he knows it. Therefore, it is apparent you have
to understand that you have a "fag" as a father. I have
used the street terms of "queer" and "fag" to bring to your
attention that society uses terms to put people down and
to control them—just as you and I once allowed your mother
to control us.

Inasmuch as we no longer allow your mother to control our lives, we do not need to allow society to influence our thinking about each other in terms that offend and
degrade one another.

I am still your father—who has always been gay—
except that I did not share that with you. I still offer to
you the deep and lasting love I have for you. God, our Creator, who loves me and provided me with the opportunity to marry your mother and gave to both of us you and
your brother, brings us together and binds us with love,
providing we open our hearts to each other and let go of
the hate man has taught us.

All my love,
your Dad

Craig, to His Dead Son

Dear Brian,
You were born in 1956 in the Republic of Singapore
where your mother (my ex-wife) and I were missionaries.
Twenty years later you ended that begun life with the aid
of your stepfather's hunting rifle in Lansing, Michigan.
You were a well-liked student at Lansing Community Col-

lege with so many vital interests, including the photography club and your church's young adult club.

There are those who have suggested that you took this route out of your desperate despair because you had discovered you were gay . . . I cannot be sure of this because communication between myself and your mother is nonexistent.

At any rate I have received the damning message from your mother, her present husband, from Dennis, Jill, and Beth—your brother and sisters—that somehow I am responsible for your death decision. At the memorial service I was treated super-shabby and walked out ever since.

I am writing this letter to you in the midst of my participation in The Advocate Experience. This Experience has been a turning point in my life, especially as regards to feeling good about the fact that I am now and have always been gay. Gay is good, gay and proud am I. I now know that it is not necessary to commit suicide if you find you love others of your same gender. It is not necessary to kill yourself if you determine your father is gay—not needful to be drenched in shame at this fact. I love you very much, I am sorry that this was needful for you at that point in time. I want others to know a "brighter day is dawning" for those who are gay and those who love gay.

Warmly,
your Dad

LETTERS TO BROTHERS

Doug, to His Brothers

Dear Ron,

     I went through a workshop this past weekend called
The Experience. It was really terrific. I learned a lot
about myself. I guess it's never particularly easy having to
closely look at oneself.

     Anyway, I made a commitment to myself to be more
honest and open to people in my life; and I intend to keep
that commitment. It is clear to me now that it is long over-
due that I come out to you. Yes, your baby brother is
gay. I'm not really sure whether or not you know that. Part
of me thinks you do, the other part says he doesn't know,
so you have to tell him.

     I find as I write this it isn't as difficult as I thought it
would be. Just so you know, I am writing a letter to Stu
as well.

Mom and Dad have known about my being gay for about eight years. They are so wonderful and supporting and loving. They said they would not "come out" for me.

I'm not sure why it has taken me so long to tell you. Fear of rejection probably. Also because of the vast difference in our ages I never felt very close to you. I was (and am) jealous of the bond you have with Stu. It's only natural you two would be close. I really look at my life sometimes as that of an only child. Hell, I'm closer in age to Ron IV than to Stu.

I really want to feel connected to my brothers. I came across a picture (which is now on my desk) of you, me, Stu, and Gertie raking leaves. I really like it a lot and it makes me feel a part of you guys.

Please know that I am happy, well adjusted, and not different from the Doug you've always known.

Should you care to share this with Tisha, please do. I think she's really neat.

Love,
Doug

Dear Stu,

This seems to be my week of writing letters to my family about unresolved business. Being the groovy kind of guy that I am, I participated in a workshop this past weekend called The Experience. It was really a wonderful place for me to come to terms with some emotional stuff I haven't particularly wanted to deal with.

I made a commitment to myself to be more honest and open with people who are important in my life. That decision was easy enough to make and is not difficult to uphold.

I want to be honest with you, because I am sick to death of having to feel ashamed of something that I'm not ashamed about. At this point in my life it is important for me that I come out to you.

Did you get that? If not, what I'm telling you is that your younger bro is gay.

It's really strange, but I wrote a similar letter to Ron with ease. This seems more difficult for me. I suppose be-

cause I remember you more in my childhood. He seemed
to leave home early on, whereas you were home more,
with you going to college at St. Mary's.

Since I feel a stronger bond toward you the level of
anxiety has risen more. I always put you on a pedestal.
You are funny, had lots of girlfriends, seemed sexy and free
spirited, a good athlete, etc. I was envious, especially "the
teen fat boy." I hated your torments and teasings on the
one hand, but welcomed the attention. Talk about being
fucked up.

I'm shocked to see some old anger manifesting itself. Actually, I'm relieved that it surfaced so I can now
release it since it's ancient history.

As I told Ron, I was (am) also jealous of the closeness you two have. I never felt that camaraderie and
missed it. I did find a picture of the three of us and Gertie
raking leaves, which I have on my desk, that I cherish
very much. Looking at it I really sense being a part of "the
brothers."

I'm sure you're wondering whether or not Mom and
Dad know about me. The answer is yes. I told them eight
years ago. They are so super, loving and supportive.

I felt like you probably knew that I was gay, but I
wasn't positive, so I needed to tell you myself.

I have to say that I am a happy individual. You know
what I'm like, and hopefully I don't fit into any stereotype you may or may not have of gay men. I feel so relieved sharing this with you. It's a real drag being in the
closet. I only wish I had the courage to have told you eight
years ago as well.

Please feel free to share this with Cheri and JJ and
Scotty if you like. I'm not embarrassed about who I am,
and I certainly don't want you to feel closeted about having a gay sibling. OK!?

Stay cool—

Love,
Doug

Tom, to His Brother and Sister-in-Law

Dear Ron and Kathy,

Without sounding ominous, I want to write to you and tell you something. I guess it should have been written before or said before but it wasn't. I'm gay and have been for about ten years now. I have this real fear about telling you. You see, I love you both an incredible amount. Standing up at your wedding back in 1968 made me a part of your life and love and gave me a sense of family I have known through college and beyond. You are such a big part of my life and my love that I don't want to lose the love you feel for me. I love the kids immeasurably and I don't want any "fear" of me to prevent me from seeing them or spending time with them. *I cannot change* those fears if you have them. I know Ron that you are "worried" about Randy. You have the most beautiful son any man could have, and please support him and love him. Create for him a place to be himself with constructive direction. I love you both so much and the kids equally. I need your support now and your love and friendship. I am in the process of writing Mom and Dad, so be prepared for some fallout and then some. It is real appropriate that I stop being afraid and be honest with people I love, and who are a big part of my life. I am real afraid that because I told you I am gay, you might not like me. I think that is bullshit. I am crying a lot writing. I didn't think it'd be that hard writing to you—but I feel I have a lot to lose—we all do— and I don't want to lose your love.

Ron, Kathy, Randy, Liza—
I love you all—Tom

SPECIAL LETTERS

John, to His High School

To South High,

It was painful, those years. Crushes and my first in-fatuation. Phil, I forgot about how important you were to me. Three suicide attempts in a short space. And I couldn't tell you, or ask you out or touch you without feeling outcast.

It was a game, I guess. The girls I was supposed to be dating and making out with and being hot dirt about. They weren't there, except as friends and companions.

I made myself feel sick about it all; worthless, futureless, bleak.

Well, I dreamed about guys in my gym classes and watched guys in the showers and locker rooms, and that's where it was at.

Phil, you were really the first of all the guys I fell in love with, and I mean hard. I never figured out what it was, outside of you being a shy, slender, self-deprecating boy. I set up a pattern with you that I repeated with everyone I fell in love with after that: play shy, be good buddies, and don't reveal any feelings. Or it goes down in flames.

Phil, we would probably still be good friends if we lived in the same neighborhood. You would know I'm gay now, and it would be OK.

And it was against the milieu of South High School that we were beginning the maturing process. So, in that white upper-middle-class environment, we played out roles and never ventured past the norm. That's what was, and each piece in the game was played according to its nature.

What fucking drew me to you? Why did my emotions burst out inside so recklessly? I know I enjoyed being moody and depressed about it, and I let it get in the way of really having a full relationship with you.

Maybe it would never have been as full as I wanted, but it could've been more open. I could've been more real with you, instead of trying to kill myself about it.

I've never really dealt with it, I see that now. I look back to South High as a source of pain, and the only pain was the wounds I created over my lack of security with you.

Phil, I was in love with you. The thunderbolt capacity, and I'm only seeing now the patterns I set up then, of hiding and not holding high hopes, and setting it up so I would never find a satisfying relationship.

I love you, Phil, that's all I want to tell you. You are a significant element in my life.

So, South High, I'm one of hundreds of your graduates who are homosexual, and that's what's so. Boy, though, did I feel like the only one then.

Beautiful, beautiful boys of South Torrance, we were lucky—I was one of you, and do I still think I am?

Do I still think I'm going to find Phil somewhere at your edges?

Maybe not.

And maybe I'll grow beyond you at last. Funny that I never said that before.

And all because I couldn't deal with my attraction to Phil against your corridors and classrooms. You're released, all of you.

I don't really know if thanks are appropriate, but thanks do go to my ability to grow up.

John

Dick, to the Catholic Church

Dear John Paul, John, Bob, and the rest of you:

I write to you to let you know that I am a loving son of the Church and wish to serve Christ and my fellow man through that Church which you represent—but you stand in my way—you and those whom you represent.

When I was a young child you tried to zip open my head and drop in a set of rote catechism solutions for me that didn't work. You could not let me love as I needed but kept saying "wrong."

I confessed to you how I shared with my best friend and you exacted of me a promise never to see him again, shouting "evil." You would only retract the demand if we promised each other not to touch and we had to fight hard for thirty years to keep that promise.

Because of you I went around the world visiting your shrines in agony that some sin might be committed with no priest around to speak my language so he could understand and give me "absolution."

You took away from me any ability I had to make moral choices—or perhaps would not allow me to learn to do so because you knew better—my feelings and intentions didn't count.

Your biggest crime (and the one I thank you for) is that you frightened me into my vocation. What is a reasonably intelligent and pious young Catholic boy to do if he knows he wants no part of marriage but comes from a locally respectable family demanding that he make something of himself? He tries the seminary.

There you created a space that was totally safe (except for the queers) and which would keep the students totally insulated from the real world. It was so powerful that its influence carried through the vacations. And you constantly threatened me with the withholding of ordination. Finally it came time for vows and you suggested I hold off for the summer because you couldn't trust me. And with this scare I had to prove myself just a little bit more than the others that I could make it.

And then you sent me out into the world to keep on fucking up minds and hearts the same way I had been taught. But I fooled you because I had compassion and sympathy even though I had not yet learned to bend the rules. I helped lots of people in their heartaches and was known as a good confessor and counselor, although you didn't like it.

But when I could no longer hold out personally you got even. You had planted the poison of guilt, and it got me onto the seesaw of "sin and repentence-absolution," love another and confess and promise never again. How contrary to Scripture!

Your unreal demands and lack of love pushed me into the care of a psychiatrist and finally the psycho ward. You offered me two nice jobs, which I could not handle for long because of fear. You still pretended to be nice to me and kept laying your trips on me, those old platitudes which have no basis in scripture, until I lost the second good job through fear and unhealthy drinking habits.

But I was determined to survive and went out into the world and as far away from you as I could get. For three years I bobbed in the uncharted sea of the secular world and got heavier into drinking, even becoming a true alcoholic. Yet somewhere, somehow, without any help from you, I discovered the love of God and the brotherhood of Christ and my sobriety and decided to return to the Church on my own terms.

Some will say I am nuts, but now I am determined to be a part of your Church whether you like it or not, and I will even be subversive if need be. I have learned to bend the rules and sweep the trivia out of the way. Now it will be my way. You can only deprive me of my employment and livelihood now.

I conclude that I have loved you all along, perhaps without cause, and you have returned this love with nothing but fear and deafness. You have handed me a stone when I asked for bread! I charge that you have not heard the two great commandments but have only bogged down in the more comfortable and less important rules made by man. And you have brainwashed others to such an extent that my very existence is a problem to them.

I want you to know that I love God and that I love my neighbor(s) as I love myself—as I love my "gay" self, with all the coloring and posturing which that entails. I also love the Church as an instrument for bringing the love of God to man and man to God. Now help me get on with spreading this love to others—or get out of my way. And I will get on with the task appointed me—that is to teach others to love God and neighbor in spite of you.

With all my love,

Dick

Paul, to a Bishop

Dear Bishop Sam,

I can't tell you how good it was to see you at Theological College a couple of weeks ago. Your face was just as bright and cheerful and full of the love of God as I remember it from your days at the Catholic Student Center. I didn't get the opportunity to say it when I saw you, but I was so very excited when I heard that you had been made a bishop. You are one of the most transparent channels of the love of God that I have ever experienced in

my life, and it is quite heartening to see you assume such a
significant leadership role in the Catholic Church.

Bishop Sam, I have been deeply troubled by something for a very long time, and I think that you might have
the ability to do something about it. I may have even talked
to you about it or confessed it to you at some point when
I was in college, yet it has continued to have a significant
affect on me even into my adulthood.

When I was about twelve years old, I was sexually
molested by a Roman Catholic priest who was stationed
in my home parish. The first time he ever touched me sexually, he embraced me from behind, grasped my crotch
with his hands, and held me close to his body as we watched
the feeding fish in his aquarium. I remember feeling extremely uncomfortable, but I pretended to be naïve, acting
like I didn't understand the significance of what he had
just done. When he said not to tell anyone about what had
just happened between us, I responded: "About what?"—
knowing full well exactly what he was talking about.

This was just the first time. There were many many
more sexual encounters over the remaining twelve or so
months that he remained in the parish, and there were even
a few experiences when I went to visit him at his subse-
quent assignments. The sexual activity never amounted to
much more than mutual masturbation, and in all honesty
the sexual experiences themselves were not that unpleasant. He never hurt me physically, but emotionally and
psychogically, the overall experience was very troubling.

The problem was not the sex, the problem is the fundamental hypocrisy in the Catholic priest, an official representative of the Catholic Church, being sexual with a young
impressionable child when the Church is so adamant in
its teaching that sex is evil and wrong and sinful in any context other than holy matrimony.

Let's stop for a moment and take a look at it. There
I was, a young Catholic boy, who had been raised in a
devout Catholic family, who had attended Catholic school
since kindergarten, and who had been taught since early
childhood that sex was something that you didn't talk about,

much less something that you did. It was something that was filthy and dirty and disgusting and evil and sinful. You could go to hell for having sex! And then there was this priest, a pillar of the Church, who was God's representative on earth and who was the ultimate authority figure in a young Catholic child's eyes. For a young Catholic, there were your parents and your teachers and the nuns and then, there was the priest. He was just below God in the power structure of the universe.

So here is this God-like figure doing this terrible filthy thing with me, and then telling me not to say anything about it to anyone. What was I to do? How could I challenge it? Who was going to believe a young child who was guilty of this terrible sin of sex? And even if they believed me, who would be the one to get punished? Certainly not the priest, after all, he was next to God in a child's mind; he would be the one to do the punishing.

So I felt awful and guilty and extremely confused, but I continued to go back and let him do it to me over and over again. But what else could I do? If I stopped going to the rectory, my parents would wonder what was wrong, and I might have to tell them what "I" had done. I was sure to be punished, and that punishment was sure to include not being allowed to go to the rectory, which would mean that I would lose all of those special treats and privileges that the priest had used to seduce me—things like taking me out to dinner or out for a hamburger and a milk shake, things like giving me gifts for special occasions or sometimes for no special reason at all, things like making me feel important by being allowed to help with the work around the church, or being able to associate in public with this very important authority figure when he would take me with him to a ball game or let me go with him to visit his friends in the parish.

So I didn't tell anybody, and I didn't do anything about it. I just continued to feel guilty and confused and to withhold my little secret. There simply was not anyone around in whom I had enough trust to share that terrible confidence. For the person who, in a child's eyes, was most

deserving of trust, had violated it, resulting in a fundamental breakdown in my ability to trust that I continue to
suffer to this very day. For I not only lost trust in other
people, but I lost a very basic trust in myself, and that lack
of self-trust, that lack of self-confidence and self-esteem
has severely hampered the development of my full human
potential. This letter is part of the process of regaining
that trust.

Bishop Sam, I share this experience with you in the
hopes that, in your role as bishop, you will be able to help
create a church that does not burden its people with the kind
of pain and guilt and self-doubt that I experienced. We
need to be able to accept and appreciate, to celebrate and
rejoice our sexuality. To acknowledge that we are sexual
beings and to embrace our sexuality as a beautiful, wonderful, integral part of our human experience. As long as
we deny our sexuality, as long as we try to repress it and
limit it and stifle it, we will never be able to fully experience the fullness of life, the fullness of the human experience, the fullness of God's love. Please help your church
to develop a more compassionate, more life-affirming, more
loving understanding of sexuality.

And help your priests to come to terms with their
own sexuality. Celibacy can be a tremendous burden for
a person who has not acknowledged his sexuality and has
not developed positive, creative, loving outlets for his sexual energies. It is all too easy for someone who is frustrated and insecure about his sexuality to direct those
pent-up sexual energies at an innocent little child who is powerless in resisting the breach of trust from such a respected authority figure.

I will be happy to do anything that I can to help further either of those objectives. I would be more than willing to share my experiences with your priests or seminarians,
or to participate in any discussions or dialogues on the
issues of sexuality, celibacy, and child abuse.

I love you, Bishop Sam, and I pray that God's love
will continue to guide you as you shepherd your people

through the experience of life. Please pray for me that I will continue to grow and more clearly reflect the love of God to the world around me.

Lovingly and hopefully yours,

Paul

One Final Letter—on the Lighter Side

Dear Publisher:

Since I am now retired and living at Leisure World, I thought you might like to know that I decided to come out of my "closet" and quit being a phony. So, I arranged flowers on the piano, baked a cake, and told my wife and three children I was "coming out"! They immediately went into a catatonic coma!

Then, I kissed our postman and the guy next door and told them I had decided to "come out of my closet," and got both better postal service and my lawn mower back!

Next, I wrote to my relatives (on gorgeous stationery!) and told them I was "out of the closet" and got privacy and smaller telephone bills!

Last summer, I went to a "gay" store and bought a T-shirt that said "gay power" and wore it while on my vacation. I had a golf fairway and a mountain stream all to myself. I didn't have to wait in line at crowded restaurants either!

You should tell your readers! Come out—whoever and wherever you are! Gay power is exactly that!

Glen (fire hot) Braem

Leisure World, California

AFTERWORD

Between the writing of this book and its going to press, a new phenomenon, called "outing" by *Time* magazine, has become a controversial issue. It has received a great deal of attention in both gay and mainstream media. Given the subject matter of this book, a comment on this phenomenon seems in order.

Outing refers to the practice of publicly disclosing people's homosexual orientation without their consent—and in most cases against their will. While generally reserved for disclosing the sexuality of celebrities and politicians who live in a hypocritical manner regarding their sexual orientation, outing can be done to anyone.

Many sound arguments have been made both in support of this practice and in opposition to it. It is not my desire to take a position here either for or against outing, but rather to encourage us all to look at outing in a larger context. For whether you and I like outing or not is less important than the fact that it is happening and is an indication of many

changes that have occurred in society during the past several
decades:

- When I began leading workshops in the gay community
  in the late 1970s, there was a great deal of resistance
  among participants to the entire notion of coming out.
  Invariably many homosexual participants would become
  angry, and initially feel threatened and less safe in the
  workshop, when there was a heterosexual present. During the past several years the level of fear and resistance
  to telling the truth has significantly decreased. Furthermore, most Experience weekends now have many more
  heterosexual participants (usually parents, relatives, friends,
  and co-workers of previous participants) and it has been
  years since the presence of heterosexuals has generated
  any concern. On the contrary, their presence is seen as
  an asset. As the years pass and consciousness is raised,
  we get to notice that regardless of sexual orientation we
  are all fundamentally more alike than we are different.
- In the early 1980s the words *gay* and *homosexual* rarely,
  if ever, appeared in the *New York Times*, the *Los Angeles Times*, or any other mainstream newspaper or magazine. It was difficult, even in 1982, '83, or '84, to get
  media coverage of AIDS, in part because homosexuality
  had to be mentioned. Today, less than ten years later,
  stories about lesbians and gay men receive far more
  coverage—sometimes even prime-time or front-page
  coverage—and films and television programs more frequently include homosexual characters, though certainly
  not in proportion to our presence in real life.
- Ten years ago, while the idea of a national day of coming
  out was clearly present for many, the time was certainly
  not appropriate for doing it. Today National Coming Out
  Day is an idea whose time has come—and it has been
  met with wonderful support.
- You may recall that in the early 1960s, less than thirty
  years ago, the fact that heterosexual couples lived together "out of wedlock" was cover story material for *Life*
  magazine. It was the source of great controversy and

debate throughout that decade. That an unmarried heterosexual man and woman were involved in a sexual
relationship was cause for consternation and was something to be kept hidden for fear of reprisal. While gossip
and media coverage about these activities among celebrities some twenty years ago might have been somewhat
akin to outing a homosexual today, such information is
now commonly accepted and taken somewhat for granted.
Most of us, the press included, don't think twice about
linking well-known men and women in sexual and romantic liaisons. While the right to privacy for these celebrities generally extends into their bedrooms, it rarely
extends into their social and romantic lives—provided, of
course, that they are heterosexual.

All of this is to say that "the times they are a changin',"
to quote the philosopher Bob Dylan. I believe that the
1990s is going to be the decade of coming out. So much has
transpired to pave the way for this:

- Thousands have already come out and are generally thrilled
  with their personal results.
- Several politicians have come out and have been re-elected.
  When they have conducted their lives in harmony with
  their political philosophies they tend to consistently receive support from their constituents.
- AIDS has indicated to many that silence equals death and
  that, conversely, honesty and action equal life.
- AIDS has also outed many well-known people in the arts,
  entertainment, fashion, political, and business worlds.

Outing could not have happened before because most lesbians and gay men were too timid or self-protecting to ever
dream of upsetting the power structure of society, not to
mention publicly declaring themselves homosexual in order
to point out someone else's homosexuality. Outing could
not have happened before because the press would not write
about homosexuality.

Outing is a clear indication of the excruciating frustration of
a community besieged by an epidemic and trying desperately

to be heard. This community, both heterosexual and homosexual, are exasperated with closeted gays in powerful positions who still refuse to recognize their own homophobia, who still refuse to recognize what value their being open could provide for many, and the self-perpetuating nature of their own belief that they will lose too much if it were widely known that they are gay. And the fact that outing has started to occur is also a clear indication of the progress that has been made in terms of increased openness about homosexuality and about sexuality in general.

While I wish that outing never had to occur, I welcome the debate that accompanies it. I welcome the learning and growth we will achieve as we view the issues surrounding outing in a broader perspective. It is important to remember that on the cutting edge of every movement there are abrasive groups and individuals, who employ tactics that generate disagreement and disapproval. While Martin Luther King is considered a hero by most of us today, when freedom marches began they generated tremendous opposition to him and the marches—not only from whites but from blacks as well. Many blacks resisted taking a stand for fear of a backlash. Many did not love and respect themselves, and thus the affirmation "black is beautiful" was born. All this, and a great deal more, was part of the process of attaining greater freedom.

It is my wish that each of us be free—that we each have the freedom to choose our own life and to determine our own actions. If all lesbians and gay men were open about their sexual orientation, outing would be totally irrelevant. Each individual can be a hero by being honest and consequently making it safe for all of us to be more honest. The men and women who contributed to this book are heros. A teacher who comes out to his or her classroom and colleagues is a hero. A student who speaks up for gay rights is a hero. An individual who refuses to support prejudice of any kind in his or her place of employment is a hero.

It is no less difficult for a celebrity to come out than it is for anyone else—for he or she too may fear reprisal. Neither is it more difficult for a celebrity to come out than it is for anyone else—for what is fundamentally required to be publicly honest is the ability to trust yourself to deal with the consequences of the truth and love yourself in the process.

I hope we can respect each individual's personal, private, and public process of coming out. I urge everyone to move as swiftly as possible through this process, because it is in establishing greater honesty and truth that individual and societal healing occurs. Coming out is a process of growth and learning; coming out proudly is a statement of one's strength and integrity.

Whether homosexual or heterosexual, we are each far more than our sexual orientation or any other limited concept we may have formed about ourselves. Each of us is radiant energy and all we truly have to give and receive is love. I hope this book provides you with an opportunity to remember that, and with inspiration to operate from that reality!

With love and respect,

Rob Eichberg

Santa Fe, New Mexico
June 1990

RESOURCE
DIRECTORY

There are several thousand lesbian and gay organizations. Since there is as much diversity among lesbians and gay men as there is among heterosexuals, these organizations represent a wide variety of concerns and interests. Included below are those mentioned in this book and a few of the larger organizations which are likely to be able to assist you in locating those of a more specific nature.

National Coming Out Day (NCOD)
P.O. Box 15524
Santa Fe, New Mexico 87506
505-982-2558

The goal of National Coming Out Day is to increase the visibility of gay men and lesbians. October 11, commemorating the National March on Washington for Lesbian and Gay Rights, is the focal point for activities throughout the country. Please contact NCOD for information about how to become involved in your community.

The Experience
P.O. Box 91626
Long Beach, California 90809
213-426-3896

The Experience is a weekend workshop about love, truth and being powerful in life. It is produced by local graduates in cities throughout the United States. Among other things, it supports participants to take their next step in the coming out process.

Rob Eichberg, Ph.D.
369 Montezuma Ave., #123
Santa Fe, New Mexico 87501
505-988-7556

To receive more information about Rob's tapes and workshops, you can contact him at the above address.

Music cassettes by Jerry Florence and Alliance can be ordered by contacting Go with the Flo at 213-651-0432 or 800-633-6688.

POLITICAL AND LOBBYING ORGANIZATIONS

Human Rights Campaign Fund (HRCF)
P.O. Box 1396
Washington, D.C. 20077
202-628-4160

The Human Rights Campaign Fund was founded as a political action committee to provide funds for elected officials supportive of lesbian and gay legislative concerns. It now includes extensive legislative and advocacy programs and has a unique component of grass-roots constituency mobilization through the Speak Out preauthorized mail program.

National Gay and Lesbian Task Force (NGLTF)
1517 U Street, N.W.
Washington, D.C. 20009
202-332-6483

The National Gay and Lesbian Task Force has created
projects and initiatives to advocate for fairness and challenge anti-gay and lesbian discrimination in specific areas of
our society. These projects include Anti-Violence, Lesbian
and Gay Families, Privacy, Media and Public Information,
Legislative, and the Military Freedom Initiative.

National Coalition of Black Lesbians and Gays (NCBLG)
P.O. Box 19248
Washington, D.C. 20036
202-265-4725

NCBLG, founded in 1978, is the only national civil rights
organization that focuses on the specific concerns of black
lesbians and gays. They publish a magazine, *Black-Out.*

LEGAL ASSISTANCE

National Gay Rights Advocates (NGRA)
540 Castro Street
San Francisco, California 94114
415-863-3624

National Gay Rights Advocates is a public-interest law firm
created to expand and defend gay rights. NGRA takes only
cases that break new legal ground. Prominent attorneys and
major law firms donate their time to NGRA's cases, clients
often put their reputations, their jobs, and their lives on the
line for gay civil rights.

Lambda Legal Defense and Education Fund, Inc.
P.O. Box 2038
New York, New York 10012
212-995-8585

Lambda Legal Defense and Education Fund, Inc., was founded in 1973 to advance the rights of gay people and to educate the public at large about discrimination against gay men and lesbians. In recent years, Lambda has also devoted considerable attention to the civil rights issues arising from AIDS. Lambda pursues test-case litigation in all parts of the country, and in all areas of concern to gay men and lesbians.

NATIONAL AIDS-RELATED ORGANIZATIONS

AIDS Action Council
2033 M Street, N.W.
8th floor
Washington, D.C. 20036
202-293-2886

AIDS Action Council is a lobbying organization that works to create sound health/AIDS public policy. It represents the concerns of community-based AIDS organizations throughout the United States.

AIDS Coalition to Unleash Power (ACT UP)
496A Hudson Street, Suite G4
New York, New York 10014
212-989-1114

ACT UP is a diverse, nonpartisan group of individuals united in anger and committed to direct action to end the AIDS crisis. The New York chapter of ACT UP can provide you with information on groups nearest to you.

National Association of People with AIDS (NAPWA)
2025 I Street, N.W.
Washington, D. C. 20006
202-429-2856

NAPWA is an organization of, by, and for people living with HIV disease. NAPWA's mission is to ensure that the needs of all people within the spectrum of HIV infection are met at every level.

National Minority AIDS Council (NMAC)
300 I Street, N.E.
4th floor
Washington, D.C. 20002
202-544-1076

National Minority AIDS Council works within racial and ethnic communities to develop leadership to respond to the AIDS/HIV epidemic. NMAC provides skill-building assistance and represents minority community-based organizations.

ADDITIONAL ORGANIZATIONS OF INTEREST

Parents and Friends of Lesbians and Gays (Parents-FLAG)
P.O. Box 27605
Washington, D.C. 20038
202-638-4200

Parents-FLAG provides a support system for the families and friends of lesbians and gay men. It also educates the public at large on the nature of homosexuality. It is a membership organization, with chapters throughout the country.

Universal Fellowship of Metropolitan Community Churches (MCC)
5300 Santa Monica Blvd.
Suite 304
Los Angeles, California 90029
213-464-5100

MCC has congregations of lesbian and gay Christians throughout the world. Its mission is to "empower people to bring

Christian salvation, Christian community, and Christian social action to the world." MCC will also provide information on how to contact local religious organizations of all denominations that provide services to lesbians and gay men.

Pride Institute Hotline
800-54-PRIDE
612-934-7554 (within Minnesota)

The Pride Institute provides residential chemical dependency programs as well as referral to local resources.

National Gay and Lesbian Crisisline
800-767-4297

The National Gay and Lesbian Crisisline provides crisis intervention, information, and referral.

National Gay Yellow Pages
Box 292
Village Station, New York 10014

The National Gay Yellow Pages, providing resources throughout the United States and Canada, can be ordered for $10 from the above address.

Black Gay and Lesbian Leadership Forum
3924 West Sunset Blvd. (Suite 2)
Los Angeles, California 90026
213-666-5495

The Black Gay and Lesbian Leadership Forum strengthens existing institutions serving Black lesbians and gay men by sponsoring an annual conference to provide necessary networking information and leadership development skills. They will also provide referrals to organizations throughout the country serving people of color.

Gay and Lesbian Alliance Against Defamation (GLAAD)
80 Varick Street
New York, New York 10013
212-966-1700

GLAAD combats homophobia in the media and elsewhere by promoting visibility of the lesbian and gay community and organizing grassroots response to anti-gay bigotry.

"By the year 2000 it won't be possible to get agreement, anywhere in the civilized world, that it is not OK to be gay!"

—A vision expressed by David B. Goodstein and Rob Eichberg, upon founding the Advocate Experience in March 1978